I0581335

Hades Sent

Book One of the Sent Series

B.Y. Simpson

Book Layout © 2017 BookDesignTemplates.com
Book Editing and Formatting by JeanneFelfe.com

ISBN 978-1-7377935-0-2 (paperback) | ISBN 978-1-7377935-1-9 (ebook)

For my boys, Easton and River. Mommy loves you.
For Jake, who always supports my ideas and loves me for who I am.
For Beth and Jennifer who read the very rough drafts and convinced me the story was worth continuing. It probably wouldn't have gotten completed without you. P.S. Jennifer, I still have the journal.

Prologue

Okay. I can do this. Really, I *can*. It's just a simple task. One short glimpse is all it takes. The mirror taunts me from across my bedroom. Why is it that every morning I dread this? Every time the sun rises across the clouds, I feel nervous and uneasy. If nothing has changed, it will! It *has* to. No question.

I swallow the lump that has formed in my throat and walk slowly across my room to peek at my reflection. Don't panic. It will be fine. Just fine. My reflection shows me exactly what I don't want to see. I toss my hair off my shoulders and breathe in deep. I'm still the same. No wings. No place here. Yet.

No place to call home anywhere, really. Laying my head down on the bedroom pillow doesn't mean this is home. It simply means shelter. These walls are empty, just like the promises the higher authority keeps telling me.

"Keep completing the assignments, and the wings will come," they say. "You need more motivation and dedication! Wings are attainable to those truly worthy." So, I complete the tasks they have for me, day in and day out. Helping people ... helping humans ... and it's okay. But after so long, one starts to think that maybe the system is rigged.

I should have left that money on the sidewalk yesterday where it was, instead of turning it in. That would be a total shock to the tally system. No one has ever tried to fail on purpose. What's the worst that could happen?

No. I shake my head to clear it. Stop it. I won't get my wings thinking like that. All those who have wings earned them without complaint. This is a new day! New people need help, and I will be the one to assist them!

I walk over and pull my white lacey curtains apart to let the sun in. It's always so bright here. Blinding, really. No storms ever come, no clouds. Just bright white light from above. We are at peace here. True peace. None of that murky, hateful stuff is allowed. Except, well ... I have trouble with that. I guess I should explain a bit more about what I'm talking about.

You see, I am an angel without my wings. Yes, it *is* tragic. I think so, too. Us young teen angels must *earn* them. I live in what humans call Heaven. However, it's not exactly the same. I am in angel heaven, not the wonderful human Heaven. Angel heaven is ... difficult. I understand that the human Heaven is peaceful and beautiful. It's a forever type of love and sacrifice.

My heaven judges and condemns you. This heaven has different levels depending on what you have earned, and the circumstances of your birth. Now that I talk about where I live, it doesn't really sound like heaven at all. And to top it off, my dad and I kind of live on … the bottom level in heaven. You know, the one right before getting kicked out altogether. It's all because Dad had an "accident" sixteen years ago and the result was me. Problem is, it wasn't with just anybody. Angels are not to have relations with humans per the command of the higher authority, and certainly not with demons. My, were they surprised to find Dad swooping back in here after a yearlong stay on Earth helping the humans with a baby in his arms. That baby was me. And yes, I am part angel, part demon. A hybrid, as they call me. Dad's an angel. Mom is a demon from Hades, although I've never met her. It's forbidden. The higher authority let us both in but punished Dad terribly. He lost his wings, and I'm beginning to think I will never get mine.

The higher authority claims I am too much demon and not enough angel. If they really wanted, I suppose they could throw me out, but I haven't given them a reason to. So, I'm trying really hard to earn my place here and move Dad and me up a level or two so that life can be better for us. Maybe I can even get Dad's wings back. Well, after I gain mine. It's all in theory.

They hate me. I look too different, I guess. Fire-red, shoulder-length hair, and one blue eye and one black eye certainly stand out. Everyone is supposed to have white hair, blue eyes, a pale complexion, and soft features. Kind of like the angel statues on Earth. I don't have that. Not at all. Besides my hair and eyes, my skin is more of an olive color, and I definitely have my mother's hands. As a demon, I'm sure she has long, pointy, black fingernails because that's what I have. They get trimmed daily. It still doesn't help.

People stare and kids talk, but that's the way it is here. They teach love and acceptance but don't follow through. Living around a bunch of two-faced people isn't easy. I'm determined to make it, only because they are so desperate to see me fail.

Chapter One

Ireland

Ireland, are you enjoying your lunch?" comes a voice from behind me. I glance up from my meal of broth and bread to see Gabriella making her way toward me. Glee shows on her face as she sits down beside me on the cafeteria bench. It's lunchtime at our school, The Academy of Female Wings, and here I am, stuck with her. Gabriella, like everyone else, is an angel that is happy all the time. She can hide her true intentions behind her goddess-looking face. I don't see how she can trick the higher authority into thinking she's kind and considerate. Everything she says is condescending. If not, then she's cold and fake.

I take another hard look at her to debate on what to say when I see what's on her plate. Envy makes my face flush. Gabriella has a beautiful array of food to choose from. Apples, cherries, wine, and rich cheese take up one side. Pasta rich in olives takes up the other. I swallow, forcing down my stale bread, and before I can respond to her question about my lunch, she continues talking as if waiting for me to answer is the most horrible waste of her time.

She tsks and says, "Such a shame, isn't it? It's not fair that the higher authority treats you so poorly. You eat this *trash* for lunch while others enjoy much more tasteful things." She pops a bright red, juicy cherry into her mouth, and I salivate. "And, to think, it's all because your father had relations with some demon woman. Pity. He seems like a smart man. You must agree, Ireland, that he doomed you from birth. And just so you know"—she regards me sharply—"I'm not judging you. I'm simply being honest. That's what *good* angels do."

My nostrils flare from anger, and my eyes grow hot. Of course, this isn't a good thing. My eyes glow faintly red when I get mad. *Thanks, Mom.* "Honesty is always the best policy, I'm told." I smile at her as nicely as I can. Apparently, Gabriella isn't fooled. She stares at me, and for a moment, appears shaken.

"You're a freak, Ireland," she murmurs before grabbing her plate and moving away.

"I am not," I whisper more or less to myself. As much as I try not to, things get to me in this place. For instance, the food options for the lower-level angels are worse than not eating. Well, almost. We get broth and bread, and on special occasions, juice to drink because we haven't proven ourselves yet. The higher the level you are, the better the food, the better the living arrangements, and you get the best missions to help the humans out. Gabriella is almost at the top level. Don't ask me how. I suspect it's because of how much she sucked up along the way. Probably has to do with her birth. Two high-up angels can set things up quite nicely for their children. Her parents are top pick around here.

I've had all I can stand of my bland food, so I tuck the rest of the bread in my school bag for later. Dad might want it. Nothing goes to waste at my house. That's an important rule. The bell rings suddenly, telling us it's time to get going to our lesson for the day. I sigh. Okay. Today will be *the* day. They must assign me a better task. Please, let them give me some kind of hard assignment.

I get up, brush the crumbs off my collared blue shirt and white pants, and head through the cafeteria doors to go to the drop-off. Every day, the lesson is different. They are not the common Algebra lessons or chemistry projects. Oh no. These lessons are the type that let us go down to Earth to help and assist someone. They are auto-assigned, and we are not supposed to help anyone else. That's hard to do. There are so many people that need to be helped with something.

The drop-off is on the outskirts of level two. It's exactly what it means. A drop-off. To Earth. Yes, I said it. We fly down from there to Earth. It's pretty much a big, open, vast space in the sky.

The Academy of Female Wings is on level three. Unfortunately, I am stuck with only females because the male angels are separated from us to avoid "conflict," as they say. Puh-lease! We are separated to prevent new angels from appearing within the levels. "No relations until adulthood," we are commanded. Well, I can't see that happening. But then, I guess, it's going pretty well considering I don't even know where the Male Academy is.

We reach each level by staircases. Each level is decorated according to who's occupying it. The bottom level has staircases of wood, ascending onward to better things. The wood on my staircase is sparse, and what is there is half-rotten. No one cares if we make it up or not. The further up you climb, the better condition of the stairs. The middle-level stairs are made of bricks and stones. The top level is grand, with marble steps and railings. Even the stairs remind me of my lack of worth.

Security is tight, and I'm only allowed up here because of school. Otherwise, I am stationed on level ... whatever. I've lost count ... perhaps level twenty? All that matters is that I'm on the bottom level, and everyone knows it. And I should leave for no reason unless it's school related. Pretty discriminating, if you ask me. This is heaven. Why are there even levels to begin with? We should all be the same, but of course, no one asked me my opinion.

Clear those thoughts, Ireland. They will get you nowhere here. Put a smile on your face! The Higher Authority demands it! I feel a twitch near my mouth, and that's how I know I've got my nice, fake smile plastered to my face. There. That wasn't so hard. Now, I've just got to keep it there, especially until I get to the drop-off. I keep walking toward the drop-off, silently hoping no one will come up and talk to me.

The path there takes all types of forms. Grass trails, cobble stone pathways, even a roadway leading to the last stairway. A normal human would be exhausted by now, running up and down the paths and stairs. Angels don't have to worry about getting tired out. We never do, at least not in heaven. I heard about one angel though that got sent to Hell. He lasted about an hour before he died. Thinking about that gives me the shivers.

But you would think some of us could fly up to each level. Nope, not the case. We must walk or run to each level, no flying. Course, I don't have wings to fly anyway. And even if I did, I wouldn't fly here. I've seen angels break the rules before, and the result was being brought to the higher authority. They control everything, and punishment is enforced. Who ever heard of angels breaking the rules? Certainly not the higher-ups. They give you two rule-breaks before you're toast. One time means you are stripped of your wings —if you have them—and sent to the lower level to live. If rule number two is broken, goodbye. You are either sent to Earth or Hell; it really depends on the rule broken or the mood that day of the higher authority.

So, why do I live here? Why would I want to? I don't really know. Perhaps, because of my dad. I can't leave him. Angels do get a lot of benefits. No pain or illness in heaven. Immortality has a nice ring to it, too. The main thing I want is to get my wings and to move up. Then, I'm sure life will be better for me and Dad. And to do that, missions have to be completed ... wings have to be earned. Sigh. And now, here we are, full circle. Except, this doesn't feel like a circle. This place feels like a cage.

"Morning! How goes it down below?" says a guard standing at the entrance of the drop-off. Kirk smiles the same condescending smile he wears every morning. He guards the drop-off night and day while wearing full military clothes, the colors bright gray. Handcuffs swing from his side as he moves to check my ID.

He knows who I am, which is why he asked me how it goes *below*. But I hand my wrist over to him anyway. If you look close enough, you can see a tiny bar code there. He scans it so that I can go in. I'm tagged in for another day. Each second, minute, and action of the day will be recorded.

Okay. I need to respond to him. "Things are good. Thank you so much for asking," I say in the best voice possible.

Kirk smiles at me in the most sour way. "It is really no problem, Ireland. Good angels always ask."

"Of course. Have a nice day," I smile as sweetly as I can and then walk through the opening to the drop-off. It's really bright here. This is the point where heaven meets Earth. It's a thin piece of atmosphere that joins us all together. Below are clouds and planes. Birds, trees, and people. Down there is freedom.

Everyone in my class is already here. I'm last. Again. They circle the drop-off, waiting patiently for their assignments from our instructor, Ms. Craven. Our teacher is a middle-aged angel wearing silk blue robes with a tie. Her hair is twisted in a bun, and she's trying not to scold me in front of everyone. Too many witnesses, she thinks. Next to her is Gabriella, who catches my eye and shakes her head in concern. I walk toward the group as quietly as I can. Ms. Craven lifts her paperwork out of thin air to run down the list of names going to Earth today.

All the girls in my class are just like Gabriella, except one. She might be my saving grace. Her name is Faith, and she does not stay with the rest of the group. All the other girls listen to every bark and command that comes from Gabriella's lips. Faith sings her own tune. She doesn't talk to me either, but every now and then, I catch her rolling her eyes, mocking the others. Faith gives me hope. She even has a different look about her. Not like me, but I swear she has green eyes that she hides as best she can with blonde bangs.

Ms. Craven clears her throat. "Okay, girls. Let's get our lessons for today, shall we?" This is the part I block out. I used to get mad when the other girls were given better tasks. Now, I try to ignore it. They all look at me, waiting for me to say something. They wait for the demon part of me to display. I'm entertainment to them. Not today, I say in my head. Not today.

Ms. Craven blabs for a while, going through the list. I catch that Gabriella gets to prevent an abduction from happening to a little child. I want to do that. Next, as always, is my turn to see what I can do today. "And lastly, Ireland. It seems that your task today is to … well … assist a bank. There's a bank robber in a semi-rural area of Tennessee. You will be going to the

United States to try to keep this robbery from happening. Sources say it is a young man, maybe twenty, who has robbed several in the area."

A bank robber. Okay. This is better than yesterday's task of finding lost money. "Sure," I answer with real excitement.

"You all will stay on your assigned tasks for as long as it takes to be completed. You are to meet back at your assigned pick-up spots each day. If you are not there at the assigned time, we will assume your task is not complete. Everyone will have a buddy partner to communicate with. You shall communicate when the task ends, and if you have any trouble, your partner can come assist you. Each partner is assigned by area, as you know. Today, Ireland and Gabriella will be partners, working together if needed," explains Ms. Craven while looking at Gabriella with pity.

Poor Gabriella is getting stuck with Ireland. I happen to think I should be the one that gets the pity.

"Oh, no worries, Ms. Craven!" Gabriella laughs. "If Ireland needs helps, I am only too pleased to assist her. I can even drop her off, being that she can't fly yet. Which, of course, is not her fault." She bats her lashes at our teacher.

"Why, Gabriella! That is very thoughtful," Ms. Craven says before I can even respond.

Yes. Very thoughtful. In fact, mind-blowing that she is willing to *help* me. I would rather fall to Earth by myself, thank you very much.

Ms. Craven claps, the sound booming throughout the drop-off. "Good luck, everyone! Remember, one mission closer to what you want. The higher authority wants everyone to succeed! That's what *good* angels do!"

If I have to hear that one more time! What good angels do! Again, I can't help but think they made that motto just for me. I'm not a good angel, so I'm not expected to get what I want. But, I am good and true. And I can suppress the demon inside me when I want to. The problem is ... sometimes I don't really want to suppress it. Like now, with Gabriella looking at me. I would love to punch her right in the face.

Gabriella looks at me as if she can read my thoughts. "Ireland, are you ready? We must be going now."

I force myself to take her hand. "Yes, I'm ready."

Ms. Craven walks up to us and pushes a device to the top of our heads. It looks like what humans use to check their temperatures. A thermometer? This device programs the missions in our minds. Details. Details. So many details about this young guy flow through my mind. The banks. The robberies that have already taken place. His exact location. Really, they make it simple. A beep sounds, marking the end of all information. "You two are good to go."

"Excellent!" Gabriella beams.

I keep ahold of Gabriella's hand because I have to. Even though she has her wings, she still gets to go on missions, I think more or less to give her something to do. And since she has the wings, she has to take me to Earth and drop me off, even if I don't like it.

We walk toward the edge of the drop-off and peer down. I take a deep breath. She will be gone in a minute. Then I will be alone again. Gabriella looks behind her as if to say something, but she stops and looks at me. "On the count of three. One ... two ... three!"

We jump off into the sky, hand in hand. Her wings unfold, stretched clear and white across her shoulders. They fluff and shine in the sun. So beautiful and I am so envious. She sees me staring. "Don't worry. Your time is coming," she shouts over the air as we fall through the clouds. Her voice is stating something as "a matter-of-fact" and not in a positive way. She knows something, and my guess is it's nothing good.

We glide for a while, feeling the air in our hair and the sense of ever-growing release. To fly would be amazing. I've never wanted something more than my wings. The view comes into place now. Green fields, pastures, and farms come into focus. Up ahead is a city, but not the biggest city I've ever been to. Then, I see water. A little lake takes in the sun's warmth. We soar over it, and I think Gabriella means to drop me off, safely on the ground. She doesn't.

"Okay, I will meet you here this afternoon in about three hours. If you are not back, I will meet you tomorrow evening at seven. Call if you need help." And then, Gabriella drops me. I go soaring down toward the lake. "Oops. Your hand slipped. So sorry about that! See you later," she calls, flying away from me.

On purpose. Everything she does is on purpose. I'm falling, feet first toward the middle of the lake. Okay. Just great. I do a little scooting in mid-air to change the angle my body is falling, but it doesn't help anything. Before I know it, my body hits the water with such force it knocks the air right out of me. The water is so cold as I sink further down into the lake, my entire body shivers. It's murky and mud-ridden. I move my arms, remembering my early swimming lessons. My arms and mind are able to make the connection, and before long, my head pops out of the water. I'm exactly in the middle of the lake, thanks to Gabriella's precise measurements.

I will figure out a way to get her back one day, I swear it. Suddenly, there's a faint beeping in my head that warns me my robber is on the move. Sometimes, my assignment works with me to fulfill the mission at hand. Sometimes, it doesn't. This time, it seems like luck is on my side. The system is giving me a heads up.

The guy is going north, and he's getting ready to make his next move, probably toward his hideout or something. That's the way these criminals work. At least that's how I would do it. I bet I could make a good criminal. The demon part of me would help me map out how to get away with things like that. I feel heat behind my eyes at the thought. Hmm ... very tempting.

No. Stop it! I will block out these unnecessary and forbidden thoughts. I'm looking for this criminal. I'm not trying to be one. Come on, Ireland! Stay focused.

The beeps continue in my head as it maps out the route the robber is taking—5th street is highlighted in my brain. The map is kind of like a GPS on steroids. I am given exact points, exact timeframes. This guy is a little man on screen. Everywhere he goes, I will follow. But for now, I've got to get out of this lake and head toward the city. My best guess is that the city is about ten miles from here.

After about five minutes of swimming, I reach the water's edge. My clothes are filthy with mud. Are my nails growing again? I just cut them this morning! I don't even know you, Mother, and yet you cause me so much misery. Oh, the irony. A demon mother causing her child misery. Never would have imagined that.

I need a solution. A good solution and quickly. When Gabriella and I were coming down, I saw a road south of the lake. Best to head there and find some person to help me.

Taking my shoes off, I run toward the road. There's no time to lose. Even a second could cause me to blow the mission. My lungs expand from the effort. Earth feels so good. The air is crisp and cool. The sun beats down through the endless trees and branches. It's all so beautiful. Heaven is ... not like this ... Earth offers its own magnificence. Cool grass under my toes, wind through my hair. Maybe it wouldn't be so bad to live here.

A truck rolls past me as I reach the side of the road. It leaves a dusty trail behind, making me cough. The beeping starts again, more urgently than before. My guy is getting closer. He will get to his destination within thirty minutes. This isn't good. Not good at all. If he gets home, he could have more weapons and certainly more options. In heaven, I am immortal. Earth is a different story. Sure, angels are hard to kill. But it is possible. And if our enemies know what will kill us on Earth, well, that's bad news.

The sound of a car traveling down the road breaks my thoughts. They only need to stop. My touch can do the rest. Best thing to do is pretend I'm hurt. Surely, whoever it is will stop to help. Quickly, I put my shoes on and lie down on the road. My damp clothes stick to me as I stay as still as possible. Breathe in, breathe out. My mission must be finished.

Soon, tire screeching fills the air. A car door slams, and feet make their way toward me. There are muddy work boats in my line of vision. One male peers down at me. My slightly open eyes catch his look of concern. He's shabby looking with soft blue eyes and stubble around his mouth. This is good. He won't fight me.

He leans in and says, "Ma'am? Hey! Are you okay?"

His rough hand brushes across my forehead and then traces down to my wrist. The male is checking for a pulse. Unfortunately, I won't have one.

Once he starts to feel my wrist, I grab his hand before he can comprehend what's happening. He tries to break free from me, shocked that I'm alive.

"What the …?!" he cries.

I let the heat rise in me. My demon blood becomes more pronounced with each second. Mother gave me a lot of ways to cause misery, but mind control isn't one of them. All I have to do is command that part of myself to take hold. Controlling my mind is the hardest part of it all because, as a demon, the male smells good. Good enough to eat. That is the part I find hard to control. I command myself to give it up ... he won't be lunch. I eat only food—food and humans are not on the same menu.

His eyes show me what I need to see. I am glowing. Not the special gold color glow you think of with angels. The demon glow is red. My whole body turns a shade of red as I stare right into those beautiful blue eyes of the male in front of me. He is pure and means me no harm. Pictures of his family flow through me ... a male of innocence and kindness.

"What's your name?" I ask in sort of a hissing tone.

He stares at me for a second, perplexed. "Dylan. Dylan Hall."

"Very good, Dylan. I need a favor. Do you think you can do something for me?"

"Yes, ma'am."

I like the male named Dylan. He is a simple type of human. Easy to control. Easy to eat.

I smile sweetly. "I need a ride to 5th street and quickly. Think you can do that for me?"

"Are you not hurt, ma'am?" Dylan asks.

"No. I just need a ride, and then you will forget all about me. Understand?"

"Yes. It will be as if I never saw you."

A laugh escapes me, but it sounds more evil than I mean for it to be. Embarrassing. "Thank you, Dylan.

You will be rewarded soon for your assistance. I'm going to let you go now. Ready? One ... two ... three."

His hand falls from me. Dylan looks lost for a moment before catching my eye again. He shakes his head trying to clear it. "You needed a ride to 5th street?"

"Oh, yes. If you don't mind, of course."

He smiles at me this time. "Get in."

Chapter Two

Ireland

Dylan drops me off on the corner of 5th and 6th with a small wave before speeding off back through town.

The city streets are busy with people and all different types of stores and shops. One shop window confirms the name of the city. According to my assignment notes, the city of Harrison is the bank capital of the United States. Hundreds of banks line the streets, housing the top financial advisors in the country. The banks and buildings also house millions in cash. Tourist revenue is high throughout the town due to the terrain and climate. Harrison comes just short of a mini paradise. The shops offer discount vintage pieces, name-brand clothes and purses with the costs cut in half or more. This is a shopaholic's dream.

My guy doesn't waste time on petty cash. He goes for the real deal. My alarm beeps again, reminding me to move on. He has already hit up numerous banks and shops causing customer complaints and townspeople hardships.

The beeping continues, telling me that he is close. I follow his trail, hoping for a quick capture. The system shows me he is just ahead, in an old apartment building above the shop called Angie's Clothes Rack.

Interesting. He's either storing something, or he lives above a clothing store. How can I be sure he doesn't know I'm here? I could go all-in and try to touch him. Then I will know his full intent, or I can wait him out and see where he goes from here. The problem is, I don't have a lot of time. It looks better if I complete my mission the first day instead of the second. Let's see, it's two-thirty now. That doesn't leave a lot of time.

This guy can't possibly know angels' weaknesses. It's just too cliché, for one thing. He's a normal human male that I can persuade to stop robbing people. Sure. Yes. No problem.

Decided, I breathe in deep and move toward the apartment. The store is made up nicely on the outside, with solid brick walls and a huge sliding glass door. A bird flies by, and its shadow makes me look up. On the side of the building is a staircase. It's a bit shabby. A few broken pieces of wood lie on the bottom step, but otherwise, it seems okay.

The system rings even louder in my head, causing lights to appear in front of my eyes. It's celebrating how close my guy is. Unfortunately, my head feels like it's in the center of a Fourth of July celebration. Stop! I try to command it inside my head. The noises fade slightly as if it enjoys taunting me. Sometimes, I feel like this system does things just for that reason. One day, to aggravate me. Another day, it's there to slow me down and try to make me fail. When I get back, I'm going to ask Faith if she has the same problems with hers as I do.

To stay focused, I place my hand on the staircase railing and tiptoe up, quiet as a mouse. The wood door is ajar, and voices from inside seep through the opening toward me.

"No, I understand," comes the male's voice within the apartment. "Father, I will complete this. *Trust* me. She will be here within the hour. Yes, I'm certain ..."

This is good. Touch him while he's distracted. Easy peasy. I tiptoe and slide through the open door to touch his back. His information is spot on. Greve Kronos, nineteen years old, black spiked hair, gray eyes, six feet tall with broad shoulders, and his arm muscles bulge when he feels my touch. Okay, that last part was irrelevant. But he's a lot better looking in person than on the screen, and for a split second, it catches me off guard.

Greve swings around, momentarily shocked at seeing me here. As soon as his eyes find me, I let my demon nature take hold. Heat rushes through my eyes, and immediately, the red outline appears around me. I can tell he's taken aback. Maybe he really doesn't know who or what I am.

Then his information comes through in my mind. Greve Kronos, bank robber, not human, can be spiteful, hurtful, and evil. His intention is to find the angel, Ireland Grace. I shudder, causing my information to stop flowing. He knows me and wants me for god knows what.

He waits until he can see it register on my face and then smiles, grabbing my hand in the process. "Your mind games won't work on me, Ireland Grace. Luckily for you, though, I've been waiting for you to come. As an angel, you sure are slow. I'm a bit disappointed." Greve tsks at me. "Maybe it's the demon part of you that you need to bring out more."

"What are you?" I ask in a mumble. No one has ever known I was coming. No human can withstand my mind control. Have I been set up by the higher authority? By Gabriella? Or is this all by fate and chance?

Greve comes closer to me, his face inches from mine. The scents of bonfires and aftershave fill the air around us. "What I am is irrelevant. You saw my intent. Ireland, I came for you, and now you are here."

"Why? I take it you're not really a robber, then?"

Greve chuckles at me. "Clever. No, actually not the kind of robber you are familiar with. Banks and money are meaningless. It's souls I'm after. And pardon me, but the soul of a part-angel is simply too good to ignore." Greve places his hands on my shoulders and sniffs me.

I automatically take a step back in response. He smells me as if I am lunch. Then it hits me ... he's at least part demon. Maybe more so. All I do is look at him more closely to see all the signs. That's why my mind control won't work. He's immune to me. Please, don't let him be able to control me.

"You wouldn't want me," I declare. "After all, I am part demon like you."

Greve runs his fingers through his hair and sighs. "Part angel is better than none at all. However, I am forbidden to eat you. I swear, the bosses really like to test my self-control. No matter, I was promised your body."

He moves behind me quicker than my mind can register. My back is to his chest, and he wraps his arms around me, grasping as if desperate to eat me now. "And I must say, Ireland, I think I will enjoy your neck first."

I feel his lips press against my neck, gentle and soft. His scent of fires and aftershave make me dizzy, or maybe it's his kiss making me lightheaded—I can't really tell which. And for a spilt second, I don't care.

Tingles run down my spine from his kisses. He whispers something I can't quite pick up on, and I think I mumbled to him in response. Control! Breathe! You don't even know who this is, and he wants to kill you, for Pete's sake! The heat in my eyes turns cold.

Greve lets me go as quickly as he grabbed me. He waves an accusing finger at me. "You will have to do better than that. Before long, the demon part of you will be all that's left. You can barely control it. I was hoping for more of a fighter."

My nostrils flare. I can be a fighter. I am a fighter. "I'm not going with you."

"How can you leave? You have no wings. You cannot fly. No one cares for you. Make this easy on me, and maybe I will ... well ... not ravish you so quickly after your soul is gone. I have orders to bring you in. You are a demon, if only part, and demons do not belong here, and they certainly do not belong in heaven."

"Listen, Greve. I have orders to bring you in. Who's to say your boss didn't set you up?"

Greve walks back toward the door where I came in and practically smirks at me. "Yeah. I don't think so. If they wanted to set me up, they chose a poor angel to get me."

I am not! I want to shout. How did I even get to this point in the conversation? What the heck am I doing wasting time talking to him? Greve is coming back with me. "Whatever," I manage to say.

"So, in case I didn't make myself clear enough ..." Suddenly, his hand is on my throat, squeezing my wind pipe shut. "You will come with me. I can kill you and deal with the bosses later."

My lungs start to struggle with no air. Sure, I am immortal on Earth, but I could pass out under the stress of no air. Then I really wouldn't know what he was doing to me. He inches closer to me, so close, in fact, I am beginning to think he likes the rule of no personal space.

The door creaks behind him, and he turns his head. I take that opportunity to knee him in the groin.

He releases me and stumbles to the floor, moaning. I collapse, almost on top of him, gasping for air. Think. Think, Ireland! What are demons hurt by? What am I hurt by when in my demon state? Happiness. Love. Laughter. Sweetness. Selflessness. Demons are inclined to feel anger, heartache, lust ... pain. Those things are what Greve lives for. Forget it! I can research him when I get back home. Time to run! Time to move!

I turn and run out of the apartment while Greve is still writhing on the floor, holding his crotch. I'll get someone to take me to the pond to wait on Gabriella. Surely, I will lose him.

My feet hit the bottom of the stairs, and I cut across the street, almost colliding with a couple of cars in the process. The drivers glare and beep their horns at me, obviously not realizing I am running for my life.

Demons are fast, terrifyingly so. Since they can't fly, they make up for it in speed. Greve will catch up to me since he is full demon and I'm only half. But maybe if I can manage to find a car, I can outrun him.

Greve shouts at me from across the street with more annoyance than fury. I keep running until a silver Camry stops in front of me. A man is in the driver's seat, waiting on the light to turn green. This is my chance. I say a silent prayer, reach the car, and pull the door open. The driver looks at me, stunned, and before he can do anything else, I tug him out of the seat. "I'm sorry!" I yell while closing the door.

Okay. Remember what to do here. Car is idling. Seatbelt is now on. Greve's reflection appears in the passenger-side mirror. Crap. I can't wait for the light to turn green, so I put my foot on the gas and floor it.

The tires screech in protest along with the poor driver I left behind. He will get the car back, I remind myself. It's just a little cruise to the pond. Yes. That's all. Greve falls behind in the distance, and for a moment, I breathe in a sigh of relief. These missions are not supposed to happen this way! Visions of Greve happily conforming to me and promising not to ever steal again leave as quickly as they started.

He was going to kill me! Well, he was going to let someone else do it. But why? What's a part-angel to anybody? Dad will know. Dad *always* knows. If I make it back to him. I glance back nervously, hoping to not see Greve running behind me. Dad told me stories of how Mom could catch up to him while he was flying. They would race for *fun*. A demon and an angel having fun together seems too far-fetched for my mind. It's basically unheard of.

The clock on the console tells me I've got fifteen minutes to get back to the pond, flee from Greve, and find Gabriella. That's not impossible, right? The car cruises along the highway now, and I figure I'm going as fast as the car can handle. I mean, speeds for me are different than human speeds. But Greve is out of sight, which means good job to me!

My joy lasts less than five minutes because when I look out at the passenger side again, Greve is running right beside the car. He smiles at me, his body completely warped with speed. "Pull over!" he mouths at me from outside the car. *Really? Pull over?*

I shake my head at him. The pond is just up ahead. He's right here, by the car, so close that I can probably pin him underneath it. Since he's part demon or whatever, he won't die. I have to admit, I would feel a bit guilty if he actually died.

Greve is still looking at me, expecting me to listen to him. I tug on the wheel, swerving the car off the side of the road. I hear a *thump*, and then the car bounces a little. My feet push on the brake and the car screeches to a stop. My breathing is labored. I hit him! One part of me shouts in victory. What have I done?! The angel part wails.

For once, I tell the angel side to shut it. I refuse to go out without a fight. The pond is there, right through the tree line. Gabriella will be there any minute. I've got to face him. I've got to face the person I pinned under the car, the person that was trying to get me killed.

Hastily, I open the car door and climb out. Sure enough, Greve lies there underneath the car, with this dumbfounded expression on his face. I can't help but giggle a little. "No offense and all, but I'm not going anywhere with you," I say peering down over him.

His eyes find me and recognition floods his face. He curses at me, but all I make out are the words "go" and "hell." He is definitely confused. Hell is where he belongs. "No thanks, Greve. Anyway, this is your own fault."

"Ireland? Where are you?" Gabriella's voice comes from across the road.

"Here! Right here! I'm coming!" I shout back at her. As I start to walk toward the trees, I feel a strange sensation that keeps me grounded. It's a tug at my middle, an unexplained sense of longing in my mind. I long for *him*. Thoughts and commands tell me to help him. To stay. To help. It's so overpowering that my knees fall out from under me. I hit the pavement, oblivious to Gabriella approaching me.

Greve's eyes lock onto me. He doesn't speak or move. He talks to me in my mind. His voice, strong and wild, tells me to stay. My body doesn't move, my nerves are frozen with confusion. I want to go. I have to go, but then, I want to stay. Greve is controlling me, at least partially. The demon part, I suspect. My hands move toward Greve even though I didn't ask them to. I struggle to stop.

"You want to be with me," Greve purrs. "Stay, and I will not harm you. Leave, and I will hunt you."

It takes minutes for me to process what he says. My mind is muttered with visions of Greve and me together. We are breaking curfew, going to parties, racing, and riding. We kiss. We lust. *Everything* I have ever thought about doing on my own, we are doing together. He is showing me all the desires my demon blood possesses, and for a split second, I want so badly to oblige.

"No," I say in no more than a whisper. "Stop it! Stop doing that. It's not real!"

Greve smiles at me. "How do you know that I'm not showing you our future?"

I shake my head. "Because that's impossible."

"Ireland, what are you doing? We've got to go." Gabriella walks over and starts shaking me. She tugs at my hand trying to get me to come. "I'm fixing to leave you here with him. Do you understand me?"

Her words hit me suddenly, and my mind feels lifted. "Let's go. Take my hand!"

She shakes her head at me, annoyed. "Finally! One … two … three …" She lifts me up across the clouds.

Wind blows in my face, clearing it. But the farther away I get from Greve, the dizzier I feel. We are still on Earth, that's why I can feel sickness, I tell myself. As soon as we break the barrier to get our heaven, I will be okay. Surely. Hopefully.

It doesn't happen that way. We pass the barrier, and the dizziness is so profound I get sick in the clouds.

"Oh, gross!" Gabriella drops me close to the drop-off and runs out of sight.

I'm alone. There's no one here. Where are the others? Where's our teacher? What's going on?

There's so much to process. I *liked* what Greve showed me. The visions all seemed so real, and I wanted it. If only for a split second, I wanted nothing more but him and the freedom. My ears ring with the pulse of my heart. Earning my wings is something I've wanted since I was young. Now, all of a sudden, the thing I want most in the world is not even here. He is at least part demon. A demon, just like what makes up part of me. Am I crazy? Am I delusional? Greve put thoughts and desires in my head, and they swirl, timid at first, only to become much fiercer. Demon blood is powerful. Angel blood is resourceful. Together, they work to override the other in my body. And I can't handle it. It's all too much. There's too much energy. It's all too demanding! My body starts to convulse right here in the clouds. "Dad!" I shout. "Daddy!" Please let him come for me ... please let him come.

Chapter Three

Ireland

Warm bed. Clean sheets. My father's voice whispers across the room. Relief flows through me along with the feeling that my mind is in a fog. My nose feels stuffy and my body aches. I didn't think this could be possible here at home. Angels aren't supposed to feel sick or weak. We are healed as soon as we cross the barrier from the outside world.

And yet ... Greve affected me in a way I never thought possible. He controlled *me*, if only for a few minutes. That time was enough to force my inner demon and angel blood to intersect. If I can't control myself around him, then I can't control myself around others just like him. The thought scares me.

I mumble slightly, more or less to myself. Dad hears me and walks over to my bed along with his friend Adam. That must be who Dad was whispering to earlier. They both look down on me, weary.

"Ireland?" Dad places his hand on my forehead.

"She feels warm to me, Adam." Dad glances over at his lifelong friend. I should have known Adam would be here, too. Thank goodness, though. Without Adam, our lives would be even harder. He's in the Higher Authority and sneaks things to us from time to time. I smile at him. How blessed we are to have him.

"Benjamin, I will run some more tests as soon as I can get the machine past the guards and down here," Adam says to Dad while looking right into my eyes. He is reading me and studying me, as always.

Dad sighs and says, "Thank you. Once again, we rely on you."

Adam smiles at me and then at Dad. "I wouldn't have it any other way. I should go before someone notices me gone. Take care, Ireland. I will be back as soon as I am able, and we will talk then."

I return the smile. "Okay. And thank you."

Dad leaves to walk Adam out of the house and then returns to me. The look on his face makes me feel ten times worse than before I woke up. When he looks at me, his blue eyes are afraid and timid. He's frightened of me, I think. How can I scare my own dad? It's true we don't look a lot alike. He has the standard white hair and blue eyes. Dad is pale with a tiny frame. But don't let his size fool you. He's the strongest person I know, both inside and out. And right now, all I want to do is tell him I'm okay. That everything will be okay, although nothing is guaranteed.

Dad sits at the edge of my bed by my feet. "Honey, tell me honestly, are you okay? Adam says you were convulsing when you came back. I've watched the recording, and I just don't understand what happened."

My stomach aches just thinking about how Greve made me feel. Surely, Dad can tell what happened if he and Adam looked through the logs. They saw the recording and heard what Greve was trying to do. Surely they did. I rub the bar code etched into the skin on my wrist. I was scanned and checked in before I left. The higher authority has all recordings and all feeds. They can tell exactly what happened. But, by the way my father's brows scrunch together, I can tell he didn't see what I witnessed.

"I'm okay." Our hands find each other. "Things are a bit fuzzy still, but nothing I can't deal with. Don't worry."

"Ireland, you still didn't tell me what happened. Why did you not apprehend the boy? You ran an innocent over, child. Please tell me ... did he threaten you? There was nothing on the tapes. Not a single indication of threats or pursuit. And you know what that means ... they will want you out."

No proof? How can that be? "Dad!" I bolt up so I can look him in the eye. "Are you serious? Of course he threatened me! He said he was going to take me. That there were people wanting me. I had to do something. It's all got to be there." I knew the higher authority was after me. They set me up somehow.

He sighs at me, tired. "Are you for certain? Are you sure you … didn't get carried away? I know it's hard for you to control yourself sometimes."

Suddenly, I feel like crying. Is my demon blood prevailing so much that people think this of me? "It is hard sometimes, but you know me, Dad. You know I would never ever hurt anyone on purpose." Well, aside from kind of running over Greve, but he doesn't really need to know that.

Dad stares at me as if trying to decide what to believe. Finally, he sighs and touches my cheek. "I believe you. The problem is the higher authority. I've seen the recordings, and there is nothing on them to suggest this boy was after you. Adam can only persuade them for so long. Even his power is limited. They will want you out. I can't bear to see my little girl plucked out of here and away from me. I just don't understand it. What did this boy want? Tell me what really happened."

I start from the beginning and tell Dad everything, leaving out no parts. When I finish, he knows exactly what happened and what Greve said, and I can tell it frightens him.

"Okay. I will recount what happened to you to Adam. He should tell the others, and we will have to see what they say. But in the meantime, you will stay put here on our level. No running around. No creating mischief. I'm afraid they have been after us for a long time, child. It's your word against all of them, and we have no place here. You understand?"

"I'm sorry. This is not how I pictured today going. I didn't ask for this. You know that."

Dad smiles and kisses my hand. "You hybrids never ask for any of this. This is my punishment more than yours. Be back in a little bit. Get some rest." He pats me on the head like he did when I was little and walks out of the room.

Chapter Four

Ireland

I wake to the sound of someone knocking on my door. My eyes flutter open, and it takes a second to comprehend someone is out there waiting on me to answer. I've been in my bed for two days trying to regroup and heal from the Greve incident. My sleep has been heavy and my dreams terrifying. More than once, Greve took me and tortured me. I shudder at the thought.

The knocking continues, so I reluctantly call out, "Come in." No one has come to see me aside from Dad, obviously. Even though I didn't expect anyone to.

The door opens quickly as Faith steps into my bedroom. She stares at me for a moment before coming closer.

"What are you doing here?" I ask, suddenly embarrassed of my appearance and my room. Faith is from the higher levels. She lives in a second-story apartment that is fully furnished with all the essentials. My room consists of a bed, dresser, and a mirror. I have a couple of books on my dresser and pale yellow walls to help decorate my space. The difference makes me so uneasy. I know she is somewhat like me because of her eyes. How is she continuing to hide her true self?

Faith shrugs at me and says, "I heard what happened the other day. The higher authority is very angry, you know."

"Yeah, why do you care?"

Faith comes closer and takes my hand before sitting on the floor. "Is it not obvious? Come, Ireland, you know we are similar. I've seen you staring at me."

I stare because you *are* different. The problem is, can I trust you? I lean over toward the side of the bed so that I can see Faith fully. "Yes, I study and analyze everyone," I respond, with more or less the truth.

"I see," she says, and her eyes glare at me. "Well, if that's the case, then I am wasting my time, clearly." Faith stands and stares at me. She's giving me another chance. Another moment before she leaves me. It is now or never.

"Wait. You're right. Your eyes ..." Please don't let her be a spy for someone. I can just picture it. The higher authority running through the house, taking me by the arms, and throwing me to Earth, while laughing with glee. A cold shock runs through me.

Faith turns around and smiles. "Yes, Ireland. My eyes ... the byproduct of me being a hybrid. That's my secret. Now, tell me yours ..."

"But you already know my secret," I answer crossly.

"Yes, I do. That demon mother of yours left you in a dire state. If she was going to give you her genetics, she should have stuck around long enough to show you the benefits."

"You ... can't be part demon," I stutter. Faith has blonde hair, green eyes, and she's pale. Nothing about her screams, "Hey! I'm part demon!" Not like me.

"No, silly." She sits on the side of my bed. I scoot my legs over to make room. "This ..." She waves her hand over her body. "What I have is human. I'm part human and part angel. You may not think you are very lucky, but you are. You have your dad."

I wait, patient for her to tell me more. So many times, I wanted and needed someone to talk to. Only when I'm sure Faith isn't saying anything else do I respond to her.

"You have both of your parents, right? Mr. Michael and Mrs. Harmony aren't you're real parents?"

Faith shakes her head. "They are cover-ups. Pure angels sure, but not like me. I have a human father and an angel mother. Dad is down there. I've seen him a time or two, believe it or not. He has helped me most, although he doesn't understand."

I can't help but notice she left out her mother entirely. Michael and Harmony seem harmless, as most angels should be. They are on the higher authority, and that's a problem. They are in my way of getting my wings. They are in the way of everything.

"What about your mom? Are you close to your false parents?" I wonder if I should have called them that. That's what they are ... fake. Everything seems that way to me. There's a big, gaping hole around me that can't be filled because the atmosphere keeps changing. Never can we, as hybrids, figure out how to fill in all the pieces.

Faith looks uncomfortable at the mention of her mother. "I don't want to talk about my mother. Maybe later, when the time is right. To answer your other question ... Michael and Harmony are everyone's dream parents on the outside. They do care for me. They also hide a lot of things, obviously. This brings me to why I really came here." She leans in closer and whispers, "Meet me near the drop-off after dark. I feel like making this relationship on more even ground. You know a lot about me already. However, I don't know a lot of what happened down there, and it's important that we talk about it. I know things. Important things. It's time we catch up."

I swallow down air. "I can't leave this room. I'm forbidden. If someone catches me ... I will be out of here."

Faith gets up as if not hearing any of it. "Like I said"—she smiles—"you have that demon blood in you. If you want to know what I know, you will find a way. Don't disappoint me."

Chapter Five

Greve

The girl wasn't supposed to get away from me. No one has ever gotten away before … and yet … Ireland Grace did. She fought against me. I don't know if I want to kill her immediately when she comes back to Earth or take her. For demons, it's usually one side or the other, lust or a kill, pain or pleasure. Ireland the angel will be back. That's not the question. My concern is what I'm going to do with her.

I throw another log into the fireplace and watch it smoke. Soon, it will catch flame and sizzle under the pressure of the immense heat. Fire. Hades, I love fire. It's the only real reprieve for me on Earth. Fire is home. And home is Hell.

Yet, I am here in this apartment above a clothes shop for women. I suppose I could go and get a drink with the humans. It's entertaining to watch them waste themselves on such hobbies. When I'm there, they tend to drink more, feel more, and think less. That could mean a fun night for me. But I find myself only able to think of *her*. She's my focus and rightfully so. My master wants her desperately. He ordered and asked for me specifically for the task of turning her. "She's half us," my master informed me. "Let's see if she can be turned to the demon side. That one is highly desirable, and the time is right for her to join her other family. You have my orders. Do whatever it takes."

I smile to myself, still thinking of his words. Corruption is my area of expertise. I poke at the fire a bit more before stretching out on the new couch I stole this afternoon. The humans never realized I was there. It's too easy. Ireland will be my most interesting prey. The girl is simply buying time for now. All prey do. They linger, while being timid. She is scared, that's all. My plan is easy. Wait her out. Wait until the mouse comes out to play.

Chapter Six

Ireland

I've been battling my own thoughts for hours, trying to decide what to do. Faith came by this morning and wants me to meet her. Dad told me to stay put for fear of the higher authority throwing me out. But what do *I* want?

I know I want answers, and I can get them with Faith. She knows more than what she told me. Somehow, she will bring me the peace and answers I've been wanting. And right now, answers are what I need most of all.

Decided, I swing my legs out of bed and stand. My room sways slightly as I try to keep my balance. Apparently, my body still isn't over whatever Greve did to me. Thus, another reason I want to talk more to Faith. She's been to Earth, and she's met her dad. Maybe she knows something about being a hybrid, too. If Dad won't tell me things, I will have to look elsewhere.

Okay. You will do this, I command myself. They have been trying to find a reason to throw me out anyway. Might as well give them an actual reason to punish me. I remove my old clothes and exchange them for a pair of black jeans and a white cropped shirt. I pull my hair into a bun at the top of my head with the idea that my red hair may go unnoticed that way.

Now, all that is left is to wait for the darkness to come. All my life, I've been waiting. Waiting for answers and wanting better things to come along. Life can't be just about waiting for something to happen. Life is too short for that. The people who really live make things happen on their own. And getting my wings will happen. Even if I don't get to have them for very long, those wings are mine.

❦

There's someone knocking on my door. Most likely, it's Dad to tell me goodnight. Darkness has finally fallen, and I've been waiting until this hour in order to make my escape to go see Faith. I hop back into bed, quickly covering myself before telling Dad he can come in.

The door swings open and Dad walks in, timid at first, before shutting the door behind him. He peers at me. "Are you okay?"

I wave my hand for him to come closer. "Yeah, just thinking."

Dad smiles. "Always thinking, my dear. Of what, if I may ask?"

Biting my lip, I answer, "Mom. Tell me … something about her." So much information has been omitted. It's only fair that I get to know her, even if it's through the eyes of my father.

Dad comes to sit beside me on the bed. The mattress sinks under his weight. He doesn't look at me at first. "Ireland, you know this is hard for me."

"But … Dad …"

"However," he interrupts, "you are almost grown. You are a seventeen-year-old girl who deserves to know more about what has happened and what is happening around you. Let's make an arrangement. I will tell you something new every day until I run out of things to tell you. Does that seem fair?"

I nod. "Okay. Yes. I will take whatever you give me."

"Scoot over," he says while lying down beside me. He puts one arm around me while my head rests on his chest. Being this close to my dad makes me realize how much I've really missed him.

He squeezes my arm. "For your safety, I'm still going to have to omit some things from you. If the higher authority knew I was telling you anything about her, you can be sure that all trust, if there is any left, would be gone. I didn't tell you earlier for that reason. It's too dangerous. Imagine if you'd been a child and started talking about her, unaware of the impact it would cause? Any talk of demons or humans is forbidden. I did enough by bringing you back with me. I couldn't stand the idea of them taking you from me. But I feel now is the time that you know and understand the real dangers of it all."

Dad swallows, and continues, "Okay ... so ... if you ever wanted to find her, you can by the name of Jade. Keep in mind that is not her *real* name. Jade is the only name you need to know. You look a lot like her. Sometimes it's hard for me to look at you without seeing her."

I stutter, "I figured ... my hair color was hers. You are saying we look a lot alike?" The thought gives me a chill. I don't know if I want to look like a full demon.

"Now, I didn't say that." He shakes his head. "What I mean is that you favor her. Your hair obviously is hers, but other things, too. Your mind control, for starters, is another. You already figured that out on your own. The way you contemplate which route to take. Which way to complete tasks. Your self-control. Your determination. Beauty, and might I even say, the stubborn part of your personality. That is your mother. Child, can't you see that she provided you with the best of her own genetics?" Dad looks sad then, thinking about Mom.

"She provided her genetics, but you provided me with much more." I lean in to kiss him on the cheek. "Thank you for sharing. You miss her, don't you?"

Dad sighs. "Every day. What we had was real. What we had didn't last long enough. Demons can change, love. We angels can change them. Your mother was a different person when she was with me."

"How? How can they change?"

"That story is meant for another time."

"Would you change it? If you could, would you take it back? She hurt you; I can see that. You hurt every day, and you live in the one mistake, the one mishap, of your life. Your choice to be with her cost you so much. Do you regret it, Dad?"

Dad shakes his head. "I regret nothing. Our love was not a mistake or misjudgment. It was *real*. So what if it wasn't right according to *them*. We loved each other at one time, Ireland. That love got me you. You can't regret following what you knew was right."

"I love you, Dad," I whisper while tearing up inside. The moisture threatens to leave my eyes.

"And I love you more." Dad sits up then. "It's time to go to bed. Who knows when the higher authority will come to talk to you. Best be rested."

Yes, but I won't be. This is for certain. "You're right. You headed to bed too?"

Dad shrugs while getting out of the bed. "Might as well. It's been a long day." He kisses me one more time before walking back out.

It has been a long day, I agree silently. More importantly, it has been a long and hard life for Dad. I intend to change that for both of us.

Chapter Seven

Greve

Days. It's been days since Ireland left. Days are what it feels like while I wait for her in this apartment. In reality, it's only been twenty-four, hours and I'm getting bored. She should have been back by now if my mind control did anything.

I shake my head in aggravation. Apparently, she's stronger than I thought. She will come, I have no doubt. It's all been arranged. Ireland won't be able to hide out much longer. Her safety net will be severed, and then she will have no choice. My heart beats faster just thinking of the moment. Her skin smells so sweet. Her blood runs both hot and frantic. She panics quickly but recovers. Ireland is ... more than I thought she would be. And I don't know if that is good or bad.

My phone rings, breaking my thoughts. I answer, not even looking at the number. He's the only one that calls me. "She's healing and will arrive within two days' time. Be ready," my master's voice croaks on the other end.

"Fine. Anything else?"

He laughs on the line. "Yes. Go find someone to torture. You sound bored. When you are bored, you act less like yourself. That's never good because that's when you become less useful. Understand? We can't be having that, can we?"

"Understood." I snap the phone shut before he can give me any more orders. He's right, of course. He still knows what I crave. Damn, he might be the best master I've ever had.

An alarm blares in my ears as the window glass falls onto the street. Being at a shopper's paradise has its advantages. There are several stores to choose from, but this one stood out to me. It's like a *Macy's* on steroids. I despise that store. Overpriced and full of over-inflated personalities ... that's probably why I slammed my hand into the glass window. Seeing it destroyed fills me with immediate satisfaction. My feet hit the store floor, heading to the men's department.

My body slides through the clothes racks, back and forth, whizzing through stacks and stacks of polo shirts and jeans. These humans all dress the same. They also follow the same routines. All work and no play makes Jack a dull boy ... and are they ever so dull right down to their clothes.

There must be something here to wear. My nostrils flare. This is taking way too long. Suddenly, a shout rises through the blare of the alarm. I scan the room to find a middle-aged cop, complete with a donut belly, jet black hair, and a sharp aim, pointing a gun at me. Perfect. As if this is a sign from below, I notice that the cop is standing right next to the suits. Right where I want to be.

My feet pick up the pace until my body is just a blur. Air rushes all around me, and every now and then I catch the man's shouts. A *pop* sound fills the air, and the projectile hits me right in the collar bone. Pain, sweet pain. The cop actually pulled the trigger. Not bad. Before the man has time to react, I turn the corner and swipe the gun out of his hand and point it right at him. "Don't move!"

The man squirms and holds his hands up, begging me not to shoot. "Please," he says, "I have a family. Kids. A wife."

I shake my head and put my fingers to my lips. "Shh. Talk any more right now, and I will shoot you. You already gave me quite a nasty hit. I don't care about your family. What I want to know is … the bad things in your life."

"I don't understand," he stutters.

Maybe he won't be what I need. Other voices come from across the street, trying to make toward the store. "Call off all the other coppers before I shoot them all dead." I point the gun at him, smiling as he flinches. This is almost too easy.

"Wait!" shouts the cop. "Stay outside! I'm coming!" he orders in his best command voice.

The other cops shout back, agreeing to stay back for the moment. Although they will come in soon—I can read it in their heads.

"Now, where were we? Tell me the worst thing you've done in your life, and maybe I will let you live," I remind the cop.

He looks at me, confused. "I tell you the worse act I've ever committed, and you won't kill me?"

I point the gun at him again for good measure. "And I will know if you lie."

As his memories and thoughts swirl in his head, I am all but disappointed to see this man isn't really all that evil.

"Alright," he pauses, "I lied to get into cop academy. I got in because of someone I knew, not on my own."

I can tell by how the thoughts flow, he is telling the truth. He feels anguish at what he told me, and that feeling is enough to at least satisfy me for the time being.

"Look at me, cop," I order, still having the gun locked on him. He looks at me, perplexed. "You will not remember me. The robber got away and ran north. You will not find him, so don't try. The anguish you feel for lying satisfies my cravings enough to let you live. Perhaps we will meet again in a much darker time in your life."

The cop looks away long enough for me to snatch charcoal slacks and a button-up red dress shirt from the racks. I glance back at him one more time, not completely satisfied. Before running to the exit, one pop rings through the air. I look around to see the source and realize with trembling hands, it was from me. Gun pointed right at the cop who's now bleeding on the floor. Bullet wound to the collar bone—a matching injury. Sometimes, I take things too far before I've realized I've done it. This is one of those times. The cop is still as stone and blank-faced, still under my influence. I let him go. Even my speed from running away isn't enough to stop his screams from catching up to me.

Chapter Eight

Greve

I step into my apartment and close the door. Placing the stolen clothes in a clean place is top priority. Once they are on the couch and away from chances of getting blood-smeared, my thoughts run wild. That was almost too easy, but nonetheless, it felt good. The cop's anguish is just what I needed to feel better. My body craves emotions, preferably ones that focus on misery or fear. I've learned over time that without some sort of intense feelings or situations to surround myself with, I begin to feel kind of sluggish. It's like when humans need coffee to wake up in the morning or goals to thrive. It's the same thing to me. Intense, burning, and raw feelings ... they are what keep me alive.

The cop helped me along in intensifying those feelings with this gunshot wound to the collar bone. My fingertip touches the spot that is covered with my blood. My heart seems to beat there for the time being, and the pain is getting worse. But I won't die from it. Nothing will happen. The spot will throb and fester until it heals on its own.

I poke the fire again. The heat will help. The ashes twinkle almost like stars when they flow up the chimney. Red and black swirl together—it's beyond calming. The fire dies back down after a while, making me feel sluggish again. My little outing wasn't enough. Sure, I had planned to go out again, which is why I got the clothes to begin with. But I was hoping I could stand to wait a little longer. When Ireland comes back, I want to be near so she can't get away from me again.

The fire hisses at me, breaking my thoughts. "Yes," I reply back to the flames. "The time has come to have some fun. You've talked me into it."

The wood logs pop and crackle with encouragement. Who needs parents when I have the fire to talk back to me? Demons do not have their own hell or heaven. We just have our own section of the Earth, and in that section, fire runs wild. We live with it, consumed in the flame. Demons can touch it and not be harmed. We can use it to heal, to communicate. Fire guides us.

Unfortunately, fire destroys things where I am now, so I cannot let the fire go free. Well, I guess I could really. A smile comes to my lips. That would be terrible ... just terrible and ... tempting. The humans would ruin it though. They have water. A chill runs down my spine. If the humans only knew … Small amounts of water are okay. I can deal with small amounts like a drink or sip of something. A quick shower becomes difficult, but because I don't have enough flame to cleanse me completely, I have to bathe like the humans to not stand out. Anything beyond that can hinder me. Demons and water do not mix. Same concept as the way humans and fire don't mix. Personally, I feel like the humans really miss out.

What are humans to me anyway? The fire hisses at me again. "Alright," I say out loud. "No need to rush me." I stoke the fire again before heading to the small bathroom. It's nothing fancy. Tub, sink, and toilet. I don't need anything more than that. If I want to get the right amount of attention tonight, I need to dress and act the part. That includes bathing the way these humans do. I touch the faucet and cut the shower on no more than a slow trickle.

Stripping quickly is impossible. My shirt sticks to the dried blood on my chest, and when it finally comes free, a big hole forms where the blood used to be. I toss it in the sink along with my pants and edge toward the back of the shower.

The water flows in soft beads down the drain. This shouldn't be too bad. Just be quick, I command my-self. My hand goes in first, long enough to make it moist. As soon as the water hits my skin, the dizzy feeling begins. That is how it starts. Dizziness happens first and then comes the feeling that the life is being sucked right out of me.

It takes about a minute to clean off the blood and dirt and to cut the water off. In that time, two breaks were needed. Going out now is necessary. It's no longer an option. Of all the things to bother me, water has to be it. I towel off and sit in front of my fire, hoping it will dry my hair quickly. By the time my hair is dry, I feel somewhat better and so does my wound. The skin is puckered now, which means the bullet is working its way out.

When I look out my window, I notice darkness is falling again. My favorite time is starting. City nightlife is chock-full of mistakes and misery. It's a time of sweet perfection. I dress in the black slacks and red button-up shirt I acquired today. Not bad. Matches my mood, I think, as I comb through my hair. Once the sun sets, it will be time. My fun is just beginning.

Chapter Nine

Ireland

The sound of my father snoring echoes through the hallway as I walk past and toward the door. He's been asleep for about an hour now, and in that time, I've sat by the door listening. When I was little, we would sleep together in the same bed. It was mainly for reassurance. Nothing compared to having my father wrap his arms around me as if scared that I would disappear. And now, here I am, doing exactly what he has always feared. I'm leaving him tonight for answers.

Maybe it's not exactly the same thing since I will be back later, but it's not so different. He's always been afraid of giving me answers and giving me information. And now, I've met someone who will hopefully give me some answers to questions I've been dying to know since I realized I was a girl without her mother.

I can't pretend I'm not excited. A hunger has formed in me, and I'm desperate to find out more. Even if it's just something to help me cope with it all.

So, I take my sneakers out of the living room closet and put them on as quickly as I can. I'm not going to bring anything else with me because I must stay in the shadows so I'm not seen. This is the test I have to pass right now. If I get caught, the higher authority will probably throw me down to Earth without hesitating.

The bar code on my wrist catches my eye as I gently close the door behind me. The higher authority only tracks us when we are on Earth, as far as I know. There is no need to track here because everyone already knows who you are. That is a blessing and one I am not likely to forget. All it takes is a simple command to make these codes activate, and I don't want to be around to see that happen.

The last level—my level—is bare. Since this is the lowest level of our heaven, we are supplied the most basic necessities. We are provided with clothes and food each month. A higher authority member, like Adam, comes down the stairs and hands out the materials once per month. Mainly it's hand-me-downs, as far as the clothes. Many things don't fit right or don't go together. They just bring out bits and pieces of this or that, white shirt here, yellow pants there. That type of thing. I guess the higher levels see us as charity, so they provide us things as a way to make themselves look better. After all, they get compensated for helping. They say it's just because they are good and true angels. I know better.

No one else dares come down here. They fear us. They fear they will become us by association. Sure, they will acknowledge our presence in public, but only because they have to. We don't feel all alone because Dad and I have neighbors—a disgraced man who once worked for the higher authority and an elderly woman who never passed any of her tests on Earth. Some say she couldn't pass the tests. Others say she refused to as a teen. Either way, she never helped a single human—a crime that calls for harsh punishment.

These angels aren't bad. They aren't good enough for the higher authority. That's how I see it. So, us four live here, and that's it. We all have our own houses, which are simple one or two bedroom and hardly furnished. Dad and I are the only ones who leave the level, though. Dad goes to work cleaning the schools, and of course, I get to go for school. Our level doesn't have any other buildings. Just three houses side by side. Night or day, they never change. I'm sure more houses will pop up if someone else was to get sentenced here. That hasn't happened in a long time.

Our staircase to the next level is usually guarded by a guy named Tim. He's the friendliest guard here and looks like all the others. He must feel sorry for us because he, at least, smiles at me in the morning. I walk around the elderly woman's house because the staircase is sitting practically in her backyard. To my surprise, Tim is standing there, staring ahead. He's expecting me.

"Ireland." He nods in my direction. "You know it's after curfew for you, right?"

Thoughts of taking him down come to mind because he is only one angel, and I am stronger because of my blood. But there's something about the look he is giving me that makes me recoil.

"Yes," I answer, not really knowing what else to say.

"So, what are you doing?"

"I ... umm ..." I bite my lip. "I'm bored. It's boring down here." He won't notice me lying because it's more or less the truth.

Tim looks at me with a slight smile. "It's boring down here, that much is true." He walks up to me and touches my shoulder. "Things are changing, Ireland. Keep your *faith*. That's all anyone needs ... is *faith*, wouldn't you say?" Tim cocks his head to the side, beaconing for the stairs. He is in on what I'm trying to do tonight.

Taken aback, I stutter, "Yes. I need faith ... more of it ... I mean."

"Good," he says while waving his hand for me to follow him. Excitement rushes through me. Faith knows a lot more people than I thought.

Tim doesn't say anything else to me. Maybe he's too scared to. I follow him up the stairs onto the next level. We tiptoe and hide around the buildings, prowling in the shadows. With each new level, it becomes easier. With more homes and buildings, we have a lot more hiding places. They increase in number every time we go up a level.

Finally, after an hour of weaving, sweating, and silence, we reach the last staircase before the drop-off. "I will wait for you over there." He points to a modest brick house a few yards from the staircase. "No need to go to the house. I will see you when you come back down." Tim leaves me without anything more to say.

Fearing that I've already taken too long, I climb the staircase as quickly as I dare. Faith is waiting on me and pounces as soon as my feet hit the top. "Did Tim help you?" she asks before I can say anything.

Our eyes meet. "Yes. He's waiting down there for me. Thank you," I answer a little too stiffly.

"Concerned?"

I nod. "Honestly, a bit."

Faith raises her eyebrows. "Good. You need to be. Come. It's just us tonight."

I follow her toward the edge of the drop-off. She sits down first, and I follow suit. The center of the drop-off swirls into a mix of clouds and the Earth's night sky. The stars shine below so brightly that they cause me to squint my eyes. "Why did we meet here?" I ask, looking back at Faith.

"Because they cannot track us as well here," she states as if it's obvious.

I try again. "What do you want from me?"

Folding her legs under her, she answers, "Much more than you are ready for. For now, I want to share. I know I said we needed to get to know each other better. I wanted to know your story. Well, it happens that I found out all on my own just by snooping today. People are eager. Too eager, Ireland, to talk about you and your dad. They spread things, nasty rumors that I know to be untrue."

"Like what?" My stomach lurches.

"Oh"—Faith shrugs—"well, where do I begin? That your dad slept with a demon of all things, can you believe it? Also, that you are a spawn of Satan. Hmm, you and your dad beg for things. Gabriella told me she caught you with a guy named Greve on your last mission, and you ran him over after you had relations with him. I tell you, how do you ever sleep at night?" Faith smiles at me sarcastically.

Heat rises in my eyes, and they start to glow. "The only true statement in what you said was that my father did sleep with a demon. That is who my mother is … a demon. Nothing else is true!"

"Relax," Faith says and pats my knee. "Honestly, are you surprised? All you have to do is pretend you are concerned about someone, and angels up here share freely. I do think they honestly feel like they are helping you. All except Gabriella. She is corrupt just like *them*. I know already about your father. I probably know more than you."

Is this really happening? "How do you know more than me?" I can't help but to secretly hope it is true. Faith could tell me what I really want to know without me having to wait any longer.

"I know more because I seek out the truth, Ireland. Plus, I suppose my parents also help. Not my real parents, but the ones I've been with since I was small." She pulls a notebook the size of her hand out of her pocket. "My notes," she explains. Faith flips to the first few pages.

"Your father was placed on the lowest level because he came back with you after a long mission on Earth. I'm sure you know that. But did you know that your dad was on the higher authority prior to this mission?"

I look at her, shocked. "I … umm," I stutter.

Faith bats her eyelashes at me. "And, if you look back at some of the records, it is clear that this same cycle has been happening for a while now." She flips through more pages. "There have been numerous cases within the past thirty years or so."

"What cycle keeps happening? The authority keeps getting rid of angels?"

Faith looks at me with anger in her eyes. "Not just any angels. They banish, isolate, or kill angels that are different. They destroy hybrids and the angels that create hybrids! And even angels that don't follow the assigned task created by the authority are eliminated in some form. It wasn't always like this, but it is now. Ireland, so many of us have been mistreated ... so many sent away for being different." Faith throws down her notebook in frustration. "Don't you see what's going to happen? Can't you see it?! Sooner or later, every one of us will be robots ... acting solely on what the higher authority wants. We will be controlled by them in one way or another!"

"It makes sense now. They wouldn't want hybrids because we cannot be controlled. I've always known they didn't like us, but I thought we would be tolerated. I mean, it's not like we choose this," I say in aggravation.

Faith looks down at her shoes, uncomfortable. "No, we did not choose this life. You did not choose to be treated like an outsider for no other reason than who your mother is. I have never been able to see my real parents because of my birth, outside of sneaking around. Ireland, there are many here. More than you know. Lots of girls scattered around in different stages of life. Same for the boys. Have you ever seen the boy school?"

"No." My face flushes. "Honestly, I don't know where it is. I've never been able to go outside my level besides school."

Faith takes my hand and smiles. "One day, I will show you. What's important now is for you to be cautious. Yes, it's true I dragged you out here. That was essential. Not only to prove how serious you are but also to make sure we will not be bothered here. Eyes are everywhere. Maybe not in the form of cameras, but in the form of spies. Don't trust your dad's friend, Adam, for instance."

I snatch my hand away from her. "Adam has been my dad's friend for years. He came just the other day to check up on me. As far as I know, Adam has always been around. If I can't trust him, I can't trust anyone."

"Be that as it may ..." Faith shrugs. "You say Adam has always been around since you were a little girl. Why? From what I heard, Adam started helping your dad after he arrived back from Earth with you. Now, why would he be interested in a disgraced angel? And one that he just met? This is not typical. Angels do help but mostly from afar as they do now on Earth and here. They give you clothes, for example. However, they don't try to associate themselves with someone who's deemed somewhat of a traitor by the higher authority." Faith picks up her notebook again. "I've heard Adam got on the higher authority right after your father was punished. He wouldn't need your father for anything. So … why? That is the question I want answered, and you should too, Ireland."

"Yes. Yes … you're right." My head spins. Could Adam have another motive? It's hard to believe. My dad has counted on him for years. I wish I knew more about how they started talking.

"So, here's what I am going to try to do," Faith explains. "I'm going to try to dig up more information on Adam and the rest of the authority, and we will meet back here at a later time."

"What do you want me to do?"

"You need to watch yourself, for one. I also heard that you are going to be allowed to complete your final mission on Earth before the trial. Something about them saying you won't return anyway from it? I'm not quite sure. This guy … this robber. You can handle him, right?"

Do I really want to get into this? I bite my lip. "Yes. I can handle him. He will be my biggest challenge, so I can see why they would think I couldn't complete it."

"There's something you are not telling me. Spit it out."

"Alright. He's not all human." I wait for a response. I get nothing. "And … he's at least part demon." Now, I've got her attention. For a second, I think it's possible for Faith's eyes to pop off of her head.

"How?" Faith asks. "How do you know?"

I roll my eyes. "Because. He has mind control just like me. That comes from demons, not humans or angels. He is part demon. That is the only problem I face." I will not tell her that he almost caused me to stay with him last time. I can control him.

"Okay … now I am even more certain that this test will be the answer to your fate. It's actually pretty clever. The higher authority has no faith in you at all. They will let you go back in hopes that he will take care of you all on his own. What's for them to lose? They think he will tempt you enough to make you stay on Earth, or they think he will corrupt you the rest of the way. They won't have to make a choice. It's already been done for them!"

"I've thought about that too, Faith. There's nothing I can do but prove them wrong. I'm uneasy about it.

Scared. Excited. All of the regular thoughts and feelings. This guy can be controlled. I just need to find his weaknesses."

As Faith starts to say something, Tim walks up the steps. "It's been too long. We've got to go down."

Faith stares at him, apologetic. "Sorry, Tim. Let me tell her one more thing."

Faith turns back to me. "Look at yourself. You are half him. What are your weaknesses? What makes that demon part of you disappear? Maybe that will help you." She stands.

"Wait!" I stand up with her. "Why are you helping me? Why do you care what happens to the rest of the hybrids?"

"Because," Faith stares down at the floor, refusing to look at me. "They killed my mother for *loving* a human man. They killed her for conceiving *me*. It's the least I can do for her. I can't save her. Maybe I can save the rest of us."

I nod because I don't really know what to say. "I'm sorry."

Faith shakes her head. "Don't be sorry. Get even." She gives me a pat on the back and nods to Tim, showing our meeting is over.

Tim waves for me to come, and I follow him. When we get to the next level down from mine, he stops.

"This is it. My shift is over. I cannot go down any farther. Do you think you will be alright?"

I look down at the stairs, hoping to find nothing when I get to the bottom. "I will be fine." I smile. "Thank you, Tim."

"No need to thank me. Just make sure you continue to help Faith out. She's all I have left."

I give him another reassuring smile. "I will." He walks back up the steps, away to meet Faith or maybe to go to bed. All I've got to do now is get down the stairs without being seen. Shouldn't be too bad.

I start down the steps going as quickly as possible. Halfway down, I hear someone whistling. It's a familiar noise, one that I've heard for years. My suspicion is confirmed when I come face to face with Adam.

He's carrying a large box and is heading up as I am going down. Adam's face is unreadable for a second. It's enough, though, to make me notice it. He smiles stiffly. "Ireland? What are you doing out and not on your level?"

There's something about his face that catches me out of character. Is it the crease on his forehead, or the fake smile he is trying to master? "Well, I got bored and thought I could just walk up and down the steps for a bit of exercise. I couldn't sleep," I explain further. "Too many things on my mind."

Adam sighs. "I understand, but you can't be doing this. I came down here to see if we could talk. You are to go back and finish your mission. I was going to tell your dad, and then I hoped we could screen and do those tests on you before you have to leave. It's important we get as much information as possible in order to make sure we can prove your innocence at trial."

If there will be a trial, I think. "Sure, we can talk about that. Dad's already asleep. I'm sure he wouldn't mind though."

Adam's eyes twinkle. "Splendid. Shall we, then?" he asks, turning back around toward our house.

I nod and follow him back to the house, all the while trying to compose myself. Faith might be on to something about him. It's hard to tell.

We get to the door, and I move ahead of Adam to unlock it. When the key gets in place, Adam tugs my arm, hard. "I might not be the next one to find you walking around. This is not the time to be adventuresome. If you're out, I need to be the one to find you," Adam whispers in my ear.

I pull the door open without replying. Does he want to be the one to find me out of concern or for another reason entirely?

Chapter Ten

Greve

Music. Sweet music fills the void I presently feel. The club's DJ cranks up the beats of the night as more and more people come in from outside. And here I am, alone, waiting on the bartender to ask me what I want to drink. It's all for show. I can hardly drink a sip without getting dizzy. But what will the folks say about me if I don't act the part they are so desperate to play themselves?

I'm Greve, the supernatural demon who's trying to act like a little human. I laugh at the thought. My laugh catches the bartender's attention, and she comes walking over to me with a full smile on her face.

"Can I get you something?" she asks while leaning over the solid mahogany bar. This girl is beautiful with brown shoulder-length hair that curls around the edges, bright-red lipstick, and green eyes. Perfection on the outside. Not what I'm looking for on the inside. She's too happy. I don't do happy.

"Just a beer is fine." I smile back at her.

She stares at me for a second. "I need your ID please."

"Sure." I make to reach into my pocket, and then I casually take her hand instead. Looking into her eyes I say, "Relax. There's no need to card me. I'm good." I let go as quickly as I touched her.

The girl shakes her head, getting rid of my thoughts. Then she walks off with no further questions.

If only it were that simple with Ireland Grace. My fingers drum the bar. No one has escaped me before. She is likely made up of more angel than demon. Her angel influence will be hard to let go of. She will have no choice but to listen to me, eventually.

The waitress returns with my beer, and again I follow what is expected. The beer hisses as I unscrew the cap and take a small sip. I've had better, I think, as the beer burns down my throat.

The city nightlife is irreplaceable with its loud music and fierce spirits. The women are especially hard to keep up with. Some are only out for a good time, while others hide behind insecurities. Some drink for comfort. Some drink to forget what's waiting at home. The women I'm interested in are the ones who want to forget. They are the ones who are hurting the most.

You would think that would be my main focus right now. Here I am, surrounded by humans, and yet ... all I can think about is her. Ireland Grace, the one I need to capture. She's the key to everything, and unfortunately, she is also distracting me.

I take another swig of beer and let it set in my mouth for a while before I swallow. I must be able to fully control her, and in order to do that, I must get stronger.

Giving up my seat at the bar, I begin to walk and search around the room for someone of interest.

One would think I would have plenty of options in a scene like this. Sure, there are a lot of women, and well, men around here to talk to, but there's even less of an option to find one worth engaging in a conversation with.

Twenty minutes pass before I spot a girl who might give me what I need. She sits in a corner booth, clutching a mixed drink in one hand and her face in the other. Her long black hair falls across her forehead in wavy strands. She appears to be crying, and what's best is, she's alone.

I need a lot of emotion, and this is the girl who will give it to me. I casually walk over to her booth and squeeze in, facing her. "Excuse me, are you alright?"

She looks up, startled that I am sitting here. She didn't hear me because she's so much in her own self-loathing to realize anything. "Oh! I'm sorry," she says and smiles timidly. "I was hoping not to draw much attention over here." Her hand tries to wipe her tears away, but all it does is smear the gunk on her face.

"Well, it's hard not to notice a lady crying. You are so clearly upset about something," I whisper so only she can hear.

She leans in to answer me, "Thanks for checking up on me. I'm alright."

I lean in closer still so that we are only a couple of inches apart. "Tell me, what's your name?"

She pauses, taking me in. The music changes from frenetic to a slow dance, and more couples are joining the floor to dance. "I'm Kayla. And you?"

Holding out my hand to her, I answer, "Greve. Pronounced like grieve, but spelled differently."

She takes my hand in return. "Really? That's somewhat dark. Were your parents humorous people, Greve?"

I smile. If only she knew. "They had some humor to them. Shall we get out of this little dark hole and dance? It might help you."

She shrugs and takes another sip of her drink. "Couldn't hurt."

It can, I think. It really can.

Kayla grabs my arm and pulls me toward the dance floor, eager to join the rest of the public. The slow tune carries on and seems to fill all the empty spaces of the club. The dance floor is filled with bodies moving and caressing to the music. Many things are happening here, and I couldn't be more pleased.

I put my arm around her waist and gather her close. She smells like all the others—roses or some other type of floral scent. Not exactly a pleasant smell, but I can make do. Our touch will help me *feel* more, so I stay with her like this just to make her feel more comfortable. "Kayla," I say, in hopes she will make eye contact with me. She does, and when my eyes lock onto her brown ones, I begin talking again. "Tell me truthfully what is wrong. I can help you."

The weight of my words holds her still. I let my voice do its work. She won't be hard to persuade.

My command more or less registers with her, and I start to feel everything she's been holding inside. Death follows her everywhere. The death of her mother is tearing her apart. To my surprise, she clings to me, desperate for some sort of understanding.

Her torture revives me. All of her worries and hurt and pain collide into me. Kayla is inside of her own personal hell of grief. The loss of her mother is something she's told herself she can't survive. A part of her is forever gone now that her mother has passed. My arms pull her close while the music plays on around us. The closer we are, the better for me and the better for her. As long as we touch, I will benefit from her sorrow. Her pain energizes me. This is what I needed most of all tonight.

The song ends, but we continue to stand on the floor. I place my hands on her face so that I can stare directly into her eyes. She focuses on me, and that is when I get the next kick of emotion. Her eyes tell everything else that's on her mind. Kayla planned to end her own life tonight. And while her life means nothing to me, I can't stand to see that happen. Death happens every hour of every day. Life goes on before the person is buried in the ground. One thing I've noticed about the world is that it doesn't stop for you or me or anyone. Money leads the world. Not feelings. Not wants. And certainly not the state of anyone's mind.

My hunger is gone. Kayla is of no further use to me. Once the initial thought and pain comes out, everything else is more or less a weakened form of substance. This is what fuels me, but I've had enough for now. "Kayla," I murmur, "you won't. Tonight will not be your last night on Earth. You will heal." Our eyes lock for a little while longer before I let her go. She's still standing in the middle of the floor. She's not looking at me. Kayla is looking for the part of herself that she's lost. And I am walking away from her. Humans are simple creatures. Kayla was anything but simple. Maybe that's why I decided to spare her.

Chapter Eleven

Ireland

Adam wastes no time tattling on me to Dad. We walk into the house together and off he goes to wake him up. Sullen, I cross my arms in front of my chest while trying to figure out what I'm going to say. It doesn't take them long to come back into the living room. Adam sets the box he's carrying on the couch and then makes a point to move away, disappearing into the corner.

He's always watching, I notice. And another thing that gets my attention is the fact that he's always here when something big happens. When I get in major trouble, he's here. When Dad and I have a disagreement, Adam sits and observes. Faith might be on to something.

"Ireland! Adam tells me he caught you coming back from another level. What were you doing, young lady?" Dad stares at me, waiting for me to answer. He tries so hard to be stern with me, but his nature doesn't allow too much room for that.

Lying to my dad is not something I want to do. Unfortunately, it is my only option. I will not tattle on Faith or Tim. "Well, Dad, I don't know! I got bored and thought I would go out and walk the staircase. I went up and down the stairs for a while. That's it. I couldn't sleep," I try to explain.

Dad walks right up to me and places his hands on my crossed arms. "You know you can't do it. You can't. If you don't understand or won't listen to me, then something bad will happen to you. We are lucky yet again Adam was here." Dad shifts his body toward his friend. "Why are you here at this hour? Have you heard news?"

Adam comes from the shadows and shakes his head, saddened. "Yes, there is news. Ireland will have to finish this test. That boy must be apprehended by the right enforcement. The higher authority feels as though she will fail, and therefore, they will see that she isn't capable of completing the requirements to get her wings here. It will be another step in outing her for sure. Especially since they are already so keen on doing that."

Dad runs his fingers through his hair. "She cannot go and do that! This is a setup. A trap. And you know it. Can't you talk to them?"

Dad doesn't see things the way I see them. They know full well what they are doing to me. And since

Faith already warned me earlier, I wait for Adam to answer my father.

"Benjamin, she has to go. There is no way around it."

"No." Dad shakes his head. "She will not go down there again and be ... be persuaded by that boy."

Adam sighs. "Then, my friend, you have doomed her. Don't you want her to go and try to succeed? If she doesn't go, they will mark her and send her down there anyway. Her chance to stay depends on that test."

"Dad"—I tug at his arm to get him to listen to me—"I can do this. He got in my head before, it's true. But he won't do it again. I am strong enough to pass. This is what the higher authority has always wanted ... to get rid of me. I won't let them."

Adam smiles and nods his approval at me. I stare at him for a second before saying, "Adam, I think you can go now. I mean, you don't have anything else to share? We need some time alone."

"I must insist on staying," Adam says with more authority. He's used to people giving him what he wants when he wants it. I guess that would serve for higher-up angels who have a lot to lose. Here, it doesn't mean much to me. I respect him for being around for Dad and me, but Faith has put doubt in my mind.

"No. Ireland is right. If the higher authority wants her to go to Earth in the morning, then so be it. Leave us for tonight." Dad walks over to the door and opens it, indicating that Adam's stay has come to an end. "We need this time. Alone."

Adam lets out a small grunt, picks up his box, and walks toward the door. "I will be waiting for your return." His eyes find mine. "Don't get too comfortable down there. You might find that you enjoy it too much." He walks out the door, and Dad closes it behind him.

I wait for Dad to say something. Anything. It takes minutes for him to speak up. "Ireland, I don't know what you were doing out there tonight, and at the moment, I don't care. Before you go, we need to talk. Really talk, child. The higher authority wants to put you in danger. That much has always been true. I fear this time, they will succeed in what they want. You know nothing of the outside world. You know nothing about demons, although it is part of who you are."

"I do know a few things. After all, like you said, I am part demon." I want to argue with him.

Dad shakes his head and points to the couch. "Sit, and I'm doing the talking right now." He places his fingers to his lips, a sign he is thinking about the past.

I oblige and sit down, waiting for him to say something.

"You think you know ... you don't. You said that the boy was at least part demon, yes?"

The boy. Greve. I shiver just thinking about him. "He is half demon, if not more," I agree.

"He sounds like your mother. Obviously, he runs fast, as you said before. He has mind control, although not full control of you. Thank your mother for that. What's his weakness, Ireland? Tell me. Do you know?"

"No," I mutter.

"Your mother's weakness was always water. Don't ask because I don't know why. Water seemed to suck the life right out of her. It takes time, though. Don't even try to get him with water as your only source because it is too time-consuming."

Water? Mom's one thing that made her recoil was water? "That's not possible. Gabriella dropped me in the lake, and I felt fine. Shouldn't water affect me too?"

Dad paces the floor in front of me. "It might have more effect once you've been out of this place longer. That happened when you came down from the drop-off. Then again, you might have gotten lucky, and water won't affect you as much. Use caution. Also, demons survive on raw emotions. Fear. Pain. Anger. Lust. Envy. All those negative feelings are what really gives them their power. Perhaps, again it may you too, but I hope not. Mom was always good to me. To other people, she was not."

"Okay." I make a mental note. "Watch out for water and negative emotions. Oh, and I can't forget the mind control issue."

Dad looks at me with concern. "Don't do that. Not now. Stop with the sarcasm and be serious."

"Sorry, Dad. Just trying to make light of the situation."

"There's nothing light about it. He may know our weakness. He may know exactly how to get into your head. You are a hybrid. A special type of breed and not everyone will be so willing to sit back and watch you live. You are fast healing. You have your own mind control, among other things. Think about that. Think before you act. Look around at everyone. I feel like there's more out there to worry about than this boy."

I look up at him to see a face I've never really seen before. Fear and sorrow etches in between the lines of his eyes. He's terrified. "I will keep in mind everything you say, Dad. I promise."

Dad nods for a minute while all his thoughts and memories swirl behind his eyes. He's remembering something else. "Don't fall in love, Ireland. If you do, you won't come back to me."

"You fell in love and came back here."

"Times were different then. They changed right after I came back with you. The higher authority saw me as the ultimate betrayer and you—a hybrid—as the result of what I'd done. Which I guess you are. But they don't see you as I do. You are *mine*. They see you and all the others like you as nothing more than a problem ... a nuisance. You are a liability. Do you understand what I am saying? If you make one big mistake down there, it will be enough to condemn you forever."

Tears well in my eyes at what he is saying. The higher authority has found a way to get even with the ones that betrayed the biggest rule of all ... having children with outsiders. The angels get stripped of titles and their wings. Then the higher authority waits until the proper time to condemn their hybrid children. That's the ultimate punishment. They don't care that the children suffer. All they care about is seeing their parents—the oath breakers—live a life without any gain whatsoever.

"They are going to kill me," I conclude. "They will kill me even if I pass this test. If not, they will send me away. We won't ever be able to be together again." This time the tears do come. They flow down my hot cheeks in pools, and before long, I break into gut-wrenching sobs.

Dad takes me in his arms. "I won't let it happen. Not to you, I won't. Adam has got to know something about all this. He's been on the higher authority since I came back with you. Maybe I should talk to him again and see what he says."

"No!" My arms pull Dad even tighter. "Promise me that you will not talk to him about this. I don't trust him. Don't go to him. While I'm gone, talk to Faith. Talk to Tim. Please don't go to Adam."

"You mean for me to go to that girl who came to see you the other day? Why?"

"Because that's who I went to see tonight. She's a hybrid like me and she knows things you may not know."

That got Dad's attention. He breaks free of my hold on him. "She came to talk to you because she's a hybrid?"

"Yes. Half human. Half angel. Her mother is … well, I would assume dead. And her father is on Earth. Trust me and talk to her. Tim's okay too. He's the guard, remember?"

"Yes. I know who he is." Poor Dad looks like he is going to burst at the seams. He's in shock.

"I wanted to tell you. I'm sure I would have before long. Now, that we have talked, it's good that Faith came to me when she did. Our time is up. I'm leaving in the morning, and we have no way to stop it."

Dad hugs me again and holds me, grasping my back desperately. "Come back to me, Ireland. Prove them wrong."

I squeeze him back. "I will."

⁂

My hair is draped in front of my face when I wake. This is it. The morning I go back to face him. My stomach flutters at the thought. Part of me is excited. I get to see *Greve* again. It's stupid of me, I know, but we have a connection I can't explain. He terrifies me. He also excites me. He brings out my other side, quite literally. The demon in me wants to come out a little for once.

I get up and look in the mirror. Old habits die hard. There were no wings magically placed on my back in the night. I shrug and then get dressed in black jeans and a cream V-neck shirt. My red hair will flow freely today. I will no longer hide who I am. In my closet, there is an old backpack. I will take that, too, just in case. No one said I couldn't.

Dad opens my door in silence. He doesn't know what to say to me. In a way, I don't know what to say either. We walk hand in hand to the front door, and he waits for me while I put my sneakers on. We will have to part here because I will walk to the drop-off alone.

"This isn't goodbye," I say trying to be stronger than I feel.

Dad hugs me again. "No, you are right. This is a new beginning."

Chapter Twelve

Ireland

Deep sadness overcomes me as I walk up the stairs to the next level. Tears flow so freely that I have to stop midway up to wipe my face. I may never see Dad again. My heart breaks and my lungs constrict at the thought of never seeing him for the rest of my life. Is this what Dad felt when he had to leave my mother? Did he feel the instant sorrow that seeps through your body, restricting your heart and lungs so that you feel like you can't even function? He must have, because he loved her once. It is a different type of love they felt, but it can cause the same devastation.

"Ireland? Are you okay?" Tim's voice registers from the top of the stairs. He is being made to escort me to the cafeteria first and then to the drop-off. Apparently, I am not allowed to walk alone anymore.

"Not really." I quickly wipe the tears from my cheeks. My lips pull into a strained smile.

Tim walks down to meet me. He holds out his hand to me. "The pain you are feeling, use it as a driving force. Prove to them that they cannot affect you. Otherwise, you know good and well that Gabriella and some of the others will eat you alive."

"Yes, you're right." I make myself take his hand. He pulls me up and pats my back. Then he goes back to the sullen Tim I've always known. He's trying to keep up his act so that people won't question his behavior. After he turns to go back up the stairs, I wipe my face with my shirt sleeve and adjust my hair, trying to make it seem like nothing is out of place. I follow his lead to the cafeteria.

Smiles follow me all the way up. Some angels say things of encouragement while others offer fake pats and hugs. I've been the talk of the place, it seems. Everyone knows what I must do and very few believe I can do it. They don't believe I will make it back, and that's why they feel like they should be nice for once. No one ignores me as I walk. All angels go by the motto, "That's what good angels do." I guess in their mind, they are doing the right thing. Now that I know the truth about what happens to hybrids in this place, I find it hard to believe all are innocent and that naïve.

But in order to not draw any more attention to myself, I play along. It's not until Tim and I reach the cafeteria that I feel a little sense of relief.

"Faith cannot speak to you," Tim whispers so low I can barely hear him. He hands me a small wooden box lacking in detail. "Put this in your bag and keep it safe. This is not to be opened until you really need it. Think of it as a backup plan for your sanity. This box is a gift that can only be opened by you. It is for *you*. And it will only open when you need it the most."

I nod and gently place it in my hand. The box takes up only about half of my palm. I quickly drop it into my bag and nod a thanks to the guy I've always known as my stuck-up staircase guard. He smiles and motions for me to move along. He will wait for me outside.

The door opens as I put my hand on the handle. Several of my classmates are walking out, already done with breakfast. Faith is one of them. She walks slowly, catching my eye. We hold our stares for a second before she looks away and walks toward the drop-off. Crap. My little breakdown earlier put me behind. Everyone is starting to leave. I walk through the door, determined to snatch a few things to put in my bag. I figure they won't say anything if Tim gave me that box to put in my bag. He and Faith must know they won't search me today. Probably has something to do with their confidence I won't be back.

Apples, walnuts, and chocolate catch my eye from the higher-level tables. If only I could get away with having some of that food before I leave. I casually glance at my level table, and the food almost makes me gag. Bowls of slimy noodles and dried-up bread fill that table. I walk over to my table and carefully place the bread in my pack, trying to not look so noticeable. Then I walk to the other table, and when no one is paying attention, I snatch a couple of apples and walnuts and three bars of chocolate and put them in my bag. What are they really going to threaten me with? They think I'm not coming back anyway.

Tim looks at me and shakes his head. He's seen me. I smile back at him and make my way toward him so that he can finish his task of dropping me off.

When I come out of the door, he walks ahead of me without saying anything. We follow the same slow movements until we finally reach the entryway to the drop-off. "This is where we part. Good luck," he whispers. Tim gives a quick nod to the guard and turns to leave.

The guard won't even look at me directly. "Arm," he demands with his own hand outstretched toward me. Here's the part where they start monitoring us again. Down to Earth we go and so the recording begins ...

I give him my arm while looking directly at him. They don't scare me anymore. There's only one option I have now, and I refuse to let any of them see the pain they have already caused me and my family.

The guard scans me for what seems like the thousandth time. The familiar dings start in my head, marking the task ahead of me. He pushes me through the gate with indifference.

My classmates all stare at me as soon as I walk through. Mrs. Craven looks at me as if she can't believe I'm standing here. *So sorry to disappoint you, Mrs. Craven.* All my classmates are standing around the drop-off, waiting for Mrs. Craven to begin assigning our missions. I walk up to the only open space available, which happens to be next to Gabriella. Even if I can't stand Gabriella, she did get me out of Greve's grasp last time. She could have left me there. This time she probably will if given the chance. I can tell by her face she is thinking the same thing. Her lips pout at some morbid thought in her head.

"Ireland," Mrs. Craven's voice snags in her throat. She clears it. "Do I need to tell you your assignment?" Her voice is brash with no amount of sympathy.

"No, Mrs. Craven. I understand what must be done," I reply with as much confidence as I can.

Mrs. Craven nods. "Good. Then let me get you your escort, and you can be on your way. He should be here soon."

He? Faith's eyes catch mine, and she gives me a look of warning. See you soon, she mouths at me. When I take my eyes off hers, I see him. Adam. I can't believe it! Surely he is not going to be my escort.

Adam's walk says everything. He struts along right up to me and smiles. He says something to Mrs. Craven I can't quite make out before turning back to me.

"Your dad requested that it be me dropping you off. Of course, I said yes. Never could say no to your father," he whispers only to me. There's a spark in his eyes that I've never seen before.

"Umm ... thanks," I manage to get out. The one thing I ask of him, and he goes straight to the man I told him not to trust.

"Shall we go?" Adam turns toward Mrs. Craven, asking for permission.

"Of course, dear." Mrs. Craven bats her eyelashes at him.

Adam doesn't seem to notice. He takes my hand. "Tell your friends goodbye," he says to me.

This isn't goodbye. Not to me. "See you guys later." I clench his hand tighter so he won't lose his grasp on me, and together we jump off the drop-off.

Chapter Thirteen

Greve

The call came in at two in the morning. "She will be there mid-morning," the male voice announces on the line. "Meet her as soon as she lands and take her by surprise." I never knew one little call could bring me so much relief.

Life is boring without someone to torment. Ireland will be my toughest case yet. All the others were so easy to turn. The other captures just accepted the fact that their demon genetics were always meant to be the dominant trait. And after the demon part stayed, I sent them on their angry way to become part of the solution for the human race, instead of part of the problem.

I will do it again even if it takes me longer. Nothing would satisfy me more than to see the angel trait completely disappear from Ireland Grace. The award for accomplishing her "restructure" will give me exactly what I need to move on with my own life.

So, here I am, standing on the corner of London Avenue and High Street, waiting to see my hybrid's silhouette appear in the clouds. I smirk at all the humans who pass me. If they only knew what I was capable of ... I chuckle to myself. Even though I've lost count of how many humans I've killed, I will never lose count of how many hybrids I've restructured. They are my specialty, after all.

The sound of birds flying overhead gets my attention. They are moving fast—as if something is coming down on them. I glare up at the clouds, watching and waiting because I know she will be here within a few minutes. My fingers flex, and I tap my jaw line in anticipation.

A bird comes down on me out of nowhere, squawking and clawing at my face and hair. I grab it while cursing to get it off of me, but before I can get it out of my hands, it pecks me and dives off, only looking back at me in disgust. Damn. Now my face is bleeding, and people are starting to look at me.

Heat starts behind my eyes, slowly turning them red. It's an unfortunate trait for demons, but considering it causes the humans to back off, it's worth accepting. All it takes are a few glances at the humans, and they all start to avoid me again.

The clouds shift over the sun, causing me to look up again. This time I do see a familiar shape ... it's going in the wrong direction. A man with wings starts ascending back into the clouds, high above the city.

An angel ... her angel ... her escort! The bird must have been a distraction so that I couldn't see her landing. And it was quite possibly a distraction for the humans so that they wouldn't catch someone dropping from the air.

Hell. Before I can scan the area for her, I feel eyes on me. My body shifts to where I feel the connection. She's behind a brick building to my right, her head reaching from behind the wall to look directly at me. Ireland has a look of sheer determination. The girl is not scared of me. All the others were terrified. All she does is tilt her head to the side, as if asking me to come to her. And for the first time in my life, I feel the pull of a command making me step closer to her.

She smiles in satisfaction. When she smiles, it breaks her hold on me. The will to step closer fades, but not the emotion I feel. Ireland Grace is playing with me. She's taunting me, and I *like* it.

Her red hair is flowing past her shoulders the next time I focus on her. She's running away, weaving through traffic and stores, causing too much distraction. Maybe that is what she wants because she knows already she can't outrun me. As long as she doesn't get into another car, I will get her. If she finds another car, things will be more interesting just like before. I don't feel like getting pinned under a car again.

My legs take off, running on their own command. I guess they didn't like the sensation of being pinned under a vehicle either. So, here we are—hunter and prey—playing who can catch the other first. The prize for winning the game means more to her than to me. I'm told she will get wings, so that makes her more desperate. This is a paycheck for me, a way to live. My bosses need me for the overall scheme they are planning. No one in heaven needs her more than me.

With every step, I gain ground. Her breathing is labored with the effort of running from me. Humans stop to gawk at us, clearly trying to decide whether to intervene or not. Ireland makes the call for them when she shouts loudly and in desperation, "He's trying to kill me!" It's her tone that gets the humans to react. Her voice is shrill and breathless, echoing, and portraying years of endless violence and terror. She's a good little actress.

A burly man in his mid-forties with white spiked hair comes to her rescue. He cuts in front of me and knocks me to the ground in one swift motion. My ass skates across the pavement while Ireland looks back at me before running off through the crowds. The guy grabs me by my shoulders and lifts me up so that my toes don't touch this ground.

"You might want to put me down," I mouth at him in warning. As big as he is, I can still break him like a twig. He seems to realize that I am no human because he lets go of me as quick as he touched me. "Get out of my way," I say, voicing with the authority of a guy twice as big as I am. After a second, he listens and scoots over to let me pass. To ensure that no one else follows, I make an example of him.

His body falls flat against the pavement as my fists pound his face. Blood oozes out of his nose. The image would be chilling to humans. To me, it's welcomed. I have an immediate desire to get inside his head to feel exactly what he's thinking right now. His pain and agony. His confusion. His lousy pride. It all makes me hungry. He mumbles something, and that's when I stop. This is nothing but another distraction. The girl is getting farther away the longer I stay here.

"Follow me, and you will end up like him," I say to the growing crowd. They look at me with hushed voices and terrified faces. Someone calls the police on their phone, telling the line to hurry, that there's a monster of a man loose in the streets. I wonder if they would be so prone to protect her if they knew she was a lot like me.

The police sirens echo in the background, and I take off, sprinting down the road before more people take up my time. Ireland's scent tickles my nose as I run by the places she's been. Warmth from the sun and lavender flow through my nose and throat, making me cough. Her scent is strong, but the lavender isn't cutting it. It's too sweet, too calming. Too much angel and not enough demon.

The farther I go, the stronger the aroma becomes. She's close. So close that I can almost *taste* her. "Come out, sweetling. I know you're out there." Her feet shift from somewhere in front of me. "I can smell you a mile away. My body can run for days. You cannot. There's no other place to go than to me." She doesn't respond. At least not in words. Her movements are slow. Her heart is beating too fast to keep up her pace. My eyes lock in on a building a few feet ahead of me. She's there, trying to hold in her desire to take off again. I keep talking while moving in close to her hiding spot. "We will have fun, you and I. You making me come to you for a second back there was thrilling. Perhaps we will work on your skill …"

The wind blows her hair within reach of me. I ease up slowly to touch her. This is what I've been waiting for. Now that I've seen her again, all I want to do is feel her. I tell myself that it's always been like this … the desire to convert an angel over fills me with longing. But I'm not so sure if I remember wanting anything as bad as I want her.

Chapter Fourteen

Ireland

The demon caught up with me. I knew it wouldn't take long, but I had to see what I was capable of. It felt great to control him, even if it was only for a few seconds. And since I was able to, it allowed me to piece together one important question—he is not all demon. If he was, then I wouldn't be able to control him at all, which means he's got some human in him. Maybe only a small percentage. Still, it relaxes me slightly.

He moves his head to the side, as if speculating how to touch me. He stretches out his hand toward me, silent. His eyes stare into mine, and for a moment, I can see a little red in them. I ignore his hand and step a few inches back from him.

"Did you see what happened back there?" he asks while leaning against the brick wall. He must be sure I won't run again.

"Are you talking about the bird landing on your head?" I ask him that even though I know he's referring to the man he beat up.

A small smile plays on his lips. "Funny. No, actually, I was referring to the man back there. If you're not careful, that could be you."

"If you wanted to kill me you would have done it already. Clearly, I'm worth more alive, wouldn't you say?"

He eyes me from my head to my feet. "Oh, yes. Definitely worth more alive."

My cheeks start to burn. The way he looks at me is unnerving. I wonder if I ever looked at someone like that before. "What do you want from me?"

Greve moves closer to me. The beeping that was once in my head is no longer there. The higher authority wouldn't dare give me any advantages.

I take a few more steps back, not realizing I've backed myself into the other wall.

Greve moves closer to me until he's inches from my face. "There's quite a bit that I want from you, but I am forbidden to do many of those acts. My boss or manager ... whatever ... wants you. And he gets what he wants, even if it's my death. If you do what I ask, you won't have to die either."

I nod like I accept what he is saying. "And when are you going to take me to him?"

"When you are ready to meet the boss, I will know. Right now, you are nowhere near what they want you to be." Greve backs away from me. His eyes never leave my face. "You will come with me. No running away this time," his voice is commanding and smooth.

His words flow through me and melt in the process. I try to block him out, to make his words mean nothing.

He repeats himself. "You will come with me, Ireland. No running away."

This time, I stop trying to ignore his commands and give in. My body is worn out from the flight down and running. When I'm stronger, I will be able to fight back.

Greve's control on me lifts as we enter his apartment building above a clothes shop. One minute, I'm focused on only walking wherever Greve is going, and then the next, everything goes back to normal. It's like he snapped his fingers, and his control slipped away.

Greve pauses to look at me before closing and locking the door behind me. "Make yourself at home. You will be here for a while."

"Why are you being decent toward me?"

Greve lets out a sigh. "If I didn't know any better, I would think you like to flirt on the wild side."

"No, all I want is to see you in jail for those robberies so that I can get my wings and help my father."

He laughs at me. It's a cold, menacing laugh. "Those feathers will never make it onto your back." He really is cocky.

"Time will tell."

"Oh, yes. In due time, the only thing you are going to want is to be around the humans for their emotions. Tell me … have you ever used them? Have you ever sucked their terrible feelings out from under them?" Greve turns his back on me to pull the blinds closed on the two windows in the living room. "It's something you will experience, that I can promise you."

I stare into his back, secretly wanting to run out the door. "You do this to everyone for a job?"

Greve walks toward me, staring intently. "No, I only do this to hybrids. More specifically, demon hybrids, lucky you. Blame your mother. Bottle it up … lash out at her … whatever. I don't care how you deal with things. All I care about is the angel part of you disappearing. The longer you try to avoid that, the harder it will be on you. I was a little scary before, I admit. But I don't have to be." He places his hand on my face. His fingers rub just underneath my eyes.

I turn my head away, rejecting him. "Yeah, well, stop trying to act like you care. Why should I even go along with this?"

Greve walks to the fireplace to poke it before turning back to me. Whatever was in his eyes moments ago is gone. Now, there is only that all too familiar spark of red. It engulfs his eyes, slowly turning them the color of blood. He takes my arm, and his eyes shift to the bar code lightly sketched across my wrist. Greve's eyes linger on it for a moment before pulling me with him to the fireplace. His arms flex with strength. He is too strong for me to break free.

"If you don't, your father will die. Your friends ... everyone you know and love will parish. People you don't even know will die. More hybrids in heaven and more humans on Earth ... the innocents ... all of them will never be able to live. And it won't be me doing it. It will be the ones I answer to. So, do me a favor and go along and pretend things will be okay, alright?"

Before I can answer, he forces my hand into the fire and holds it there with a look of sheer determination.

Chapter Fifteen

Greve

The heat feels so good I don't notice Ireland's face when I stick her hand in the fire. She screams and tries to pull her hand away from mine. This has to be done. The bar code must be destroyed.

"The heat can feel good to you too. You just need to embrace it," I murmur to her while focusing on the flames.

"You're crazy!" she screams again, less urgently.

Her skin stays spotless except for the skin that houses the bar code. It slowly starts to shrivel under the heat of the flames. Ireland looks in disbelief that her hand and arm haven't caught fire or that the flames haven't caused any burns.

She breathes in and out, glaring right at me. "What are you doing?!"

"Killing the link to your world. With this code thing gone, they can no longer track you. I don't want any unannounced martyrs coming to your rescue." My fingers rub the spot where the code used to be. The fire ate it all away, and Ireland's skin is still as smooth as it was prior to getting into the flames. She flinches away from my touch.

"Tell me what you feel," I order while keeping a firm hold on her. Our arms are linked together in the flames. The heat makes my body come alive. It brings power to my veins ... making my body so eager to enjoy it.

She looks at her hand and then back at me. "I don't know what to feel. I feel like I hate you."

"Hate is a strong word and emotion. Good. But I meant, what do you feel in regard to the fire?"

"It doesn't hurt," Ireland says in surprise. "I mean ... it doesn't feel great either. It just is a little uncomfortable."

"Go on. Tell me more," I say in no more than a whisper. She has to concentrate on what is happening.

"One minute, I feel strong, like someone gave me a jolt of energy. But then, the next minute, I feel the opposite. Like part of my body is working against itself." Ireland seems surprised that she has even spoken to me about it. Her face shows that she's curious. She's also terrified.

"Get closer to it," I order.

She looks at me, startled. "No! Let me go!"

"No disagreeing," I warn. Her hand grabs mine tight. I pull her close until she has no choice but to look me in the eyes. My chest touches hers, and that is when I feel her heartbeat against my ribs. So fast. So urgent.

"Put your whole arm in the fire and focus. Focus on the heat. It will force your body to work hard on bringing the demon part out of you."

Her eyes go slack after my command, and she puts her arm completely in the fire without another word.

I nod my head in approval. "Good. Now, keep it there." With her arm completely in the fire, she turns her head toward me, afraid to get her face any closer to the flames. My arm joins hers in the fireplace, eager to not miss out on the fun.

Our skin touches and combines as the flames lick our skin. I tingle. For Ireland, it is a new sensation altogether. Her face shows concentration as she bites down on her lower lip. I'm not sure if she's counting the minutes hoping for it to end or if she's trying her best not to show how good it feels. Demons need and crave the fire. It brings us back to where we belong—in an endless circle of flame and pure heat.

Minutes pass by in a blur. My senses are heightened. My visions are stronger. The thoughts of every human I've ever talked to fill me. Even the cop I came in contact with days before comes to mind. Every horror and sadness. Each time they've had extreme lust or failure, every single negative thing that's ever happened to them does good for me. I am opened up and ready to ingest it all.

Ireland's arm moves slightly as she starts to see what I see. We are connected in this moment. She has nothing but good things to share and that is to be expected. Before long, she will have her own human experiences to add to mine. Our skin tingles together, making her flustered.

I smile a convincing smile at her. "Let it go and open up to it."

She shakes her head, terrified. I remember the first time this happened to me. My mother's own sadness filled my head, shining in front of my eyes. Her pain of losing me and my father was too much for her. For a while, it was too much for me to bear. Then, my father showed me how to use her pain for our needs. We are demons, he told me. I was to never see her again because of the way demons live. I cried for days, maybe even months. However, in time, my human thoughts and emotions went away, and they were replaced with what demons long for.

Ireland is experiencing what I did in a different way. Her eyes shine with the tears of knowing she can never be the same as she was before. She never will be what her father is. Demons are not meant to be any-where else but where we are stationed. Our lives are not free. Our lives are meant to be handled by others. It's not fair to be sure. Life's not fair though. Not to humans. Not to demons. Not to anybody.

I look at Ireland again to see how she's handling the new experience of being freed by fire. Her mouth is frozen shut, as if she's scared the emotions and feel-ings she feels from me will invade her body. That's not so. It's all in her mind. She has to see that she cannot be afraid of the fire. Her demon blood will protect her. The only way to show her is to take drastic measures. So, I place my hand on her back and forcibly push her upper body into the fire, head and all.

She screams and wiggles, trying to free herself. I hold her, determined to make her see that the flames will not harm her. After a few seconds, her screams stop, and her movements slow. She breathes in deep and strong, finally letting the smoke and heat sur-round her. Her body and hair are untouched. Call it magic from the blood or call it a curse, but regardless she is unscathed. Her shirt, on the other hand, is an-other matter entirely.

The fabric burns and turns to ash in less time than it took for her to calm down. The fire welcomes her bare skin in unison as if it has found some long-lost love. The tips of the flames surround her chest and face as if it licks and kisses something more beautiful than itself. Her demon blood has finally found its place.

I let go of her and draw back, careful to make sure Ireland realizes it is not me holding her in the fire any longer. Once, she understands I am no longer holding her, she rises out of the fireplace. Goosebumps appear on her arms and chest from the drastic temperature change of hot to cold. Her shirt is gone, only soot and ash remain. My eyes rise from looking at the ash and soot to the sour expression on her face.

"You could have killed me!" she yells, accusing me.

I roll my eyes at her. "No, I knew you wouldn't be harmed."

"I bet you did, but I didn't!" Ireland moves fast, and before I know it, she whacks me hard across the face.

I stand back away from her, stunned that a half-naked girl just slapped me. So much for the angel part of her being modest. I wonder if she has even connected that her shirt has turned to ash.

"You hit me before you put another shirt on. I guess the fire did wake up your inner demon." I smirk at her as she realizes her chest is bare.

Her face turns solid red as she tries to cover herself with the backpack she placed on the floor when she walked in. "You should have told me."

"When? While you were slapping me across the face?" I laugh at her pained expression.

"I'm not sorry."

"Good. Don't be. You will learn to control yourself, Ireland."

Her nostrils flare. "I know how to control myself!"

"No, you don't. You're high off the flames. You're high off the power it gave you. Right now is the best time to move forward with this whole process." I look at her and see the red behind her eyes. Her nails have grown at least two inches while in the fire. Her red hair shines more brightly. All ways to know her demon blood is strong.

"I'm not going anywhere." She looks at me, determined.

"Oh, yes, you are," I murmur, trying to get her to calm down. "We are going out tonight. You're going to get a shirt of mine." I take her hand and lead her to the bedroom. I pull out a basic blue t-shirt and hand it to her. "After you put that on, we are going downstairs to that women's dress store to get some clothes."

She takes the shirt from me but still doesn't put it on. She's waiting on me to finish.

"Then, we will come back, get all dressed up like you women like and head out." I smile at her while waiting on a response.

She turns her back to me and puts her bag down on my bed. "I'm not like other girls." She slips my shirt on and faces me again.

I walk up to her, closing the gap between us. "Clearly," I whisper, hoping to make her recoil. She doesn't. In fact, she continues to stare at me, eyes dilated, until I'm the first one to look away.

Chapter Sixteen

Ireland

He's a nutter, I think to myself as we both head downstairs to the clothes shop. First, he shoves my hand in the fire and then my head! Obviously, he knew I wouldn't be harmed ... I try to make reason of it all. What scares me the most is the fact that he is right. I *do* feel different. Besides my outer appearance changing slightly, the inside of me feels strange. One minute, I'm dizzy and tired. The next moment, my heart hammers out of my chest, shooting adrenaline through my veins.

Is this what I am supposed to feel like as a hybrid? That my body is fighting against itself, the demon and angel sides hating each other, struggling to connect to the fact that it is supposed to work in unison? If so, I want no part of it. Bodies are not meant for inner turmoil, least of all angel bodies. We are not supposed to feel pain or weakness in heaven. But I guess I'm not like them up there. I am me. The angel who is also something frowned upon. They don't believe I have a place around them. Hybrids, to them, are nothing more than a problem. The result of a mistake. Maybe I would have a better life without them.

The doorbell clangs as Greve opens the door for me. "After you," Greve waves me through.

We made it down to the store without me realizing it. "Thanks," I mutter, sullen. The workers take one look at me and wince. Do I really look that bad?

Eventually one of the workers comes forward after realizing I'm not leaving. "May I help you?" she asks, trying to smile. The woman has blonde hair tossed up like a beehive on top of her head and blue eye shadow across her eyelids.

"No," Greve answers for me while sifting through shirts on a nearby rack.

My head swivels around, glaring. "I can answer for myself, thank you."

The woman gives us a look and shakes her head before leaving us.

"Is that so?" Greve asks after the woman is out of hearing range.

I walk over to a rack that's full of summer attire and start sorting through them. "Yes, I do believe the woman was talking to me. I can handle it."

Greve follows from behind and glances at the selections I've chosen so far. He rolls his eyes and pretends to gag at the beige cotton dress that falls below my knees and a gray silk skirt I have secured around my arm. "These aren't going to work. I know you are from drabville and all, but we are working toward your inner ruthless genetics and behavior, right? You can do better than those." He holds his stare for a moment, daring me to argue in front of the workers.

"I am not a slut," I announce a little too loudly. The workers glance our way again, not daring to look at me directly. My cheeks begin to grow hot.

Greve looks at me, serious, before a small smile plays on his lips. "You have a colorful vocabulary for someone destined to be white and glorious."

"I've been around humans enough to pick up a few choice words. Shall I tell you some more?"

Greve takes the clothes I have picked out and places them back gently on the rack. "I admit that I am liking this more ... outspoken you. However, instead of giving me lessons about how the human race speaks, I am more interested in your mind-controlling ability since you've dabbled in the flames."

"What are you talking about?" I ask while walking over to another rack. This one has more formal attire. A soft emerald-green strapless dress catches my eye. I pull it from the rack and hold it up next to my body. The material falls right down to my thighs.

Greve looks at the dress and gives me a nod of approval. "The answer to your question is simple. Once you get done picking out what you want, you will take it and walk right out of the store."

My stomach lurches. "No," I whisper, not wanting to drive attention to myself again.

Greve takes the dress out of my hand and then pulls me toward the dressing room. His eyes make contact with mine. "No back talking. You've got to try this on first anyway. Make sure it's perfect, but I don't want to see it. Not yet."

Suddenly, I feel the familiar pull of a command. His words circle my brain, enclosing it. All that's left is what he just told me to do. At this moment, nothing else matters. "Okay," I mutter. He smiles, guides me into the dressing room, and closes the door behind me. Then the dress comes over the top for me to catch. The hanger pops me on the head, sending pain through my skull. The pain releases Greve's words away, leaving the area in my head with fog. For a second, I forget what I'm supposed to do, but it all comes flooding back. The dress has fallen off the hanger, only to land by my feet.

He wants me to try it on, I remember now. He wants me to steal it. My heart hammers in my chest. My arm extends to pick the dress off the floor. The soft material caresses my hand as if I'm calling out to it.

I pull off Greve's shirt and my pants and put them on the bench. I extend my arms and pull the dress over me. When it's in place, I tug at the bottom, not satisfied with the length. The dress hugs me, perhaps too tightly across my chest and legs. I shiver, cold from how thin the material is.

My reflection shows ash and soot across my collar bone and all across my back. He just had to put me all the way in that fire. My eyes zero in on the place where my wings should be. My shoulder blades look abandoned, as if a body part could ever feel that way. I bite my lip. Maybe it's not my shoulders feeling that way. Maybe it's me.

The dress's green color catches my attention. It really goes great with my hair and skin. For the first time in my life, I feel beautiful. And for the first time in my life, I don't have to feel ashamed because I am different.

Satisfied, I pull the dress off and place it back on the hanger. After I'm back in my regular clothes, I open the door, holding the dress in hand.

"How did that work for you?" The saleswoman smiles up at me from behind the counter.

"Great. We'll take it." I smile back at her while walking up to place the dress on the counter.

Greve silently walks up behind me.

"Anything else?" she asks me, trying to be polite when she just wants me to leave.

"We aren't done yet," Greve interrupts. "If you would be so kind as to hold onto it for us, we won't be too much longer." He takes my arm again and pulls me away. His touch sends heat through me.

"You need more than a dress. Pick out some jeans and shirts first, and then you will do what I said."

The heat Greve sent through my arm arrives at my face. "Fine," I spit out. I take an assortment of shirts and jeans, not bothering to look at much of anything aside from the size. I place them gently on the counter, trying hard not to scare the sales woman with my beet-red face and eyes.

She stares at the abundance of clothes and starts scanning them without saying anything. Greve comes up to me and places his hand on my back as a reminder of what he wants me to do.

I swallow and refuse to look at him. Sweat forms on my brow, and my nerves are on edge.

He leans in so that the sales lady can't hear what he is saying. "If you don't try out your mind control, I will hurt her." His breath is smooth and quiet, no more than a whisper. And yet, by the tone, I know he means it.

Do I fight this? Do I fight him? Honestly, the thought of doing something wrong terrifies me. The higher authority will find out, and then, my wings won't matter. But it probably won't matter anyway because they don't think I'm going to make it back to them. And it's not like Dad never did anything anti-angel, and he is a full angel.

Greve stares at me for a while, letting me sort this problem out in my head. For a minute, I glare right back at him. Maybe my eyes are trying to challenge him. Perhaps it's because I want to see what's behind his mask.

The sales lady clears her throat, trying to get my attention. I glance her way, and she's waiting on me to pay. The numbers on the register show two hundred fifty-three dollars. My heart sinks. That's a lot of money for me to steal and a lot of money this woman is going to lose.

Her hand stays planted on my pile of clothes while she waits for me. My hand reaches for hers and I lightly brush her skin. The contact is enough to get her to look at me. I take that opportunity to focus on only her. "The clothes have already been paid for. Please bag them for me. You will miscalculate your drawer tonight. Nothing is missing," I whisper. "Forget me," I add at the last second.

Her eyes fall to her hand and then she looks back at me confused. I smile sweetly, and say, "I was saying, ma'am, that you have such smooth hands."

"Thank you, dear," she responds while trying to smile back. Her hand hesitates over the clothes, and for a second, I fear that my mind control didn't work. Then she shakes her head, clearing her thoughts, and begins packing the clothes into the sales bag.

I take the bag and wave as Greve and I walk out of the store. My heart rate slips back into normal function as I climb the staircase to his apartment.

"You were exceptional," Greve says while climbing the steps behind me.

"Don't praise me for that," I spit out. "They will lose money because of us."

Greve sidesteps me to open the door. His arm brushes against my elbow, causing me to shiver. "And what of it? That woman will have to deal with it. That is what life is all about, isn't it? Shit comes at you, and you work through it." He steps through the doorway, leaving me outside.

His frank response leaves me hanging in the doorway. My feet carry me in the rest of the way, and I set the bags on the floor. "But we shouldn't be making her life harder by our actions."

Greve shrugs. "If we don't, someone else will. In case you haven't noticed, most humans are vile creatures."

"Not all of them," I argue. "I've helped a lot of them on my missions here. Besides, you're a demon. Humans can't be any worse than you."

Greve hikes up one eyebrow. "You really think so? I guess you will find out then, won't you?" The question comes out as a challenge.

"I'm not scared of you," I lie. Fear does come to me when Greve is around. I can't quite grasp what type of fear it is. Do I really fear that he will hurt me? Or do I fear the emotions that are coming out so strongly?

A low chuckle comes from deep within his throat. "It's not me you have to worry about. I would not hurt you even if I was commanded to. Hurting women is not my forte'. But that does not mean those people out there"—he puts out the window—"wouldn't hesitate. You are too naïve, Ireland. Not everyone is good. The sooner you realize that, the better off you will be."

"Perhaps ..." I trail off.

Greve walks up to me, demanding attention. "Perhaps nothing. You'll see that here, you have to watch out for yourself." His fingers lightly trace against my arm. He hesitates with the touch but doesn't seem to want to let go.

My breath becomes ragged. My thoughts become watered down. Is this his mind control? Is this my body's response to his touch all on its own? Everything is terrifying. His touch. My reaction to it. The demon part wants more. *I* want more.

"They are harmless," I mutter. My eyes fix on his. He has me completely with just one look. As his lips find my face, I can't help but wonder ... who will protect me against him?

Chapter
Seventeen

Greve

She did well down there. Ireland Grace made mind control look easy. Not one single mistake. The saleswoman complied with hardly any hesitation. I should be proud of her, and well ... I am. But still ... she's too good this early on.

Sounds of water from the shower fill my ears. I shudder. Ireland is in there getting cleaned up, and the water doesn't bother her at all. It will be my turn next, and I haven't quite figured out how to make sure she doesn't see how much water affects me. It is a weakness. My only weakness, and I intend on keeping it to myself.

After she got in the shower, I went down and got more wood out of the storage compartment that's under the stairs. The wood pops and cracks as the flames take it. Heat rises to fill the living room, and my breath catches in relief.

Even though my body can function fine without the flames nearby, the same can't be said for my mind. I've either got to be near fire or near raw emotions to function the way demons are supposed to. Otherwise, I guess I would become more human, like my mother. And since I'm part human, keeping the demon trait more prominent is difficult. If I slack, my father will know, and then things will turn ugly.

He hates me, I conclude. My father hates every one of his children aside from the ones that are full-blooded like him. That's how demons work. They use their half-bloods for whatever purpose they see fit. We all share the same fate, including Ireland. Her mother will see her eventually, and that will be that. She will be bound to her mother like I am with my father. It's unavoidable, and the best thing I can do for her is to get her ready for whatever task they will throw at her.

It's what I keep telling myself time and time again when I have to destroy the human or angelic side of someone. If it doesn't happen ... if the demons see that their child isn't evil enough or strong enough, they will kill them right then and there. I swallow the grief that's formed in my throat. It's happened only once since I've been doing this. One time, I couldn't get a girl prepared enough, and she died because of it. The girl's mother plunked her up and ate her right then and there in front of me. The demon said her daughter wasn't strong enough and that I hadn't gotten her prepared. That I *killed* her with the love I had shown her.

Her words still haunt me. I see the girl sometimes when I'm in the fire. Her last few moments play over and over in my head. The fear. The sorrow. Her mother's terrible laugh and my father's warning right after. He told me to never lose focus again, and especially not with a child of Jade.

Ireland clears her throat, breaking my thoughts. She stands in the doorway with a towel wrapped around her. Her red hair falls below her shoulders, and she's staring at me almost too intently. "Your turn," she says, making her way toward the newly acquired clothes.

I nod, still looking at her while trying to shake the feeling that she looks more familiar to me now than she did only moments before. I've tried to block out the girl who got killed. To completely forget what happened, what she looked like, and how she acted. But now it all comes flooding back to me. Ireland reminds me of that girl. It's like someone opened the flood gates that contain my memories. The images start slow, only to gain speed behind my eyes. Then they drown me with the realization of what's happening.

This is a test. Not just Ireland's test, but mine as well. My heart begins to pump faster, shooting adrenaline through me. He wants me to fail. This is Father's way of killing me off. He expects me to lose, to not have her ready ... to forget my task. One question will settle it for me. One question will let me know if what I fear is true. Who is Ireland's mother?

I clear my throat, trying to be calm. "Who's your mother, Ireland?"

Ireland pulls the green dress out of the clothes pile and stares at me. She answers as if the name makes no difference to her. "Some demon named Jade."

Chapter Eighteen

Ireland

Greve stares at me, all the color drained from his face. "Have you ever met her?" he asks me, no louder than a whisper.

"No, never. Why?"

He shrugs as if I've just given him the worst answer possible. "Nothing. It doesn't matter."

Greve leans over against the flames. He looks shattered and vulnerable for the first time since I met him. My legs carry me to him, and before I realize it, I'm sitting across from him in my towel. He barely notices me.

I don't know why I reach my hand out in comfort, but I do. "You know her, don't you? Did she hurt you? Will she hurt me? You know something, Greve."

He looks at me for the first time since I answered him. His eyes are dark red, shining with hatred. "Don't touch me. Go get ready because we are still going out tonight."

I flinch, somewhat scared of him. Then I remember his lips on my cheek only minutes ago. He leaned in, and I thought he was going to kiss me. I had hoped he would for some reason. Instead of landing on my lips, he landed on my cheek and lightly brushed up against me. It was a gentle moment, and because of that, I don't fear him. If he wanted to hurt me, he would have already. "If this is about my mother, I want to know," I say with as much authority as possible.

Greve waves his hand toward the bathroom, trying to get me to go away.

"I'm not leaving. Something about her name just about sent you over the edge. I need to know."

Greve laughs at me. It's a cold laugh, full of anguish. "Oh, you will find out eventually. We are nothing to them, you know that? *Nothing*. You should have stayed up there."

He carries on for a few more minutes while both mumbling and cursing incoherent sentences.

Not knowing what to do, I slowly back up to get away from him.

He smirks at me. "So, you are finally scared of me? What's more terrifying, Ireland? My eyes? My fear? Or is it the fact that you can *feel* my anguish?"

"All the above," I admit. Everything he is feeling, I feel too. It's all about closeness and vulnerability. For the first time, I understand what he means about taking the emotions of others for gain. My stomach turns in excitement. Once again, the dark part of me is shining through. His anger is my release.

Greve takes my hand and places it on his face. Beads of sweat emerge from his forehead. "Second lesson. Focus on what you want from me. What emotion makes you stronger? Is it my fear? Sadness? Anger? I know you want more. Get it from me."

My hand shakes from the contact. "I ... I don't want more. No! I don't want this!"

"Yes, you do. You want the power. It's understandable to want control. Control is necessary even for people like us. Our bodies crave it. We want to have a little taste of the control we aren't able to have in our own lives."

It's true even though I want to deny it. All of what Greve said is true. I've never been able to make my own decisions. Never have I been able to choose how I've wanted to live. It's always been someone else. The higher authority. Dad. Adam. Someone or something to prevent me from getting what my body craves. Right now, all I want is more ... more of the feeling that I can choose. That I can feel strong. And I'm learning just how demons get to exorcise what they crave. They take it.

My eyes connect with Greve's as we form a connection between our bodies. I'm peering into him, forcing his mind to give me what I want. He allows me to enter his thoughts. They swirl around me, swallowing me with the grief he feels.

There's a girl that he's thinking about. The girl has strawberry blonde hair and mismatched eyes. She has the same facial expression I often convey when I'm mad. We are similar, but then we are not. She's fragile and timid. Thin, but determined. The same task I finished downstairs, she cannot complete. Her mind control is off, and she knows it. Over and over again, she tries until she's no longer able to tell the human what to do. It's too confusing to her. Too forced. She will never be able to do what the demons want her to do. Then the girl smiles and hides her thoughts as a shadow comes around the corner. She's determined to not show how lost she really feels—

Suddenly, Greve pulls his hand away and forces me out of his head. I'm dizzy and breathless from the experience. My body is wired, like I just acquired a jolt of boundless energy. His mouth starts to move to produce an odd combination of words I can't quite make out.

Greve backs away from me to get closer to the flames while talking. "You fail. I pushed you back out before you received all I had to give. It's also better to focus on anger as the primary emotion you want from people."

"You told me I could choose what emotion I wanted from you." My voice is strained. "And I chose guilt."

Greve shifts his head around to look at me. "So you did. Find anything appealing floating around in my head?" Without waiting for me to answer, he dips his head and chest into the fire. It's the same position he put me in only hours before.

"As a matter of fact, some things did pique my interest a bit. The girl with strawberry blonde hair ... she was another one of your assignments?"

My hope for an answer fades because Greve has shut me off completely. The flames hold all his attention now. He wants to be surrounded by it, to feel encased by something stronger than him. For a moment, it starts to draw me in, too. I ease up to him and the flames, only to stop when the girl shines back behind my eyes. She's a part of his past he can't forget. We are connected somehow—the girl and I. Even if he hasn't told me, it's in plain sight. We favor each other ... if only by certain characteristics. So, what happened to her? Why is Greve building his wall back up to close me out?

I place my hand on his back to get his attention again. As soon as I do, his shirt dissolves from the combination of flame and touch. So much ash covers his back that when I pull my hand away, flakes of it fall at my feet.

He pulls himself out of the flames to face me. "Sooner or later, you will want more than what you have received. You're going to want more power. More freedom. If you stay with me and learn who the girl is ... you will lose what little freedom remains. There's no hiding from fate. It's a lesson the girl you saw had to learn, and unfortunately, she died before she could get a chance to prove her worth. If you don't want to end up like her, I suggest you become a little more focused on becoming more like your mother and less like your father." Greve's voice is quiet and stern.

"And since we are being all serious right now, I'm going to let you in on something else," he whispers.

I nod, hopeful I will get some new way to make sense of all this confusion.

"You need to know I am here for one purpose and that is to teach you to use your demon genetics in the way *they* want you to. What you want or what I want is irrelevant. I've had several assignments I've had to complete over the years. All of them for the same purpose. If you don't listen to what I need you to do, then there will be nothing I can do for you when the time comes to show the people who really matter. If you need to know something, I will tell you when you're ready. You are a project, Ireland. My assignment. I have no intention of furthering our relationship once the time has come to part ways. So when you feel some sort of inkling to know what's wrong with me, ignore it."

I force myself to look at him. Not just a glance, but to take him in and search what's on his mind. I look deep into his eyes and conclude he's told this speech hundreds of times before. His eyes show the repetition he feels. Same old assignment, new hybrid to fix.

I flush at the thought of only moments ago trying to comfort him. If I am only a project for him, I see no reason to offer any sort of conversation. "Only if you give me the same. If you stop being touchy with me, then I will stop asking questions. You say you want our relationship to stay as ... professional as possible, yet you have crossed the line more than once. It can't work both ways."

Silently, I'm battling in my head how I really want him to answer. I'm scared to be touched, and yet I like it. I've never known a boy that way. Any kind of basic contact was forbidden, especially with the lower-level individuals. I don't even know where the boy school is up there. Part of me wants to continue to see how far Greve will push me. Will he think my inexperience with boys and men a weakness? I cannot be considered weak, least of all by him. My cheeks flush all over again, but this time from embarrassment. Did I really just try to bargain with myself that his contact is okay?

Greve stands there studying me. The corners of his mouth start into a smirk. "You're blushing. Why?" He completely ignores my counteroffer of no contact.

"Not blushing ... I'm mad," I answer, though in a lie.

Greve's eyes grow big as if he's only just realized something important. "You are completely, without doubt, innocent." He lets out a sigh. "Yes, you are an angel, of course. However, you've had missions down here. Have you ever had any relations with others? Ever had friendships with humans? Love?" Greve is more or less talking to himself without fully coming out and asking me. "Never have I dealt with someone who has been *this* innocent. No human contact aside from missions ... no relations with boys of your own kind. You don't have to tell me. I see it written all over your face."

I don't know whether to feel ashamed or proud. No, I've never had any real connections with anyone aside from my father and maybe Faith. Although, my friendship with Faith is stretching the boundaries a bit. I feel the need to explain myself so that Greve understands. "All those things are forbidden for me.

Surely you know that rule by now? You've dealt with angels before."

"Yes, I have. Most of them, though, have been human/demon hybrids. I've taught a few angel/demon hybrids, however, most of them didn't seem so keen to follow the rules to begin with."

I raise my eyebrows, not really believing him. "I see."

Greve points his finger at me accusingly. "You are not as modest as you think you are. I've seen you with no shirt, and now you've got just a towel on. Obviously, you have a little of what they had in them. All of you hybrids have a weakness at first. It might be a lack of social skills or control. Maybe you have too much desire or lack of understanding. In the end, it all comes full circle for you. I do whatever it takes to make my students aware and confident. So please tell me that this is your only weakness."

My breath does a sharp intake. "I have several, as you probably have already heard. You mentioned a spy being in my world. Surely, that person has let on to what weaknesses I have."

"Strategically, I do know. You battle control of your needs and your mind. Socially, people intimidate you. These things will get better. There's also something else you need to let go of before you can really concentrate on what's important. I'm going to help you with that."

Greve walks up to me and doesn't stop until his chest is at my eye level. I glance up, almost too scared to look at him. He places one hand on the side of my cheek and tilts his head down at an angle so that our eyes lock. "This makes you uncomfortable," he states as a fact. "My touch. My closeness. It all confuses you. You don't know whether to run away or see how far we can go. I know. I've been in your place before. It's a hard place to be, but let me help you decide."

I close my eyes as his mouth closes in on mine. Our lips connect in one swift motion as his chest touches mine. His skin is pure fire against me. His kiss makes me eager. Scared that the towel will come off, I merely touch his chest and neck. It all feels right. Greve's mouth becomes more urgent as his lips press hard against my throat. My mind tells me to stop, but my body tells me not to. I command myself to look at him so that it's easier to break away.

This is happening too fast for me. My body is shaking from both nervousness and excitement. When his eyes lock on mine again, I see that his are dilated and red. His breath is ragged when he finally speaks. "I said I was going to help you get over your confusion about me. Don't worry. I won't try to kiss you again. I don't even like you." His eyes turn cold when he releases me.

He doesn't ... like ... me. The words form a hard reality in my mind. He doesn't care about anyone aside from himself. Greve is truly lost. And as his words repeat in my mind, all I can do is forbid the tears from coming as he walks away from me.

Chapter Nineteen

Greve

Her touch lingers on my lips as I head toward the bathroom. Once there, I shut the door so I won't have to see the hurt on Ireland's face. It had to be done. She has to think that I don't like her. It's for her protection.

My father wants me to fail. He wants me to develop feelings toward her so that he can have an excuse to get rid of me. Ireland's main focus has to be her mind control. It can't be me. If Father knew she started having feelings for me, he would try to kill her too. Demons don't *feel* like that.

Some days all I want to do is tell my father to fuck off. This is my life and, therefore, my choice how to live. He shouldn't be able to control me this way. He shouldn't be able to tell me that I can't love or that I can't live the way humans do.

A shiver runs through me when I remember that I did actually tell him that once. The results were nothing short of violent. He threw me up against the wall and choked me in front of my poor mother. He said that I would never talk to him like that again, or I would die. Point blank. I believed him. The only thing that saved me that day was the way he looked at Mom. She was begging and sobbing, and he gave in. That's the only time I've seen any type of weakness in him. And probably the only time I ever will.

Ireland's mother will be like my dad. She killed the other girl while I looked on, helpless. It will not happen again. Ireland will live. She may not be the person she wants to be, but she will live. Maybe that's all I can hope for and all she can ask. Living is better than being dead. If you're alive, you can hope. When there's hope, there's a way.

The floor creaks outside the doorway, and for a second, it sounds like Ireland might be thinking about coming in. I hold my breath, not really knowing if I want her to or not. The sounds fade, and the bedroom door shuts instead. She must have decided to finish getting ready in there, which means I must start getting ready in here.

Water trickles out of the shower faucet, drawing my attention to something else that must be done. This again. Water. The shower. I shudder before turning the shower on to a slow spray. The water hits all over the tub before I can talk myself into getting in. I pull the curtain, bracing myself for this degrading experience.

After a few minutes of standing in dread, I pull off the remainder of my clothes and get in. My back connects to the back of the wall in an effort to not touch the water. A warm mist touches my face, making me dizzy. The same old feelings come back to me. Dizziness. Weakness. Fatigue. My body tries to fight away the chemical makeup of water.

Out of nowhere, the bathroom door slams open, and Ireland walks in. Her eyes are red from crying, and her hair is tousled on the top of her head. She wears the emerald-green dress we picked out, and it fits her perfectly. She's beautiful. Her eyes catch me looking at her. "I heard you."

My body is growing weaker by the second. It takes me a moment to process what she said. "I didn't say anything."

Ireland stands at the mirror, working on her hair. "Not out loud, but in your head. I was right by the door, and I guess our little kiss made me more connected to you. Plus, I already got a read on you from the test."

Her body is relaxed as she talks to me. Did she really hear me? "What did you see in my mind?" I want to know. I want her to be telling me the truth.

Ireland continues to look at herself, fussing and sighing at what's becoming of her hair. "Don't you think you should get out of the water? I've been told it's your weakness." She turns to look at me, more or less as a challenge.

"I'm fine," I lie. She cannot know it. There aren't many people who know what water does to me.

"You are not fine, Greve." Ireland states it as a fact. "I'm not getting into what I saw just a few minutes ago. But I will say that I understand why you said you didn't like me. And I respect why you thought it was the best way to handle me. I'm a big girl, Greve, and I can handle solid facts." She turns to look at me. "You don't have to worry for me. I understand that we are likely to die if I don't focus on what you want me to."

I nod, grateful I don't have to explain about my past. I'm not ready to share yet. Ireland hasn't figured out that the girl is her sister, which is also good. It will only scare her. She will also be scared if I don't get out of this water right now. My body may just shrivel up to nothing as she stands there doing her hair. "Can you go in the other room?" I ask in a faint voice. My system is slowing down much too fast. The water is like poison running over my skin, starving me of what I really need. My knees give out and hit the tub before I hear her answer. Water pours all over me as I struggle to get back up. Am I really going to die here in the shower? And while a girl looks on, confirming her knowledge of me and my weakness?

My eyes get heavy. My head aches and burns under the attack. Just when I think I can't take another second, the shower stops.

Ireland peers over me and quietly says, "Do you still want me to not care about you?"

I want her to care. God, I want someone to care about me. "No," I croak with weakness.

"Okay," she says in neither happiness nor surprise. "Stay here, and I will go get some towels."

Chapter Twenty

Ireland

Beads of sweat run down my face from the effort of dragging Greve's body back to the fireplace. He fainted on me the moment I brought back the towels. His body, so pale and cold, looked so vulnerable and weak that I couldn't bear to leave him. I don't know why. It would have been my only chance to escape. As I looked from the front door to him, I just ... couldn't go.

Whether he wanted me to or not, I saw some of the memories he has kept buried. His father is an evil man. Greve claims my mother will be the same way. I can't grasp the concept of a parent being cruel to their child, but I suppose it is true. Greve is living proof of that.

His body shifts under the towels to get closer to the fire. It's his instinct just like it is partially mine. Greve needs it to heal, and I need it to build strength. However, right now, Greve seems to need the fire to both heal and to grow strong again. He seems to agree because he mumbles and tries to push his way into the hearth.

"No." I grab his arm to stop his body. "If you go back in there you will have to deal with the water again."

"Need it," he murmurs.

"Stay right by it. I know it will help you by being close. I can feel it too. We don't have to go out tonight to do whatever task you had in mind. Just stay here and grow stronger." My body shifts next to him so that I am facing the flames and him, but my back is against the couch.

He doesn't respond to me for a while. I can tell he's thinking about what I said about staying here. Finally, he looks at me and says, "No time to lose. It must start tonight."

"What? What must start tonight?"

Color is returning to Greve's face. He even manages to raise an eyebrow at me. "More mind control. It will help you, and it will help me. Don't worry about me. I don't have to sit here all night to start to feel better. Go ahead and get ready."

There he goes again. He's trying to push me away. "Okay fine. But, Greve ... people will not care about you unless you let them in. You say you want me to care, and I do honestly believe that to be true, even if you don't want to admit it. In order to understand, you have to be willing to give." I take his hand to show that I'm not going away. Not yet.

His eyes look down at our entwined hands. He doesn't take his away. Instead, he squeezes mine tightly. In this moment, he has lost his entire tough persona. Greve faces me, completely raw of emotions. "I don't know if I can."

I smile while trying to hide the pity I feel for him. "Well, we are likely to die if you don't, and I'm not ready to die. I want to live. So find a way to make it happen. We both have to work together from now on to insure that we both live. It's really pretty simple. You can't act like you don't need me. You need me. I need you. Together, we just might be okay in the end."

Greve nods and briefly smiles at me. It's forced and fake. He's already given up. He *can't* give up. Not on me. Greve saw something in his memories that makes him want to recoil. That can't happen. If he can't get it together, then he won't be able to teach me. If he can't teach me, I won't live.

I lean closer to him to make sure he's listening. "Whatever happened to that girl won't happen to me. I'm stronger than her, and you know it."

Greve leans up closer still until his face is inches from mine. His eyes start to burn a dull red color. The old Greve is returning. The fire is bringing the demon back around, and I don't know whether to be scared or relieved. "Damn right it won't happen to you," he whispers. "They want us both to fail. You saw it in my head. You know how *he* acted toward me. Prove it to me, Ireland. Show me, tonight, what you can do."

Chapter Twenty-One

Greve

The club is full of dancing bodies when we arrive. The air is moist and thick. The lights are dim, and the music is blaring. My shirt clings to me from sweat, and I've only been here for half an hour. It feels different in here tonight. Maybe it's because Ireland is with me. It's been a while since I've brought someone willingly into this type of place.

She seems okay though, considering the new elements. I glance at her from across the bar. So far, she's been too busy eating food to bother to do anything else. Guess I can't blame her. Her body has to have it. Mine doesn't. That's something I will have to keep remembering. And right now, it's quite a different change in pace for me. I am actually watching a girl eat a hamburger and fries and wondering if I am really missing something. She's practically ravaging it. I can't help but laugh.

She catches me. "What? I haven't eaten like this in months. Bread and cheese don't go too far. It's dull and boring to eat the same things day after day. And it also gets *old*."

"Yes, I would imagine so. Although, it is hard for me to imagine eating without feeling faint."

She dabs her mouth with a napkin and crosses the space between us. Her dress moves with her body and clings to it. Perfection. Ireland is a mold of sweet perfection. "Let me explain what it is like, Greve." Her voice catches me off guard. "Imagine you getting the flames or a person's thoughts just long enough to survive but never long enough to live. Think about getting to watch someone else be able to get what your body needs, and all you can do is watch because of your station. It all is forbidden to you because of how you were born and your genetics. You and I are a lot alike. We didn't ask for this."

I take a sip of my now warm beer that's been sitting on the bar since we arrived and make myself swallow. "No, we didn't." I could say more, but I'm more anxious to see what else Ireland is going to say to interrupt. Let her build. Let it all build up around her. If anything, it will help when she has to read someone.

"It makes me sick," she continues. "When I was up there, everything seemed okay. As long as Dad was near, I felt at ease. Not happy, per se, but compliant.

Now that I'm here, there's an empty feeling. It's like seeing the forbidden fruit and wondering what all I have missed … and once you finally taste the sweetness, you don't want to take a chance of it leaving. That's what I feel right now." Ireland moves her hand closer and snags my beer. She takes a long swig, not bothering to ask for her own. "And I don't know if I want to continue to be compliant. Not for Dad or *her* and her demon counterparts, and not for you. This is my life. I just want to *live*."

I take my beer from her and wave the waitress over for a refill. "Your emotions are jumbled up right now, Ireland. Of course, you want to live your own life. That would be nice. You want your wings, too, and in order to have what you want, we've got to work together, remember?"

Ireland smirks at me. "And what would you say if I told you I don't want my wings anymore?"

She's so confused. This has happened before. The angel and demon sides are conflicting with each other. She's focused but on the wrong things. Temptation is getting to her along with the potential of freedom. The problem is that we hybrids don't have any freedom. But if I have to skirt around the truth with her to get her to stay focused with me, then so be it. "Then I would call you a liar," I whisper. "You want those wings more than anything. You told me so. You want the freedom that comes with wings. What I don't remember quite so clearly is what you've got to do in order to obtain them."

"You know." Ireland glares at me. "You know what has to happen."

"What? You have to lock me up in the human jail? Will that please them so much up there that they will just bow down to you and give you what you want? Me—the bad robber locked up tight and booked. Ireland—the savior of the human race who stopped one person from taking something that isn't his. Think about it! I am one person in this big, tainted world. One guy among millions who do wrong. Do you honestly think they really care about these humans or you or me?"

"They did once." Ireland's voice is certain. "I've been told that it hasn't always been like this. I don't know why things changed, but missions used to mean something."

"Every good thing ends somehow. Someone ruins the good and replaces it with the bad. Corruption is what caused it. There's someone up there who's changed things to their liking."

Ireland bites her lip. She knows I'm right. "Perhaps ..."

"No!" I touch her face to force her to look at me. "I'm telling you again, there's a spy up there. Things will not change unless the people responsible get removed."

"Why are you telling me this?"

"Because as I already said, you need to think about the bigger picture here. Wake up before you lose your life. Nothing good will come from you completing your mission. If anything, you will bring more attention to yourself. Your mother already has her eye on you. Isn't that enough?"

"How can I be certain you're just not saying that to me because you don't want to go to jail? How do I know that you are not the cause of all the corruption?"

"You don't." I sigh. I want to tell her that I'm not the one to worry about. That it's not me who wants her dead or wants to see how much they can use her before she cracks. If she makes it past her mother's inspection, she will then go on to be taught more horrible things. And those are far worse than what I have to show her. This is the first step ... the first test out of several more that will have to be completed.

A lock of Ireland's hair falls across her face as she waits for me to say more. My hand catches the red strand and guides it back to behind her ear. "Here's something for you to consider. Jail doesn't bother me. I mean ... I can just tap into a couple of minds and get out. But the only way I will go for you is when we have a prayer of becoming something other than tools. Otherwise, there's no point in it."

"Maybe you feel like it won't make a difference. It will to me, Greve."

No, it won't! I want to scream at her. It won't make one bit of difference if she gets her wings and completes her mission. It won't happen because she's already marked. She's already been noticed and seen by too many. Having them won't change the fact that even up there in heaven, there are creatures even more sinister than me.

"Okay." I nod, hoping to move her off the topic. The air is uncomfortable around us now. When she stares at me with those mismatched eyes, it brings out a lot of emotions. Pressure surrounds me, making my muscles tight and tense. I can't be doing this. I can't let her get close because if I do, they will take her from me.

"So ..." she says with eyebrows raised.

I shake my head, trying to clear my thoughts. "So ... let's get going now that you've refueled." I take her hand. "Follow me."

Chapter Twenty-Two

Ireland

Greve's hand wraps around mine as he pulls me to the dance floor. His grip is strong and secure against my hesitation. I've never really danced before and certainly not with a male. Greve doesn't notice me staggering to keep up with him. All he wants is to get to the center of the dance floor. It doesn't matter if I trip and fall in the process.

Once he is in the center and surrounded by people, he pulls me closer to him and points toward a guy leaning against the far wall. The man is thin and frail with dark circles under his eyes. The blue shirt and faded jeans the guy is wearing fit so loose, they look two sizes too big. The man's face looks pained, but every time someone comes up to talk, he hides the pain behind a mask of contentment.

"I think you can handle him," Greve says in my ear. "Go read him."

My heart hammers in my chest. I'm nervous and excited at the idea of reading someone else. But I'm also scared because I don't know how to approach him. "Hmm ... I don't know."

"You don't have an option. Try it," Greve responds hastily.

"Okay, but come with me."

Greve squeezes my hand. "If I do, it will scare him off. Besides, I'm going to go read someone else while you read him."

"Fine. Where we meeting after?"

"I will find you," he answers. Greve pulls his hand away as a signal to get me to walk toward the man. As soon as he lets go, I feel disappointment. No matter how Greve acts, I know there's some good in him somewhere. Maybe that's my way of making excuses for him.

I wait until Greve walks toward the back before I start stepping toward the man in the blue shirt. Okay. I *can* do this. Really, it can't be that bad.

Before I reach him, he notices me. The pain in his eyes disappears and is replaced by a forced smile. Poor man. He and I are so similar.

"Hello," I say in greeting. "Are you doing okay?"

He looks up, startled. "Yes, I guess so. Observing is something I prefer to do, you know?"

"You like to just watch the crowd? I can understand that. It takes a lot of the pressure off," I respond.

"Yes, I suppose it does," he says, turning his head to the side. He's trying to get a read on me. Can't say I blame him.

The music slows down to a crawl. People are joining together for a slow dance. I take the opportunity to glance around the room along with my new companion. Couples are arm-in-arm while staring into each other's eyes. Some are sober, and some are half drunk. I wonder how many of these couples are actually dating and how many are just together for a night? Either way, the atmosphere in the room is heating up. I swallow, feeling more uncomfortable by the minute.

"Hey, umm ... what's your name?" the guy asks me, trying to break the silence between us.

"Ireland." I try to smile. "And yours?"

He stretches out his hand for a handshake. "The name's Levi. Can I ask you something?"

I return the handshake. "Hmm ... okay."

"That guy you were with on the dance floor before ... is he your boyfriend?"

Oh, god. Don't get upset. Don't get embarrassed. I shrug. "No. Why?"

Levi nods toward the back of the dance floor. "Well, because he is now hugging up against another woman."

"Oh," I mutter. My eyes follow Levi's to where Greve is dancing with a blonde female. He has his hands on her face and is whispering something to her. The woman seems to be enjoying the attention and is not at all in distress. In fact, she seems to be enjoying him a little too much.

My face immediately gets hot. I can feel the heat returning, making my eyes turn red. I blink a couple of times, trying to get rid of the obvious color change to my pupils. They still burn with heat, letting me know they are turning red regardless. Why should I care that he is close to someone? We don't have a label. I don't know him that well. And he told me he was going to read like me. But ... still. Seeing him like that with her fills me with emotions I am not familiar with. The only way to combat it would be to make us equal.

I take Levi's hand and start walking toward the dance floor toward Greve. "Come on. We are dancing."

He hesitates. "Look, I'm not getting in the middle of your lover's quarrel."

"There's no quarrel to get involved in. You will dance with me," I order.

"No," he says while jerking his hand away.

I hate to make the guy dance with me if he's that afraid. However, my feelings toward Greve are affecting me so much that I don't really care one way or another how Levi feels. Turning toward him, my eyes make contact with his. If he wasn't scared before, he is now. My eyes, red from my anger, terrify him. "Be quiet and take my hand," I command while keeping his eye contact.

This time he does not hesitate. We walk hand and hand toward Greve and the woman. I don't say anything. Levi's hands find my waist, and I make myself wrap my arms around his neck. We start off dancing oddly, neither of us comfortable with the other. Then the slow song ends and is replaced by another which is even more invasive and slow.

Greve eyes me for just a moment. His happiness is replaced by a smirk on his face. I ignore him. If he can do it, then so can I. I stay with Levi, dancing by all these people in the hope I can read him.

I move my hand closer to his neck, mainly because that's what Greve is doing to the girl. Levi's breathing picks up as my hand rests firmly on his skin. "Relax," I say, trying to soothe him. "Let me in. Tell me anything," I whisper while never taking my eyes off of him.

Levi relaxes and sighs. The sound represents something close to relief. While looking into his eyes, I swear I can see a tiny part of his soul. It blinks at me from behind his lids, waiting for me to come and take away all the bad things in his life.

And it takes only a second for that part of his soul to start sharing what terrible things this man has gone through and seen. Visions of death and sorrow come first. They surround us in misery so strong it makes me light-headed. His mother, father, and brother are all dead. His girlfriend was murdered a few years after them. Then come the memories of drug abuse and periods of self-loathing as a result of all that's happened. I see Levi spiraling down into the depths of his own personal hell.

He wakes only to get that high. He lives in the streets with nothing but the shirt on his back. Levi is hungry and miserable. He's torn and addicted to all that is evil. The last memory comes on me fast, without warning. An elderly woman, around the age of seventy, approaches the broken Levi in the streets, and without one word hands him a stack of cash. She tells him to get better and to get past the chaos that he has become. That was the moment that started Levi back on the right path. That was also just two days ago.

My breath catches in my throat. This man is still so broken. Without thinking, I throw my arms around him for a hug. My fingers run down the bones that make up his spine. He's so weak both mentally and physically. As the mind control comes to an end, I feel many different sensations. My mind swims in all that is Levi. His hurt and pain. His addiction and anger. It's all my body can handle. The demon is relishing in all the negative feelings while the angel part of me feels sad and hopeless for this man. It's all so confusing, and I still don't know how to handle it.

Tears form in my eyes as I release Levi from my control. He looks at me, confused. Before he turns away from me, I take his hand again. If I can make this better for him, then I'm going to try to do my part just like the elderly woman did.

"Take the money you have and go to rehab. Check yourself in and focus on breaking your addiction. Get your life back on track for yourself and for the rest of your family. Get out of this club with all its temptations." All these things I say as a command. My voice goes into the deepest parts of him, including the little blinking light behind his eyes. I hope he will become a better man with my help. If the elderly woman saw it in him, then I believe I can see it, too.

Levi nods with understanding before walking away from me. I stand there letting him go in the hopes that I've done the right thing. My heart pounds from excitement and adrenaline. I can feel the blood pulsing through my veins, but my body struggles to cope with the sudden shift of power. Dizziness overcomes me so fast I barely have time to find a booth. As I sit, my vision comes in and out of focus. Then the nausea starts, and I feel like I'm going to get sick.

Where is Greve? I haven't seen him since he was with that girl. We need to leave before I faint. This is all too much. He's supposed to be here with me. Isn't he? My vision goes out, and for a second, all I can see is blackness. When I come out of the darkness and back to the present, I notice Greve coming out of the bathroom.

He sees me but makes no effort to come over. Instead, he stays put while a lady with red hair approaches him. The woman has sharp features with bold cheekbones. My vision starts to blur again, but I force myself to stay awake. Greve and the woman are talking somewhat forcibly. He's uncomfortable with her because the woman demands his full attention. After a few minutes, she glances my way. I see her eyes, and a shiver runs through me. Her eyes, large and intense, glare at me. I have a moment of pure awe looking back at her. My eyes are staring at me. My eyes show me hatred. No! Not my eyes ... *hers*.

The realization of it all comes crashing down on me, and I can't take it. Instead, my body drowns in it all, and everything goes black once more.

Chapter Twenty-Three

Ireland

I wake up to the sounds of screams so sharp and shrill the noise hurts my ears. My body rises fast off the bed to figure out where the sounds are coming from. Sweat covers my face and hair. The dress that I last remember wearing clings to my body. It's so tight that any fast movement might tear the fabric.

Greve rushes into the room with the look of utmost concern. He stares at me, silent.

"I heard screaming," I say. My voice comes out hoarse and weak.

"It's okay. No one is here," Greve replies softly. He comes to me and sits on the edge of the bed ... *his* bed. He must have put me here after what happened at the club. It's all slowly coming back to me.

"Someone's here. I heard screaming," I murmur, still slightly confused.

Greve shakes his head. "That was you. You've been screaming on and off in your sleep."

"Me?" I ask, not believing him. My body hurts, along with my head. Everything aches with tension. Mostly, I think my heart hurts worst of all.

"I'm sorry," he says. "I must have pushed you too hard, too fast."

"Maybe." My head starts to spin again. I fall back into the bed to try to get it to stop.

"If I don't push you, you won't make it," Greve states as a fact.

After seeing the look my mother gave me, I believe him. "I know. I saw her. She hates me. That was my mother, right?"

Greve doesn't confirm or deny anything. He just studies me for a while. "We can go slower if you want, but I think we still need to keep up the pace. This isn't just about mind control. You have to learn more."

I turn over to face him. "I asked you a question. I think you owe it to me to answer."

"It will only make things harder."

Tears form in my eyes because I already know the answer. I just need to hear it. "Tell me. God! I have to know!"

Greve runs his fingers through his hair. "Fuck, relax. I will tell you." He takes the opportunity to lie on the bed. We are side by side, facing each other. The space between us shortens as he moves closer to talk.

"Your mother was at the club last night. It was sort of your initiation. She wanted to see how you would do."

Tears come at the realization that the woman who stared at me with such hatred is my mother. I just let them go, knowing that, right now, it is what I need most of all. "And she's disappointed in what she saw?"

Greve winces at the sight of me crying. "Honestly, she's taken aback at you. I don't think any of her children have favored her as much as you do. But, just so you know, demons are always disappointed. It comes down to *how much* their children disappoint them."

"They are disappointed because we are not full like them?"

Greve nods. "Yes, that's it. We will never be what they want. And if they are very disappointed and offended by us, that calls for death in their way of thinking. Don't ever cry for them, Ireland. They would never cry for you."

I wipe the tears from my face. He's right. "Nothing will ever be the same. She won't let me go back home?"

"I'm sorry," Greve says.

Those two words confirm my worst fears. I will never see Dad or Faith. I will never be able to do what I want. The first thing I want to do is cry all over again.

But it won't help. I will find something that will. My mother may think she has control over me. I'm going to show her one way or another that she doesn't.

"I'm sorry too. But I am one child she will not control in the end. I will find a way to get out of this."

Greve smiles at me. "I hope you do get out of it. Don't be trapped like me." His smile is unnerving.

"Why are you being nice to me?"

Greve leans in closer so that what little space there was between is now gone. "Because I'm tired of being mean. I've discovered you work better without me being crude. It's all I've been taught to be. It's not an excuse, but I've gone through what you have. I've been on the other side and was taught to be spiteful and manipulative. Dad taught me to be cruel. That's what he wanted of me, and for a long time, I had to obey. Meanness becomes a habit. Might not make sense ..."

"No," I whisper. "I get it. If you are taught to be that way, it's hard to learn to be different."

"Yes. I've learned some kindness from others along the way. Maybe that's why I'm able to change. I want to change. I don't want to be the person I have been."

"Then, don't be," I encourage. "Don't be the trapped person anymore."

Greve sighs. "Dad will find a way to beat me back down. It's happened before. I feel like the whole situation is repeating itself. He's setting me up, and I'm afraid I will fail. Last time that happened, I wasn't the only person to get hurt."

Flashes of the girl come to mind. The girl, who couldn't handle mind control, that Greve remembers so well. "Did she die? The girl I saw in your memories?"

Greve bites his lip, as if trying to determine what to tell me. "She did die but not by my hands. I didn't kill her. Her mother did."

"She wasn't good enough?" I ask. Greve has been so willing to share. I can't help but to want more information.

"Not in her mother's eyes. She was a good person. She cared a lot for the people around her." Greve looks at me as if he's experiencing his own grief.

"Tell me more. It will help to talk about it."

"No. I can't and what I have to say will only hurt you further. What happened is something that I will have to deal with for the rest of my life. It's the ultimate symbol of failure. I can't talk about it anymore. Not right now."

"Okay," I respond. Greve looks at me with both pity and sadness. We haven't even scratched the real surface of what all he's been through. Still though, seeing this little piece of the real Greve is comforting. He's just the result of influence, much like Levi at the club. And with all things lost, there will come a time that he will be found again. Greve needs help finding who he is. After all, he is a victim like me.

"I like you like this, Greve. This was what I was talking about when I said you needed to open up to me. It's okay to feel something besides negativity."

Greve laughs. It's the first time I've heard him make the sound. His laughter fills the room, making me laugh along with him. Greve responds, "You like me like this? Are you saying that you like me?"

I place my hand on his side to make him take me seriously. His skin feels hot underneath his shirt. Like me, he hasn't changed from last night's adventure. "Yes, I like you. I believe you are good even though you don't see it. I like this nicer you ... the more open you. We can learn from each other."

Greve places his hand on mine, not caring to move away from me. "I like you, too, as you very well know. I just don't show it the way I need to. I'm worried about them finding out that we are getting close. That was my downfall before. I fear they killed that girl because we became friends."

"We can't let it happen again," I agree. "They won't kill me," I promise.

"You don't know that," Greve mutters. "They might kill us both."

I shudder at the thought of dying. I know it could happen, and to die at the hands of someone who is supposed to love me is terrifying.

"Come here," Greve says after he sees me shudder. He wraps his strong arms around me as my head rests on his chest. His heart hammers against my cheek. His smell relaxes me, and for one second, I forget where I am.

I release him, worried I've overstepped yet another boundary in this place. "If we die, we will die together. We will die as friends, as victims, and as people who only wanted a life of their own."

Greve nods in agreement. "Don't back away from me. I need this, too."

I smile. "What do you need? Do you need me, or just the touch of someone?"

Greve puts his arms around me again. He's a man who has surrendered. "I need you, and I need this."

He leans back to cup his hands to the side of my head. His lips hover over me in hesitation as he fights with himself. I make up his mind for him and bring my lips to his. Our kiss is soft and slow. It is full of confusion and excitement. My heart aches for him. I ache for us. All that we've been through. All that haunts us. We are two people with the same reality.

His lips part to breathe me in, and then he stops. "I think you more than like me."

I smile. "I think you may be right."

Chapter Twenty-Four

Ireland

Days pass by with Greve and me following the same routine. We sleep during the day and go out at night. With each night comes a new task. I've read more people than I can count, and there's still more to learn. Greve insists that things are going well, and I have no reason to believe otherwise.

My mother hasn't reappeared as far as I know. Also, Greve has been completely honest with me about why I'm learning the things I am. Now, mind control comes easy. People do and say what I command of them. It's not just about reading and remembering their thoughts anymore. It has more to do with understanding who they are. After that, I learn I can manipulate them quite easily.

Not that I like controlling another person. I don't. The act makes me feel dirty inside. The sad thing is that I'm not making them do anything bad. Most of the time, it's making them walk to me or to Greve. It's making them forget me. Things like that. It's nothing like what Greve says my mother will make me do.

I'm terrified of what my life will become. Will I be able to convince her? Does it even matter? I don't know that it does.

In the other room, I hear Greve's phone begin to ring. This is nothing new either. The spy who lives alongside my dad calls to check in at least twice a day now. It seems to me that the spy is getting anxious.

Greve comes walking in with the phone in his hand. "Yes, Ireland has gotten better. Yes, she can do that," he mutters into the phone. He isn't concerned about letting me hear the conversation. I've tried to place who might be on the other line, but for some reason, I can't hear the spy well enough. One time, Greve put the phone on speaker, and the spy knew instantly and demanded to be taken off. We haven't tried to do it again.

"Her mother has seen her already," Greve continues. "I think she was put off by the resemblance. Yes, I intend on doing that. No, her mother won't refuse her. I understand ..." His voice trails off. A second later, he clicks the phone off.

"So ... how did it go?" I ask, curious. If only I could place who that is. Apparently, he's been over this type of hybrid trafficking operation for some time now. When I find out, I think I will kill him myself.

Greve sighs. "Same old, same old. The guy is worried. It is curious because he's never been like this. Usually, he just trusts me enough to take care of all the hybrids and deliver them when the time comes. It's as if he knows something is different this time." Greve smiles at me. "He knows you're different, and he doesn't like it."

"Perhaps," I respond, not thinking that's the case at all. "You've never seen him before? Never even a picture or another person who knows what this spy looks like?"

"No picture. All the people who would know what the spy looks like are dead. So, you see, it's easier to go along with the phone conversations and not question. When people question, they come up dead in a ditch somewhere. You haven't heard of anyone, Ireland? I mean, surely you've heard some rumors?"

"A friend did warn me about someone. He's been a friend to Dad since I was brought to heaven. I don't know really because I was never able to pry around. They kept me pretty much secluded aside from school."

Greve walks around his bedroom in frustration. "Of course. Seclusion is a good weapon to use against the weak. Well, let's just say the spy is a man. The voice sounds like a man even though I've been surprised in the past. Sometimes, the voice that calls is a woman. Maybe they like to keep things spicy. At any rate, we should get going now that the call is out of the way. I have something special to teach you today."

"You always say that, and it is always more mind control," I grumble.

"What I have to show you today will be the most important skill of them all. I do believe it will come in handy." Greve flashes his teeth at me.

My stomach turns to knots when I see him smile. We haven't kissed since that night after I saw my mother for the first time. Greve is being cautious of the whole situation, and I, on the other hand, am not. We've come close since then, but Greve always pushes me into focusing on something else. All I want is to feel him again. This might be my only time to truly feel something for someone.

Greve's hand brushes up against my arm. "You okay?" he asks.

I shake my head, trying to clear it. "Yes. Okay. Do I need to bring anything?"

"How about the bag you brought with you the day you came? It can finally be used for something other than holding crap food," Greve teases.

"Alright," I say while getting the bag off the floor.

Greve doesn't wait on me. He walks back out of the room, leaving me with my thoughts. I hear him put another log on the fire before everything goes quiet.

Since we are going out in the daytime, we can't be going out to the bars and clubs. My heart hammers in excitement. We are going somewhere new!

I take a look in the bag and find food. Everything is ruined except the chocolate. I can't believe I forgot about the food being here. My days have been crammed so full of new and frightening things that I just forgot about it. The mind I had when I first came here is not the same mind I have now. I'm wired to be a little stronger and a lot more focused on what is important. The constant battle between my angel and demon parts exhausts me before each day is done. I have little room for remembering the past, even if it was just a few weeks prior to this. I turn the bag upside down so that the food can be tossed out. As the food falls, a small box falls along with it and hits the floor beside the bed. The box seems important, but the memory of it is distant. What was this for? Can I trust Greve to know?

Greve shouts at me in an effort to leave. For now, I won't tell him. Deep down, there's a reason why I kept it safe in the bag. Greve says that my brain will start to process things again like it should. I try to think of it as a temporary problem compared to all the other ones I already have. Everything is still there ... all the memories and knowledge. It's just that the mind control has made my demon part stronger than my angel part. It's all about finding a balance. And with me focusing more on mind control, it makes it very hard to focus on anything else.

Decided, I place the box back in the bag. It's important to me. I just wish I knew what use it will serve. Greve comes around the corner again, waiting.

"Alright. I'm coming," I say, giving him a brief eye roll. He's so impatient.

He nods. "Good. Tie your hair up and out of the way before we leave. We don't need any distractions. Not even from your hair." Greve hands me a rubber band.

I take it and maneuver my hair into a bun on top of my head. "Better?"

"Not really," Greve answers. "You look much fiercer with your hair blowing behind you." He looks at me, serious, but then can't keep the act going. He smiles at me, teasing.

"And you look much better with that smile than when you frown," I reply.

His frown still intimidates me. Greve can scare off a room with just one look. His face can turn cold and frightening. It's as if he can read all your dirty little secrets, and he is getting ready to call you out on every single one of them. Which, in a way, I guess he could. He reads like me. However, his smile shows much more promise. When I see that smile on his face, I know it's only meant for certain people. People who he wants to care about. It's meant for me, who he's trying so hard to trust.

Chapter Twenty-Five

Greve

The transition phase is underway. Ireland is changing. She's forgetting who she is so that she can become more like her mother. It's a scary thing to be a part of. I'm seeing a hybrid change over to become more like her absent mother than the father who raised her. It's a sad and unfortunate thing. It's also very necessary.

Ireland will not lose herself completely, though. The real her will be there, underneath all the unbalance. I've tried to tell her that what it comes down to is finding a balance in what her body needs. For her, it's more difficult because she is not part human like me. To find a balance for her, she will have to have both positive and negative influences. For me, it's easier than that. I am part demon and part human. I live on Earth with all the other humans. That is my balance. Between teaching and mind control, it's enough to make me feel somewhat whole. Of course, being more on the negative side of things makes it hard. I will always struggle to keep the demon part of me underneath the surface.

Ireland's genetics are more complicated. Her body is like a scale. One side is weighed down with acts of kindness, honesty, and love. All the things that are pure and good. The other side is weighed down by pain, dishonesty, and addiction. She gets all those things from the people she reads. And all the things that are negative float inside the scale, weighing the bad against the good. Without being in heaven, Ireland has to find that balance here with me. And let's just say, using humans for positive is a lot more difficult than she anticipated.

I can't say I'm not worried. Ireland has gotten through things faster than any other student I've ever worked with. She's tough and quick. Her mind soaks up the information with no problem. All this would be great if I wasn't so concerned that all of it will come crashing down on her. There will come a time when she will break. They all do. I just hope it happens when I'm around to fix her.

"Greve, we're here," Irelands says from the other side of the cab car.

I look around to see we have indeed stopped. The ride over should have taken longer. At least an hour should have gone by. Surely I wasn't zoned out that long.

"How long have we been riding?" I ask her while opening the door.

Ireland looks at me confused. "Maybe forty-five minutes or so. Is this the right place?" She opens the door and swings her legs out. As she stands up, the sun hits her face, and she quickly places her hand around her eyes. Ireland always has a shield around herself. Even if it is just used to keep the brightness away from her face.

I stop looking at her to glance around the area. A tall brick wall looms in front of us. Behind the wall, two rundown buildings stand. They are used to house weapons and various machinery and supplies. We are in the dry plains of the region. Hopefully, we are far away from prying eyes and even nosier demon parents.

"This is the place," I confirm. "Let's get going." I shut the cab door and wait for her to come around the side of the car.

"Aren't you going to pay the driver?"

"Wasn't planning on it. He's been told to forget about the money."

Ireland shakes her head at me while folding her arms around her chest. "Pay him," she says, more or less as a command. "You say I need to maintain a balance of good and bad things. Well, I need some good things to occur around me. Let's start with you actually paying this man for his work."

I blow out a sigh. "Fine. Whatever." Ireland holds out her hand to take the cash. I give her the money and wait while she pays the man. If this will keep her sane while we go through this process, then I'll deal with it. She won't need to know when I go out and steal some more to make up the difference.

The cab driver thanks us and drives off, leaving us in a circle of dust and smoke. When the air clears, Ireland steps my way and takes my hand. I pull her close, although I immediately regret it. It's not like I don't want more. I do—so badly. It's just that ... I can't let it happen again. She's so close to being ready. Thinking about me will do nothing but make her backtrack.

We walk hand and hand toward the brick wall. The space around us is vacant. There's nothing here aside from the wall and the two buildings behind it. A blue sky looms above us. A hot breeze flows past us, burning our faces. "Wait here for a second," I whisper.

Ireland lets go of my hand and waits patiently without saying a word.

I walk over to the wall and place my hand in the secret compartment that's located a few inches off the ground. The scanner within the brick wall checks my identity. When it matches my fingerprints to the ones on file, it dings in approval.

The door slides open to allow our entrance. I motion for Ireland to come through before the door locks again with us now on the other side.

"Why are we here?" Ireland asks, looking around. "Why is this place so secretive?"

"Ireland, go to the first building, and then we will talk. It's the one with the black door and no windows."

"Alright," she says. "After we get in, I want to know what we are doing."

Ireland follows me to the entrance, and I repeat the same process of the scanner checking my prints. After a few seconds, we walk through the threshold. I hear Ireland suck in her breath, and I can't help but smile. Today will be used to turn our luck around.

"As you can see, this building is home to many different types of defense equipment." I turn to watch Ireland take it all in. "The building is one massive space designed for learning shooting techniques and battle defenses. A shooting range takes up the whole middle space with booths of various guns and equipment taking up the rest."

Ireland raises her eyebrows. "It's … impressive and nothing like what the outside looks like."

"Yes, I'm glad you think so. We have the building to ourselves today. I made sure no one will disturb us.

Ireland, you are going to learn to shoot, and most importantly, you are going to learn how to defend yourself. Depending on how well you do, we might get into the other building which is used mainly for defensive fighting."

"No, I … I don't think so," Ireland stutters. She looks at me, frightened.

This is out of her comfort zone. It makes sense for her to be scared. Unfortunately, her mother won't give a damn about her feelings.

I take her hand to force her to focus on me. "Look at me," I say, hoping she will calm down.

Ireland tries to jerk her hand away. "I said no. I'm not looking at you either. You will try to use that mind control again."

Our hands stay locked together, and I use that to my advantage. I pull her close to me so she has to look into my face. "Never again will I use mind control on you. You are more than that to me now. No more are you my project or someone for me to use. Ireland, you can trust me."

"This is against my nature," she sputters. "I don't have it in me."

"This *was* against your nature," I correct her. "You are no longer up there. You are down here on Earth. Say what you will, but I know you can learn how to use them. Policies and rules don't apply to you anymore. *Their* policies have no bearing on you now."

"Why are you making me learn to shoot?" Tears start to flow down her face. All her life, Ireland has been told to never hold or use a gun. The angels are taught to fear them. Never could they use a weapon against another. Never could they rightfully hurt a human. This has always been the hardest part of teaching them. If they know how to use a weapon, it will shred and change everything they've ever known about the world above. They will no longer have the fear to keep them conformed.

"Why am I making you?" Because of your mother, I think. "Because you have to learn to defend yourself against anybody who threatens you. Humans are not all kind. Demons, obviously, are more sinister." I run my fingers through my hair. "Let's just say, if your mother wants you to fight someone ... could you do it? She will test you somehow. What if it isn't mind control that she wants? What if it has to do with weapons? The day you go to her, it can work in many different ways. You've got to be prepared for anything."

Ireland bites her lip. "No! This is too much. You are asking too much of me. If the higher authority found out about me learning to use weapons like these, they would never let me back in. And regardless of what you say, I will be going back somehow!"

I back away from her to put more space between us. "Yes, you say will go back home. How, may I ask, will you manage such a task?" I turn my back to Ireland without waiting for a response and walk through the first door to my right. Once in the room, I snatch the nearest gun off the shelves and load it with ammunition. The gun is nothing to speak of. It's simple and small with a short, narrow barrel. However, it does pack a surprising punch. For now, this will be enough to get started.

Ireland's footsteps echo off the walls before I see her. She comes through the door as I start to walk out with the gun. "Don't just walk away from me, Greve."

"I didn't walk away from you. I walked away to get the gun we are practicing with."

"Whatever," she says while crossing her arms. "Look, when I'm up in heaven, I won't need weapons. Angels are immortal for the most part. No one has weapons either. We were taught at a young age to avoid force when on missions. The higher authority drilled it into us to be scared of such things as guns. If we kill someone, it calls for immediate departure and loss of status."

I roll my eyes. "And please tell me how your status isn't already like that? Here we are, once again, at the same old problem. You are too naïve. Honestly, I might not know who the spy is up there, but I can promise you one thing. The spy has a weapon! It might not be a type of gun the humans use. It might be something only harmful to hybrids or plain angels. He or she isn't just sitting up there with nothing as a backup. That is one thing I promise you is true."

"This isn't going to happen! I'm not the person you think I am." Ireland starts waving her hands around to get her point across. "You ask me to read people, and in the process, you make me get closer to the demon part of myself. All my life, I have fought to remain in the background. All I've ever wanted was to bring happiness to my father. To help ... to sacrifice ... those are the things imbedded in me. You want me to destroy the only sane part I have left!"

"That's not true, Ireland!" I walk back into the main room in hopes Ireland will follow me. She does. In fact, she practically stomps on my feet all the way back. I put the gun on the ground, away from us both, so that maybe she will listen to me.

"You're right. You are becoming more like your demon counterpart. Things will never be the same for you. You've spent too much time on Earth with me to be fully immortal. The longer you stay here, the less immortal you will become. And yet still ... you honestly think someone won't hurt you?"

"Oh, please! Like you care. People will hurt me. They've been hurting me since I was a child. Maybe not physically, but emotionally is another story," Ireland lashes out at me. "You know nothing about me! All you do is play on emotions. You think you have it all figured out. You think all hybrids are the same. Well, I'm not! I'm tired, Greve. I'm tired of being used. If my mother doesn't want me for who I am, then she can just kill me!"

I walk up to her with arms out wide. "Damn it, Ireland! If you are giving up, they might as well come kill me, too. And while they are at it, the spy can take care of your dad and whoever else you are close to. If you don't do this ... you will kill us all!"

Ireland shrugs away from me. I can see her mind working underneath her frightened appearance. She drops to the floor and begins to cry. "I'm feeling too much. My body is overworked and confused. It's battling itself on the inside. You may think I'm okay. And I may even think I'm alright, but I'm really on the edge, Greve. Do you hear me?!"

I bend down to touch her. "Yes, I hear you and understand. I've been right where you are. My human mother was almost killed by my father. I had to agree to go through the training, too, in order to save her. I get it, and I wish I could say to you that you won't cross over the edge. I want to say to you that everything will be okay. That you will be okay and you will rebalance. But I can't do that right now. What I can say to you is the truth, however hard it may be. Ireland, you are capable of so many things. Don't let fear overcome your ability to hang on to what matters."

"I don't want to lose him," she sniffles. "Dad is all I have left."

"Then, fight for him. Every day, think about him and why you are here. You are not good to anybody dead. Not to your father, the other hybrids, and not to me."

Ireland shakes her head. "You don't care about who I really am."

Her chin rises as I place my fingers underneath. "There are two people in this world I care about. One of them is you."

"Who's the other one? Yourself?" Ireland sneaks a smile. She's coming around finally.

I smile back at her. "Funny. No. The other person would be my mother. Maybe you can meet her sometime if we ever get out of this. After all, I've already met yours."

"Lucky you. You got to meet her before me."

My smile fades. "Yes, well ... back to that. Help me learn to help you. What can I do to make this easier for you?"

"Make it go away," Ireland replies. She leans in closer to me and rests her head on my shoulder.

"I can't. We are both trapped in this hell."

"Then help me forget. Even if forgetting only lasts a few minutes." Ireland looks up at me, tears still shining in her eyes.

I've never seen anything so beautiful. God, I just want to forget the demands and stress. I don't want to worry about people's lives being in trouble. For once, why can't time stand still?

I lean in close to kiss her. Ireland joins me halfway, and when our lips connect, it feels as if we are both on fire. The heat spreads across our bodies, forming a flame so strong, I doubt it will ever go out.

Chapter Twenty-Six

Ireland

Greve hesitates to let me go. Our lips disconnect slowly, forcing reality to surround us again. Greve looks at me with soft eyes. "That's better," he says as more of a statement than a question.

"A lot better," I agree. When Greve kisses me, I get lost in him. His scent captivates me. His warmth comforts the most eradicated places within my mind. He is my escape. But even when you escape, reality comes back to find you. And it doesn't take long for me to remember why we are here.

"Are you okay?" Greve asks while still holding me. "Do you understand why I've got to ask you to learn?"

I understand ... I'm terrified. I nod. "Yes, I get it. What if I lose myself completely? What if I can't find my way back? This might upset my balance too much."

"No, it won't. I do not believe for one second that this will hurt you. Mentally, you are capable. Ireland, you were meant to be more than what they have al-lowed you to be. What's the worst that can happen if you do shoot? They kick you out? It's already hap-pened."

"I'm just scared," I whisper into his shoulder. "Promise me that if something happens and I start to forget who I am that you will try to save me. I need your guarantee that you will try to bring me back."

"We've already made it this far," he says. "You will be okay."

"That's not what I want from you. I want you to say to me that you will promise to do what I asked. You don't understand. I feel like a nut! My mind is con-stantly going back and forth between feelings and emotions. One minute, I want solitude and peace, and the next minute, I crave negativity. This can't be what my life is meant to be."

"Alright," Greve says while taking my face in his hands. "I promise to do everything I can to ensure you will not go crazy. And if you make it back to heaven as you want, I will promise you something else. If we get past this, I will help you get your wings."

I smile. "So you are saying that you believe we have a chance of beating them? Of beating our parents?"

Greve shrugs. "It's possible, but you've got to learn to shoot. Even if you won't hit anyone, just being able to use one as a threat will come in handy."

"I will try."

Greve bends down and lightly kisses me. "Good, because I know you can get past this."

He has forgotten his own rules. His rules consisted of not getting close to me. Greve wanted to stay as distant as possible because he was scared to let anyone else in. If he can get over some of his fears, then I can, too.

"I need to get past my doubts about everything," I say more or less to myself. "It's time for me to accept certain things."

Greve looks at me before placing his hand on my right thigh. He comes to me slowly, timid that his touch will be too much. The heat from his hand travels to my face. I blush from the contact, but it feels too right to pull away.

"What do you have to accept? Me?" Greve asks while staring at me. The beginning of a smirk rests on his mouth.

"I ... umm ..." I stutter. Get it together, I order myself.

"There are so many things that don't include just you," I retort, knowing full well he is one of the things I have to accept. Not just him, but the idea of becoming close to someone who I thought was going to hurt me. How can I accept that what Greve does is okay? He works for the people who want to hurt me.

Greve nods. "I know where you are coming from. It wasn't too long ago that this situation was reversed, and *I* had a guy telling me how to live. He told me what to learn and what my life was going to be like. It doesn't matter that he was my father. He brought me up to take his place. And here I am, focused on training and changing hybrids into what I've become."

"Which leads me to exactly my next concern," I say. "If we are being open with each other, tell me that what you are doing with me is different from all the others. Make me believe that you aren't playing me. How do I know this isn't just part of the game? How do I know you haven't repeated this same stuff to all the other hybrids?" I take his hand that's still on my thigh and hold it up to my face. "Tell me you care more about who I am than what I am."

Greve places his other hand on my face and kisses my forehead. "Damn it, Ireland. I don't know how to convince you. I've never cared about the others like I do you. You have changed me. Before, I didn't care because all I saw were shells of people. You fought back against everything I've told you to do. You keep me grounded and focused. All your actions have woken up the human part of me. I was lost for a long time. Maybe it wasn't the other hybrids that were shells. Maybe I became the shell after years of living in hell. Your spirit has cracked open my bitter remains, and

I'm finding my way back. Even the girl you saw before in my head couldn't do that."

"She was your friend though," I whisper.

"Yes, she was. She was a friend I wasn't strong enough to save. She died because I was still too far gone. I'm not making that same mistake again."

Suddenly and without warning, the security system blares. The lights flicker and go dim as the sound of a door slamming echoes around us. Someone is here, and whoever it is wants to make a scene.

"Get behind me!" Greve orders, while offering his body as my protection.

My heart hammers in my chest from shock. "I thought this place was locked up?"

"It is locked from humans," Greve whispers while feeling the floor for the gun he put down. He would have had it if not for me.

A pair of footsteps run down the hall and into the range. The silhouette of a man fills the doorway. He is burly and broad-shouldered, and his voice sends chills down my spine when he finally speaks.

"Is there ever going to be a time when you won't disappoint me?" The man steps into the room as the alarm shuts off. The lights come back to full power as he stands there, arms crossed over his chest. Tattoos cover his neck and trail all the way up to his skull. His chin and lip are covered in black hair arranged in a defined goatee.

Greve's father. I recognize him from seeing inside Greve's head. This also means he is a demon. And for someone who has always lived in heaven, the sight of a full-blooded demon is enough to make my skin crawl. However, it's not just his outer appearance that scares me. His tone of voice and his body language terrify me more. This is a man who's come to destroy what's left of his son.

His eyes burn red as blood as he takes in the sight of me. "You are definitely a child of Jade. Even if you are a weak, watered-down version of your mother, you are still of value." He looks at his son next. "You, however, are of no value. I'm tired of trying to teach you. I'm taking over this endeavor."

I shift around to stand beside Greve instead of behind. We will face this monster together. Greve's eyes lock into mine. It's hard to say what I see behind them. He reminds me of a scorned, battered child who has suffered from years of abuse. His eyes also show that for the first time, he is ready to be more than that.

"Edgeman, I'm taking care of her," Greve says to his father with as much will as possible.

Edgeman?

His father laughs at him. Even his laughter sounds evil. "It's about time you call me by my real name instead of calling me Dad. You and I both know I am not father material. Nevertheless, I was made to breed. Thus, here you are ... another child in my way. You all have always been a pain in my ass. None of you ever took the hint that I don't give a shit about you."

Edgeman shifts his feet, scooting a little closer to us in the process. "Ireland, is it?"

I stare at him, waiting for him to continue, only to realize he means for me to reply. I nod because I can't quite make myself speak.

"The spy is concerned. He's worried that my son doesn't have the skill or ability to teach you. And now I've seen all I need to know that it's true. Greve is more concerned with sex than he is the cause. Of course, you're not the first hybrid he's fallen for, so don't flatter yourself too much—"

"That's enough!" Greve interrupts. "The only thing that comes out of your mouth is hatred and lies!"

My heart flutters in my chest. It hasn't always been just me, this I know. Greve has taught hundreds to be the slaves their parents want them to be. Somewhere along the line, he was bound to develop feelings for others. However, there is a part of me that had hoped he cares for me more than the other girls.

I clear my throat. "We don't keep secrets from each other. Greve has told me everything about the other hybrids so your tactics aren't going to work with me." Greve grabs my shoulder in warning, but I pull away. I don't care if Edgeman knows I'm the one lying. Greve hasn't told me much about the others. And he certainly hasn't told me about the mysterious girl I've seen in his head.

Edgeman pulls his lips tight into a forced smile. "I really hoped you were smarter than that, Ireland. After all, your mother has expressed a heightened interest in you. Usually, she doesn't care about her spawn." He comes closer to me while ignoring his son. Edgeman bends down so that we are eye-level. His breath stings my face. "If you were anyone else's child, I would have already taken you. Your mother demands you to be unharmed, which is a pity because keeping you unharmed is no fun at all. I like to play with little hybrids like you. Jade allows me full control of the ones that fail and believe me, there's not much left after I get through with them. So, you see ... your mother is actually doing you a favor already. She ordered me not to harm you, so I won't. Not a lot of hybrids get an option as sweet as that."

My eyes try to shift to Greve, but I find they won't move. My eyeballs snap back into place so that Edgeman never leaves my line of vision. Edgeman looks at me while licking his lips. My heart beats nervously as I wonder if he is going to try to force me into kissing him. Then a familiar tickling sensation starts in my head. The feeling starts slowly at first, like a light brush across my skin. After a few seconds, the tickling feeling becomes more of a squeezing sensation. A sudden wave of nausea hits me and my knees give out.

Greve shouts, "Get away from her! You're not going to fucking do this again! You're not going to control *her*. Not like this!"

I see a movement of shadows on the floor, and that's how I know Greve means to come toward me. His words terrify me. So this is what it feels like to have a full demon read my mind? Edgeman has merely scratched the surface of my thoughts and yet ... I feel like I can barely keep it together. Greve wasn't like this. He was gentle, even in mind control.

Edgeman takes his focus off me to face his son. His shadow moves farther away to meet Greve. "If you come any closer to her, I will kill you," Edgeman declares in an icy tone. "We are past the courtesies. I am past giving chances and seeing my spawn fail. I'm the laughing stock of all demons because they think I can't control a hybrid nitwit."

I try to stand up, only to fall again. He is still reading me even from over there. My stomach rolls and I begin to dry heave. Pressure fills my head as Edgeman continues to caress my inner thoughts. God ... please make it stop! I hear Greve mumble my name, but I can't make out all the words. He wants me to stop moving. That should be easy enough because I can't even tell what's up and what's down anymore.

Greve turns his attention back to his father. "You're the laughing stock of all demons because it is you who fell for love. They consider you the *freak*. You ride me because I care? You ride me because I loved before? Guess what?! I'm the half-human! You are a full demon and yet you still managed to love my mother. She's the only one who did it to you. The only one you care for still to this day. The demons call you a freak and call you weak because you fell in love. I am the product of your obsession with my mother, it's true. But I am tired of taking the blunt of your cruelty!"

"Just SHUT UP, BOY!" Edgeman shouts. His body moves closer to the other side of the room. The air around them becomes charged. It won't take much more for one of them to attack.

All I can think about is the gun on the other side of the room. Edgeman is slowly moving closer to it. Why can't Greve see what his father is doing? I feel a slight release as Edgeman leaves my brain to shift all focus on Greve. It's in that split of time that I'm able to look at him and mumble, "Gun. He's going for the gun."

Greve whips his head in my direction as his father makes a break for the weapon. He looks at me with concern before running after his father. Before Greve can get to him, his father picks up the gun and points it at Greve's chest.

"I'm going to kill your mother first before I kill you," Edgeman says through clenched teeth. "You can watch her die in agony before you leave this earth. Then you will know exactly what type of distress and anger you've caused me. You know what? Talking about all this makes me even more frustrated. I've changed my mind. You'll die first." Edgeman pulls the trigger, releasing two bullets into Greve's stomach. Greve drops to the floor, red blood dripping off of him as he falls completely down. His head makes a loud crack as it hits the floor. His shadow moves no more. His father's, on the other hand, moves closer to me again.

"No," I cry, weakly. "You killed him," I say a little louder. Edgeman picks me up by my hair and tugs me upright. I scream at the pain shooting down my neck. His harsh eyes find mine.

"The only person responsible for this is you. He's falling for you," Edgeman hisses. I feel a sharp pain at the back of my skull as he tightens his grip on my hair.

"You're not the first, and you won't be the last. You will do good to remember that he has loved before, and in the end, you mean nothing to him. You mean nothing to me or Jade. No one will save you here."

My body starts to shiver and convulse from the combination of pressure in my head and the feeling of pain from my hair. This is what he wants. Edgeman wants to see me die in front of his eyes. While I look into his face, there is a moment when I want to oblige him. Why not die? Why not let it be all over?

Then I remember what he said about my mother protecting me still. "You said Jade wanted me unharmed. Are you really going to kill me against her orders? You are hurting me. You are *damaging* me," I say as my throat burns from the effort of talking.

Edgeman releases me slightly as he lets my words sink in. Power turns to fear in his eyes. "Perhaps I got carried away."

"Yes, you have," says a voice that doesn't belong to either Edgeman or me. "Drop her," the voice commands from behind Edgeman's back. The sound of the person talking brings me immediate relief. I know who this person is. I just can't believe she's here.

Edgeman waited too long to respond to the woman's command. Suddenly, a huge gush of water surrounds him, and he releases me in frozen shock. The water makes contact with him, causing sudden weakness in his body. I drop to the ground, and Edgeman stumbles over my body as water continues to pour on top of him.

My head feels weak and tired, but I make myself hold on. My eyes find Greve's still body on the floor, and that's all it takes for me to start moving again. I don't care what's happening with Edgeman. All I want to do is get to Greve. I want to save him even if I don't know how.

Slowly, my body finds itself beside Greve. I touch him, hoping to feel his body hot under my touch. His skin is not hot anymore. I lay my head on him and cry. He can't be dead! It's all too much to take. My brain is tired. My body is weak. I collapse onto Greve's body, not even caring if I wake up.

Chapter Twenty-Seven

Greve

The next time I wake, I am surrounded by flames. The heat has charred away my clothes. A cold sweat forms on my lips as the smoke circles all around, flowing straight into my nostrils. I breathe in through my nose as the scent fills me with relief. However, the relief doesn't last long, and when it's gone, the feeling of fear and panic comes to take its place. Where am I? Most importantly, where is Ireland?

I try to shift my head around to see where I am. It's a useless thing to do because my head is in so much agony. I can't stand to lift it an inch off the ground. If I can't lift my head, maybe I can use my arms as a means to move around. I try to move them with no success. No matter what I try, I can't move from this place.

I remember my father being at the range. How he got in is a mystery. How I got here is even more so. My whole body hurts, but nothing hurts and bothers me more than the thought of losing *her*.

If he did something to her, I will kill him. The sick son of a bitch hasn't seen the last of me. A sound close to a growl escapes my lips. He threatened my mother, too. He said he was going to kill her and make me watch. My stomach gets queasy because he means what he says. All he has to do to destroy me is kill my mother. He knows my weaknesses, and I'm tired of him using them against me.

"Damn it!" My voice rattles off the fireplace. This wasn't supposed to happen again. All I had to do was pretend to be the robot they wished me to be. No one would get hurt that way. Instead, I became senseless and selfish. I became *needy* of my own desires. Now, my mom will never get to live out her days unharmed. And I've pretty much sentenced Ireland to death. She didn't get to prove herself. She would be miserable with her demon mother, but she would be alive. Ireland would have had a chance. And since she's nowhere in sight, I have to assume he took her. My father *took* her and ran off without a second glance to god knows where. All the while, I am stuck here. Unable to move. Unable to think. Not about to save them.

"Damn him!" I scream into the fire. "Damn all of the demons!"

Just the thought of losing anyone else is enough to break me, and he knows it. Father knows how to get to me. I'm such a fool! Every person I get close to dies. In my presence, the hybrids learn, but in my friendship and love, they die. That is my ultimate torture. Because my father loved, he feels I cannot. He doesn't want me to experience acceptance because if I'm always alone, he has more control of me. It's all making sense now. Even in this fiery pit with my head throbbing, I am able to make the connection. The point is though ... what am I going to do about it?

I have got to get my ass moving because just lying here isn't helping anything. Thinking about life and how it should have been different doesn't do a damn thing to change my outcome. I've been handed a deck of cards that consists of jokers instead of kings. But this is what I've known all my life. I'm not going to let it consume me now. Get over it, I tell myself. Get over it so that I can save *her*.

Determined, my body remains still in the fire. In a few hours' time, my arms should be able to move. The rest of me should follow soon after. Fire heals me but only after so much time. My body is still weak from the encounter with my father. It has nothing to do with the gun shots either. Oh, god! Ireland didn't know I picked out a paintball gun as her first practice weapon.

Edgeman shot me with paintballs, which I'm sure he was aware of. The paintballs hurt slightly. After the shot went off, the blow sucked the air from my lungs, and I fell. My head slammed into the floor on impact. That is what is causing my problems. It left me almost paralyzed. Again, something my father knew. It was all done for a purpose. They wanted to get her away from me. Nausea forms in the pit of my stomach at the very thought of what could be happening to Ireland. *Hold on. I'm coming for you.* Those thoughts form in my head. If only there was a way for Ireland to hear them.

Chapter Twenty-Eight

Ireland

The sound of her voice wakes me up enough to realize that she really did save me from Edgeman. My mother came and blasted Edgeman with water to make him stop hurting me. I guess I'm more shocked by that realization than anything else. What I'm not shocked about is the fact that I'm bound to a bed so that there's no way for me to escape. She saved me just so she could have full control. Not very surprising.

Cold, hard steel wraps around my wrists and ankles, securing me to a bed much like those used in hospitals. I've got a needle in my arm drawing blood and a strap around my belly screening for god knows what. One thing is for sure—my mother knows how to get my attention.

She also knows how to get the attention of everyone around her. Once she sees my eyes open, she orders everyone out of the room. Her curly red hair is tied up in a bun on top of her head. The familiar red of her eyes glares down at me as she stands over me. Her posture is rigid. Her body is perfection, and while people say I look a lot like her, I don't see it.

She apparently sees something in me though, because she would have killed me by now otherwise.

"Hello, spawn." My mother's tone comes out icy.

Here's the deal. I should be feeling a lot of different things. My thoughts should consist of several different feelings like excitement, fear, annoyance, or curiosity. The problem with me is that I don't feel anything. My mind is numb. It's like Edgeman nibbled at all the good stuff in my brain, causing me to completely shut down.

"Jade," I answer in the dullest tone possible. "You demons can't seem to get enough of me."

She smirks. "Nor will we ever get enough. Hybrids like you are in top demand." Jade takes one vile filled with my blood and exchanges it with a fresh empty one.

"What are you doing to me?"

"Tsk," she answers while placing her hand on my mouth. "All you need to know is that you are too important to die right now. I mean that in the most sensible manner. We need your blood and your mind skill. You are just another form of fancy, high-demand merchandise."

Her fingers smell like burnt charcoal. It's a far cry from Greve's familiar, homey smell. My heart aches at the thought of not knowing if he's alive or not. I want to ask, but I'm scared to bring attention to him if he somehow got away.

Jade's fingers move to the top of my head. They stay there, twirling the strands of hair that have fallen on my forehead. "If you weren't so weak, I would read those petty little thoughts of yours. I'm afraid, though, that Edgeman got too greedy with you already today. Pity. I want to see what your life has been like."

"Why do you care anyway?" I ask through clenched teeth. "The first time I saw you in the club, you looked at me with hatred. Now, you look at me as if I'm a science experiment. I'm nothing to you."

Jade tightens her hold on my hair when I try to twist my head away. "There are things I need to know that only you can tell me. I would much rather fish for it myself instead of waiting for you to answer me. And while I would love to say you are nothing to me, that's not exactly true."

The strap around my stomach beeps, concluding its scanning process. Jade switches the strap off and releases it from me.

"Back to what I was saying ... you, as a whole, are very important. We need your body and genetics to aid us in finding better ways to control ourselves with the humans. What we don't need are your personal opinions, beliefs, or values. Basically, I don't care *who* you are on the inside. None of us care what you've been through or what you want."

"So really you just want a shell," I conclude.

Jade smiles so big her front teeth extend out over her lips. It's the first time I notice the pointy edges of her front teeth. They look like they could tear flesh quite easily. "Yes, that's all I ask of you. Think you can give that to me? I did give you the gift of life, after all. And you've gotten some good years in, so it's about time for *repayment.*"

"You gave me nothing," I spit out. All my life, I've never known her, and now that I've seen her, I don't want to know anything else about her. Jade makes me miss my father. She makes me realize how lucky I am to have him. The thought of him and what he could be doing is enough to bring tears to my eyes.

Jade sees the tears and mistakes them for something she caused. She laughs at me. "Tears won't do anything for your cause."

"I'm not crying because of you!" I jerk my body, forgetting for just a moment that my arm is having blood taken from it. The needle embeds itself farther into my skin, causing pain to shoot down my arm. The blood stops seeping into the vial probably because the needle moved out of my vein.

Jade jerks her head in the direction of the needle, looking at what I've done. Her nostrils flare as she looks me dead in the eyes. "Stop moving. Stop talking. You will mess everything up."

A tingle runs up my spine, into my head. Her control takes hold of me. My body is now rigid and unable to move.

"When I want you to do something, you will do it one way or another. Either by your own actions or by mine," my mother says as she pulls the needle out. "You will do good to remember that."

Jade places the vials of my blood into a cooler-like container before she comes back over to me. "I've gotten what I need from you for the time being. From what I hear, Greve has told you of many tests you will have to endure. We are fixing to start the most important one. If you survive this, then I will know you've got enough of me in you. If you don't, well then … you have other siblings I can focus on."

She looks at me while placing her hands on each side of my face. Her touch makes my heart jump. Jade whispers, "Eventually, the demons will have enough hybrids in place to control the United States government. Once we get the president under our mind control, we can move on to the other countries. I tell you this because I don't expect you to live long enough to do anything about it."

Her lips touch my forehead. This act does not calm me. In fact, as soon as she pulls away, a dull ache starts exactly where her lips left my skin.

She makes eye contact with me again. "You may move now. You can scream and try to break free. I give you full range," Jade's voice washes over me.

My mind eases back into control, and soon I can move all the way from my fingers and toes.

"I want to hear your pain," my mother continues. "I want to see your reactions and hear your discomfort. Seeing my children struggle is half of the fun."

"What are you going to do to me?" I ask quietly. The ache in my head is getting worse. My body is already weak from blood loss, and my mind feels out of sorts.

My mother presses a button on the bed, ignoring my question. The bed rotates under me and raises me into a sitting position. Then the back of the bed folds together, leaving my back exposed. The sound of fabric tearing fills my ears, making me realize Jade has ripped and torn my shirt off.

"Such sweet, innocent skin," she says in a soothing voice. "Not a scar on you. I knew your father was going to be way too protective."

"You didn't answer me, Jade. What are you going to do to me?" My voice sounds louder now than before. It's probably my imagination because, in my heart, I am terrified.

Her long, ridged fingernail scrapes across my skin. She runs her nail all the way down my spine, cutting deep.

I force myself not to scream. Blood trickles down my back as she repeats the same motion as before.

My mother doesn't reply until her nail reaches the bottom of my back again. "I'm making you achieve your full potential. After this is over, you will be as much demon as you can get. If you live, then I will give you back to Greve. Perhaps you will kill him for us so that his father will have to find a more suitable hobby."

She places both hands on my back and pushes her nails into my skin. My flesh burns like I'm being cut open. My mouth lets out a scream.

"That's it, darling," my mother coos. "Let's make you into the demon you were born to be."

Chapter Twenty-Nine

Greve

I'm awake, flexing my arms and neck when Ireland arrives. She is being carried in by a short, plump man who's struggling to keep upright as he walks into the room. Jade strolls in beside him, neither looking at the man nor her daughter. She looks straight at me. Her eyes bore into mine, showing no emotion whatsoever.

The man drops Ireland on the floor between the couch and fireplace. His hands, as well as the clean, pressed blue suit he chose to wear today, are covered in blood. The man doesn't look appalled by this revelation. In fact, he appears to be excited. He's so excited that instead of washing his hands, he licks the blood off instead.

I shudder and look at Ireland's body on the floor. Cuts go from her neck to the bottom of her back, making it appear she has been mauled by an animal. What clothes she has on are barely held in place by strings of fabric. Her beautiful red hair is now matted with dirt and sweat. She's pale and silent. For a split second, I think she must be dead.

Anger swells inside me, so strong I try to get up before realizing that I am still anchored to this hearth because my legs aren't moving. The fire has healed my upper body, making my head, arms, and torso usable. With my brain clear, I realize I was dumped back at my house. Jade picked the perfect time to come. My body is healed enough to realize that she's here, but not enough to try to do anything to her.

"What did you do to her?!" I spit.

Jade bends over to get a better look at me. "You know what I did. You went through the same thing, yes?"

I bite my lip, forcing myself to not think about when I went through it. "She's alive, I take it. Otherwise, you would have eaten her by now."

Jade shrugs. "Obviously."

"What do you want me to do now, Jade?"

Jade flicks her nails at me. "Babysit her. I've got what I need for the time being. She's alive, but barely. Ireland needs to be put in the fire to heal. She's been gone for too long from heaven to heal on her own."

"I'm not a babysitter. Ireland is more to me than that."

"You are telling me stuff I already know. The whole community knows what you've been up to, thanks to your father. I do wish you would just die so that he won't be so distracted."

"Why don't you kill me now and be done with it? It would be so easy since I'm wounded. Isn't that what you all like? Helpless victims?"

Jade smiles at me before bending closer to my face. Her eyes flash red. "We don't kill each other's spawn. Your father would do good to remember that. Ireland is mine to kill. I made her, therefore, I can kill or devour her as I see fit. That goes for your father and you. I cannot kill you. But you know I don't mind killing my own children."

Jade places her hand on my chest, right above my heart. "After all, you witnessed first-hand what happened to Abigail. Would you even say that you were at fault for her death?"

My chest begins to ache at the thought of Abigail. Abigail, the girl who consumed me before Ireland got here. She's the girl I couldn't save. The girl who wasn't strong enough but would have made a great human being. Fate made her a hybrid though. And her own mother squished her like a bug because she didn't like her. "You killed her. It was all you." I snarl at Abigail's murderer.

Jade shrugs. "Whatever makes you feel better. How do you think Ireland is going to feel once you tell her about Abigail?"

I push Jade's hand off of me. "She already knows about her."

"Oh?" Jade stands up to move closer to Ireland. "So she knows everything? She knows who this girl was to you? That the girl you so desperately pine over was her sister? I don't know about my daughter here, but most women wouldn't feel comfortable knowing the person they are with loved their sister first."

My nostrils flare. "I didn't love her. Not like that."

Jade laughs at me. "I guess she will be the judge of that. You will tell her," she orders. Jade nods toward the short man as a means to signal it's time to go. "You will tell her, or I will. I suspect that might be all it takes to completely break her."

"I will tell her everything she needs to know. You are wrong about her, Jade. She will not be the fully deprived angel you want her to be. Ireland will not go wild, and if she does, I'm going to be here to watch over her," I say more confidently than I feel.

Jade pats the plump man on the back and nods toward the kitchen. He walks off, heading to the sink without comment. I wonder if he can even speak.

"Ireland will become *me* in the closest form possible," Jade whispers. "The angel in her will fight, but the demon part will win. I hope you are healed before she wakes. I suspect she will be quite a handful."

The man returns from the kitchen with a soup pan full of water and stands beside Jade. He is waiting for her next command.

"I know what it's like," I say as a reminder. "Doesn't change what my stance is on her current situation."

"How charming. Well, I must be going. Things to do. People to control." Jade flicks her wrists at the man.

He walks up to me, stands there, and pours the water all over me and the fire. Immediately, my mind starts to feel the effects. I'm spurting and cursing, trying to climb out of the remaining puddle on the floor.

"Pity your fire went out," Jade says. "Maybe you can figure out a way to start it again before your girl *dies.*"

I'm still coughing and spurting when she and the man close the door. They leave me alone with a beaten Ireland with no fire and no help. Shit! Of course, they would have, though. I should have seen it coming.

The water seeps into my skin like poison. Every limb and muscle becomes weak. Fatigue hits too, and I struggle to stay alert. They are not going to make this easy on me. But there's no room and no way for me to give up.

My arms are still strong enough to allow movement. I slowly scoot out of the fire pit and onto the living room floor. My legs drag behind as my arms carry me toward the bedroom to where my lighter is hidden. I always thought that using lighters to start fires made people into pansies. Especially half-blood demons who know how to light one using better skill than that. Now, I can't complain. In fact, I am not so silently rejoicing the fact that I have a cheap lighter. Ireland needs fire and quickly.

My body works through the nausea and pain to get back to the fireplace. Luck is on my side because the logs my ass was on are basically still dry. The rest of the logs, not so much. My fingers flip the handle to produce a thin flame. Just the feel of heat makes me hunger for more. My body craves it more than ever, and I have to fight myself to keep focused. With shaky hands, I gather some of the smaller logs, which are still dry, and keep the lighter under them. After what seems like several minutes, the flames catch, and smoke encircles the hearth once more.

The fire starts slowly at first, kind of like my relationship with Ireland. It's weak and selfish, wanting to make its mark on everything it touches. Now, as the flames expand to consume everything in its path, so do my feelings for her. I would kill for her, though I haven't known her that long. There's something about her I can't give up. The logs keep the fire going, making it expand and crackle with desire and need. That's what Ireland does to me. She makes me want more for myself. I want to grow, just like those flames. Ireland is my fire, and I am the smoke, weaving in and through her, wanting and needing, until we finally combine into one great big mass.

As soon as the fire grows big enough, I make my way to Ireland. She is as still as stone. A little pool of blood surrounds her body from the cuts on her back. They are festered and red. Most likely infected, compliments of Jade's demon nails. Her chest falls in shallow, rugged breaths.

"Hold on," I whisper in her ear.

As long as I can get her in the fire, she will be okay to make it through the rest. The task of moving her is tedious. My arms strain from my own weakness as I roll her over to the hearth. One last shove forces her in, and I squeeze myself in alongside her.

Ireland groans a little, so I take that as a decent sign. She will be all right. I brace myself for a long night in the fire. At least I won't be alone. I've got her back, but I just hope she still realizes who I am when she finally wakes up.

Chapter Thirty

Greve

Ireland's moans wake me up. She thrashes and screams against the nightmares that consume her. We are both in the fire trying to heal. I glance around at her, trying to figure out how long we've been in the flames. From the looks of her cuts, I determine that we've been together for a few hours tops. Her screams make me want to wake her. I fight against the instinct. Waking her too early will not help.

She mumbles something about a box. Her box, she says. My mind races fast to try to remember what she might be talking about. She had a box? What does she mean?

Ireland says it again, a little clearer. It's like she wants me to know something. Box … box … the memory just doesn't form. Her body thrashes up against me. Our skin touches, and for a second, I feel lightheaded. The poison in her back leaks into my chest. She's in danger. The fire might not be enough to heal her completely.

Hopefully, that won't be the case for me. First, I wiggle my toes and discover they actually obey. Then comes my legs, and much to my relief, they move around. I rise, trying to get my legs fully functional when I notice that Ireland has gotten quiet.

Her eyes are open. There is a film in her eyes. When she looks at me, she doesn't *see* me. "Box," she says again. "Box. Bag. Need!" she repeats, more urgently.

"Okay. Box. We will find it, Ireland."

Ireland smiles briefly and falls back into her rhythm of thrashing and moaning. The poison has to come out quicker than what the fire can accomplish. Maybe she knows the cure? Is it in the box ... in ... her ... bag? And then it hits me like a lightning bolt on a tree. The little box was in the bag that she had when she first came down. Ireland had it with her when we went to the range. The box must be important, which is unnerving. If my father figured out what it was, it is surely gone with him.

Ireland can't stay like this. She's being healed, but at what cost? I crawl out of the fireplace to test out my moving abilities. My muscles are slow to remember their job, so my legs move painfully slow at first. It feels good to move again after a few steps, and then the ability comes back to me as if nothing ever happened.

My mind hums with energy and hunger. The demon part of me is more active now that I've fed it with the desire of fire. It wants more; something I can only get through the desires and thoughts of others. I want nothing more than to run away and grab a human in order to read their minds. It's a fight to remain here, watching Ireland struggle.

I make myself busy rebuilding the fire to take my mind off my own temptation. The stronger the fire, the less time Ireland will have to stay in there. And hopefully, the less time it will take to heal her. Once that is done, the hunger doesn't seem so bad. It's faded slightly so now I can refocus on what else needs to be done.

Ireland is here, and that's the best I can do for the moment. My mother can still be in danger, and I owe it to her to check up on her. She's too far away to visit, so I search for my phone and dial her number. On the fourth ring, she answers.

"Hello, son. Everything okay?"

"Mom! Are you okay?" I answer. My heart races at the thought of her being in danger like Ireland.

"Your father stopped by," she answers. I can hear dishes banging in the background.

"Fuck! Did he hurt you?"

Silence is followed by more dishes banging around. After a few seconds she says, "The only way he could hurt me would be to do harm to you, son. You know that. I am fine. I did ask about how you were though."

"I'm glad you are okay," I say after a few minutes.

"Are you okay, Greve? Honey, I'm concerned."

I sigh. "Things are complicated. My stress level has decreased now that I know you are fine."

"Your dad will never hurt me physically. I've learned to handle the mental part over the years. Has he touched you?"

She says he won't hurt her physically. I know better. "Yes, he's been around. He immobilized me for a bit. Father also hurt a friend and threatened to kill all of us. That includes *you*. Come here, and we will figure something out. I don't like not being around you."

"I miss you terribly, but you know us being together would be the easiest way for your father to cause harm. I'm sorry, son, that I've put you through this whole mess." Mom pauses and clears her throat. "We loved each other once. Your dad and I. That's before I really knew what he was."

I pace around the apartment as a means to stay focused. "You've told me before. And I've told you not to apologize to me. We are in this together. He's a horrible man."

"In the past, he wasn't so bad. I wouldn't change a thing because if I did, I might not have you. We are in this together along with the girl you referred to. Is she another hybrid, Greve?" Mom's voice is pained.

She has asked me time and time again to stop converting hybrids. Dad has other opinions about the subject. His instructions are clear: do what he wants, and no one gets hurt. Mom doesn't fully understand the temptations and obligations I feel trapped in.

"Yes, she is." I glance over at her to make sure she's all right. "Her name is Ireland. She is part demon, like me, and part angel. Ireland is different than the others. She's powerful and strong. They want her. Like really want her to be converted over to them. I can't let that happen."

"Of course, you can't," Mom agrees. "I don't expect any less. Tell me, son, why do they want her so badly?"

"She looks a lot like her mother for starters. Her mother is the demon. Ireland has been through the first test."

"Oh no," Mom whispers over the line. "The same one they made you do?"

"Yes."

"I'm sorry." Mom's voice begins to break. "No one should have to go through that. You shouldn't have had to."

"Not your fault," I say, trying to keep the subject on Ireland. "Help me, help her. You got me back, Mom. Somehow, you saved me against my own personal hell. You got me back to being me. Not the demon me, but the hybrid. The *real* me. Ireland will not be herself. Not fully. I did some horrible things when I came out of that test. I would like to spare Ireland the memories of guilt and torment I have."

"Is this because of Abigail?" The sound of a door slamming echoes through the phone. Then comes the wind blowing into the receiver. Mom went outside to escape possible prying ears.

Anger and guilt swell up inside me at her question. "Abigail will always be a friend I lost, that much is true. There's not a day that goes by that I don't feel like I could have changed her outcome."

"So, it is about Abigail?"

"Ireland is Abigail's half-sister," I mutter into the phone. "The way I see it, the relationship means nothing. It's just a coincidence. Ireland was just a project at first. She was something to change and turn over to her mother or whatever. As I said, she's different. I've fallen for her in the most unexpected way."

"Love has no boundaries, honey. It comes and goes as it pleases while it touches the most sacred places inside us."

"Yes. I'm beginning to understand."

"Son, you asked me how you can bring her back. I really don't know what to tell you. Show her love and sacrifice. When she fights you, throw kindness in her face. That's all I know, dear. I wish you the best. Bringing back hybrids isn't a dull affair. Just don't lose yourself again, okay?"

"Okay. Love you, Mom. Thanks for the talk. Won't you consider coming to stay with me? I will keep you safe."

Mom laughs at me. The sound plants a smile on my face. "Focus on bringing that girl around instead of worrying about me. I'm okay."

"Alright, Mom. Be careful."

"Likewise, honey. I love ya."

"Love you," I say back as the phone clicks off.

My heart rate decreases slightly now that I know Mom is safe. I like to think Mom is right about Edgeman not hurting her. He might not kill her, but he would certainly hurt her. She is too naïve. Always has been ... and yet ... she never overlooks the reality of having a half-demon child. I owe everything to her. She not only gave me life as a newborn baby, but she also brought me back to life after my father destroyed me. "Someday, I will get rid of him for us," I mutter to myself.

Ireland stirs in the fire, which brings me back to the present. Mom said to help her by giving her kindness and love. I can try to do that, but I don't think I will be successful on my own. My mother was barely able to help me, and she's my *mother*. My own flesh and blood had trouble getting me back. Ireland needs more than what I can offer her.

I pace around the room in thought. Ireland wants that box from her bag. It must hold some sort of importance. Maybe it holds the answers.

Ireland groans some more in the fire. Her body is healing, but at what cost? Not knowing what else to do, I prepare for the fastest trip to the shooting range possible. Ireland will be out for a while longer, but I want to be here when she wakes. The world has to be shielded from her.

I turn to leave with one last glance toward Ireland. The door shuts, and I lock it even though it won't keep Ireland from getting out. The staircase creaks as my feet run down them. Shadows of people flow through the streets. The last few minutes of light fade behind the tall buildings across from me.

A short, plump woman makes eye contact with me when she comes out of a nearby store. She looks at me with concern before taking out her phone. I see myself in her thoughts. Bloody, torn clothes ... wild crazy eyes ... a young boy looking absolutely scary under the harsh sunset. No wonder she's thinking about calling the cops. I probably look like a killer. Well, I am a killer, *technically*. I'm just not one today.

When our eyes lock again, I demand her to stop thinking about calling the police. Immediately, her arms go slack. The woman stands there, looking at me without fear.

"Damn people," I mutter to myself. Humans always have to interfere. I don't have the time to command everyone to stop noticing me. When you need help, no one comes around. But when you don't need anything, they come meddling, asking questions.

I stand on the side street, debating on running to the range when a silver Escalade comes screeching to a stop in front of me. The windows are tinted black so it's hard to see who's in the car. My feet lurch back in preparation for a fight.

The passenger-side back window rolls down enough to make out the top of a head. Blonde hair peeks through the window crack. My mind rushes to determine this person's interest. When my mind reaches past the window and into the car, it's met with the thoughts I've wanted to hear.

Whoever this is knows Ireland. She's a friend.

"Get in," the female voice says. "You don't have much time."

I reach for the front passenger door handle, and it's locked.

"Back seat with me," she says.

People are starting to stare again, wondering if I'm trying to hijack the car. Horns start to blare at me. People are talking among themselves. Hurriedly, I run to the opposite side, pull open the door, and crawl in. The Escalade pulls off the curb, blackening the road behind us.

A man is in the front seat, not bothering to look back at me. With just a look and a smell, I realize he is full human. The girl, though, who keeps looking at me without saying anything, is a hybrid. Not a demon hybrid type of combination, but a hybrid, nonetheless. Her green eyes burn into me with curiosity. She doesn't trust me and rightfully so.

No one should trust me.

Eventually, she sighs and pushes her hair out of her face. "Ireland is needed at home," she says as if she has known me forever.

"No kidding?" I cross my arms in front of my chest. "Who are you?"

"I am half angel/human. *Who* I am is not important. I have something you need."

"How do you know I *need* anything?"

She rolls her eyes at me. "Please. You need all the help you can get. I know your type."

"You know nothing," I whisper, softer than I intend.

The girl laughs at me. She's making fun of me. "I do know a few things." Her index finger pokes my chest. "You have connections to the spy who lives where I do. He's out to sniff out all the angel hybrids and deliver them to their demon parents. Of course, *you* know that because *you* work for him. Such a shame. Of all people, you should know what it's like to be forced into something."

I snatch her fingers away from my chest. Anger builds inside me. Heat pulses through my eyes and face. "If this is all you are going to do or talk about, just pull over. You're wasting my time," I say through clenched teeth.

"Careful, daughter," comes the man's voice from the front seat. "We don't have a lot of time. Give him what you mean to give him so that we can be on our way."

The girl's head whips around to look at her father. "I want him to understand the outcome of his actions."

Her words spark outrage inside me. I can't control it. My arms reach for her neck. Just one little squeeze, I tell myself.

Her head smacks against the window glass as my fingers wrap around her throat. The action feels good. Almost too good, I realize.

The car screeches to a stop. "Let go of her, you evil creature!" the man screams from the front seat.

"I'll kill her," I hear myself say. My voice hums with anticipation. "Keep driving, or I will kill you both."

The girl looks at her dad and nods. She's not struggling. Not yet. The car bumps back into traffic as he reluctantly agrees.

"So let me get this straight," I whisper in her ear. "Do you honestly think you can be the one to make me realize anything? I didn't come here for a damn lecture. You know Ireland. Tell me how."

"Ireland is my friend," she answers. She looks right at me. "You know how it all works. The missions. What happens to the hybrids. Well, it's not going to happen to Ireland."

Her green eyes peer into me. She is not afraid. "Ireland needs to come home," she repeats.

"You've established that. Unfortunately, she is not fit to go home at the present time." My hand slips off her throat. It's hard to make myself do it. My cravings are becoming hard to ignore. I want to feed on someone. The need for human thoughts is clogging my brain.

The girl shakes me off at the first opportunity. "Then get her ready. Things are getting worse, and the spy is getting desperate. Even though Ireland's barcode was destroyed, the higher authority is still getting their information from the spy. They know everything that's happened. They know you are not in jail, for example."

"Is me going to jail really going to make a difference? If they want her to fail, she will fail. I have nothing to offer as a resolution." My voice drops lower to hide my curiosity.

"If you go to jail, you give her more time. If you do not, you give *them* more reason to see her as a failure. This is what the higher authority wants. They want to see her fail. They are all being controlled, but deep down, they know what's happening is wrong. There are few that can change the course for her. My adoptive parents can help her, but they've got to have a reason to strike against the spy. No jail for you means there isn't a reason to help Ireland. You go to jail. She passes the mission. Her *last* chance to get her freedom depends on you."

The girl shifts around and takes something out of her pocket. Her hand encloses the object so that I can't see what it is. "I don't understand the struggle you and Ireland have dealing with the imbalance of control. I can see you are struggling to keep from hurting me or reading my father. But, if Ireland is still with you, I have to assume you care for her more than the rest of the hybrids. And that's why I've decided to give you this." She unfolds her hand and shows me the box.

My breath catches. Ireland's box is exactly what I need. "How did you find it?"

"I went where my adoptive parents told me to go." She shrugs. "They really want to change things at home."

I nod and take the box from her. "What's she supposed to do with it?"

"She was never told what to do with it. She was just told to open it when she really needed it. It will not open until she's ready for it. It's a tool to get her back. Someone will come down and get her. Make sure she's available to meet them."

"Tell me your name so that I can tell Ireland," I say, uncertain if I should trust her or not.

The girl smiles. "She knows me by Faith."

"Alright," I answer while taking a mental note. "What's your dad's name?"

"Why do you need to know that?" Faith glances at her father.

"So that I can mentally remember you for the future." I smile. If I have their names, I can track them. Humans are all traceable. Even the hybrid ones.

"My name is Sam," answers Faith's father.

"Now that I have your names, I can track you anywhere. You understand that if trust becomes an issue, I will have to find you."

"It won't come to that," Faith says.

"Time will tell," I mutter to both of them.

"It won't," she repeats.

"Good. Now, let me out." I scoot back to reach for the door handle. Time is ticking, and Ireland might already be awake.

Faith reaches for me and grabs my arm. My eyes drift downward, and I struggle to keep from snatching her hand off. She doesn't know when to stop. My mind snaps to attention, desperate for thoughts. I bite my lip to fight it.

This girl gave me the box, so I have no reason not to trust her. Still, I've got to get out of here before I hurt her or her father.

Faith clears her throat. "You are not as cold as I thought you would be. I've seen you before, and the Greve I've seen in the past is not the Greve I see now. You might have changed Ireland, but she's changed you, too."

Our eyes meet for a second before I nod. She's right, but can I make myself remember? Will I be able to remember what's true and fair when the time is right?

The car stops long enough for me to climb out. Faith waves at me before pulling off, out of sight.

Nighttime has now fallen, and the city lights cast shadows on the buildings in front of me. The club crowds and bar hoppers are starting to emerge. It won't be long until the streets are filled with the kind of evil I crave. All the more reason to get back to Ireland.

Chapter Thirty-One

Ireland

When I wake, I think of only one thing. The pain. My back feels icy cold even though fire surrounds me. A deep throb runs through my spine as I try to move around. It feels as though my flesh is being ripped apart. I shudder to think that maybe it actually has been ripped apart. And by my mother, nonetheless.

What happened comes back to me in sequences. Her nails slicing down my back, leaving gaping holes and sores. My mind bursting with resistance as my mother beat me from the inside out.

Even now, my thoughts are sluggish. How could a mother be so cruel? But then I hear myself laughing. She's a damn demon. How else should I expect her to be?

My veins burn as her poison finds its way through me. She's taking over my body, and my mind-and there's nothing I can do about it. One look around the room proves that I am truly alone. Greve's house stands empty. He's forgotten me. My mother despises me. My father is better off without ever having me in his life.

Jade was right when she said I would wake in pain. But I never expected that it would hurt this much.

Greve's eyes meet mine the next time I wake. Instead of pain, I feel numb. Actually, I feel dead. I'm dead inside. The pain is still there though. It comes in waves, sloshing in and out of my muscles and nerves. Her poison is still busy, making sure the angel part dies forever.

"You're awake," Greve whispers. His voice breaks me from my thoughts.

"And you were gone," I answer, remembering the first time I woke up.

Greve looks at me uneasily. "Only for a while. I went to get your box back."

"Box?" The memory barely comes to me. Oh, yes. The box was given to me *up there*. It's supposed to help me somehow. "It's too late for all that now. I don't want it."

Greve looks at me for a second, as if trying to decide what to say. "Then I will put it away until you do want it."

"Might as well throw it out," I mutter while flexing my arms and legs. My body is tense. My nerves feel on edge. Everything is off-balanced.

Greve leaves for a minute to put the box where he thinks I won't find it and then returns with a towel. "Let's get you cleaned up and dressed. Then we can decide what to do next."

One glance at the towel reminds me of water. And that's something I don't want. My body shivers at the thought. Only ... water used to not bother me at all. Am I really that far unbalanced that water will hurt me?

I realize I must be because otherwise, water has no effect on me. This, of course, is what Mother wanted all along. I am becoming *her* in all aspects. The scary part is that I no longer care if that happens. The part of my brain that is responsible for making rational decisions is being overrun by her poison. I can *feel* it.

"The fire is dying," Greve points out in my silence.

Flames that used to cover me are now only smoking embers. My throat clenches. Fire. I've got to have fire.

Greve sees my reaction and raises his eyebrows at me. "It's okay. I need it too. Get out, and I will work on it." He throws me the towel.

I catch it in one swift motion before it touches the embers. My legs protest the feeling of crawling as I make my way out of the fireplace. Ash and soot cover me from head to toe. It's everywhere. But even though I am covered, I still feel my face grow hot due to the sudden realization that I am naked.

Greve doesn't seem to notice how embarrassed I am. He bends over to tend to the fire, not caring that the girl beside him is naked.

A growl escapes my lips, and it takes a moment for me to realize I am the one making the noise. That all too familiar feeling of heat and anger rushes through me, and I don't know why. *He doesn't notice me.* That is stupid to think. I didn't want him to notice me a couple of seconds ago. Why does it matter now? Of all things to think about, Greve noticing me and my body shouldn't be high on the list.

Before I can even think about what I am doing, I clear my throat to get his attention. He should desire to be with me. Greve should *want* me.

He spins his head around and gives me a troubling look. "You're not in the shower," he says more of a statement than a question.

"Nope. That's because you aren't in there either," I hear myself respond. What am I doing?

Greve coughs. "Hmm ... what?"

My legs move without my mind giving consent. It's like I'm being controlled by an outside force. My toes struggle to stop my feet from moving farther. Regardless of how much I try, Greve now stands directly in front of me.

My hand gravitates toward his face. "You should want me, but you don't."

Greve stands still, piecing together my words. His eyes grow wide when he finally connects the pieces. "I can assure you that is not a problem." His eyes grow red. "But, Ireland, your mind is going to gravitate toward sin. We will not be a byproduct of what your mother's poison is making you do or think."

Deep down, I am thankful for his words. There's still a part of me the poison hasn't reached yet, and I credit that with being why I feel slightly thankful for what he just said. Greve is right. My body and my mind are gravitating toward sin, and the temptation is almost too strong for me to fight.

Greve takes my silence as a win because he wraps the towel around me. His hand touches the small of my back and that brings back instant thoughts of lust. Thoughts of him kissing my lips come through the entire muddle inside me. In this moment, my mind is focused on him and only him. Nothing else matters. I'm hungry. *Starving*, in fact, because my body is so unbalanced. My body needs the sin in order to keep my demon counterpart in control.

"Help me," I pull the words out of me before throwing myself on top of him. Lust. Need. Temptation. Embarrassment. Shame. All these feelings pour out of me as my lips touch his. Greve returns the kiss, and for one blissful moment, we connect in want and need. Heat traps inside my head as the demon part of me becomes satisfied.

My mouth runs along his neck. The scent of him invades my senses until I reach his chest. I stop to catch my breath, and that's when he pulls me away.

Greve's hands wrap around my elbows in an effort to keep me off. "You are making this difficult," he murmurs under his breath. "How can I help you when you keep tempting me?"

"I ... I don't know what's happening." My mouth lets out a whimper. So many thoughts. So many feelings. My mind is in information overload.

"I'm dizzy," I hear myself saying as the room starts to sway. My face grows hot. My mouth becomes dry. A sharp pain starts in my toes and slowly moves up until it reaches my head.

Greve rushes to get behind me as my head falls toward the floor. He catches me in time so that my head lands on his shoulder. I see him move me, but I can't feel him. I can't feel anything.

My body sways in Greve's arms as he heads toward the bathroom. The swaying motion makes me nauseous. That spirals into me becoming sick all over the floor. Whatever this is will be the death of me.

"You are going to live," Greve speaks to me. "Thank god you are only part demon. The angel part of you does not want to let go."

What if it does let go completely? I want to ask. What if I can't fight any longer?

"I'm losing," I say, my voice trembling. "It's losing," I clarify, referring to my angel self. And just to make sure my angel side *knows* it is losing, the demon side multiplies the pain.

Searing pain pulses at my temples. The ceiling light burns my eyes. Greve's footsteps echo across the floor. My eyes flash to the familiar bathtub, and my stomach roils.

The poison screams inside me. It doesn't want the water. My body begins to thrash against Greve, hoping to get away from what is about to come.

"You are about to be fully controlled by the poison. I may kill myself in an effort to keep you alive, but that's the risk I'm going to have to take."

Greve takes me with him into the bathtub. My body presses up against his as Greve gets ready to turn on the faucet. He takes my arms in his hands and secures them in place. Then gently, he starts the water trickle.

First, my ears hear the noise. A slow gushing sound travels through the pipes, forcing the water out. Then my eyes see the droplets falling down toward my feet.

My heart hammers in my ears. Time slows before me as my lungs try to keep up with the forced breathing inside me. I am terrified.

One droplet connects with my flesh as it slowly trickles down my foot. My skin sizzles against the cool touch. Soon, the room is filled with my screams.

"You're okay," Greve whispers in my ear. "Everything is going to be fine."

He tries to convince me that his actions are necessary. The water is the only way to get rid of the unbalance. No matter what he says, it's not enough.

I'm *not* convinced.

I will die if he turns the water up. "Going to die!" I proclaim in thoughts and rambles.

"No," Greve responds, voice firm. "Not while I'm here."

"You can't control it. You can't control *her!*" My eyes have the sensation of forming tears, but they do not fall. Instead, they burn worse than before.

"I'm getting rid of your mother's influence," Greve says. He reaches over and turns the faucet on full blast. Water flows everywhere. It covers my legs and feet and starts to flow toward Greve.

Greve hisses as soon as the water comes in contact with his skin. It soaks through his pants and is rising toward me.

"Don't," I mumble while the pain takes me places I've never experienced before. In heaven, I am immortal. On Earth, the immortality fades. But as an imbalanced angel, death can come all too quickly.

Chapter Thirty-Two

Ireland

My eyes flutter open only to see that I am still floating in water. I blacked out. That's the only explanation. The pain was too much for me, so my body did the only thing possible—it shut itself off from everything.

Greve breathes into my ear with ragged, pained sounds. His arms no longer hold me in. They are lying still in the water that used to be clear.

Now, the tub is filled with a foamy black substance. It floats to the surface as if it's struggling to keep itself separated from the pure water below.

Must be the poison. Oh, god. That's what was inside of me! The foam pops and moves of its own accord, struggling to stay together as one big mass on top of the water.

If it can, it will find a way back inside me. I can't let that happen. If it gets back inside me, there will be no going back. I couldn't get lucky twice.

My body shudders from weakness, but also from just thinking about what happened. The pain was something I could never experience again. Of that, I am sure. And not to mention the fact that it was controlling me.

What happened comes back in bits and pieces. The sensation of being pulled a million different directions, and I had no way of stopping it. My mother tried to kill me on the inside so that she can take me over on the outside. All it would take would be for me to break. For my body to go so weak that she would have no problem using me and abusing me even worse than what she already has.

And then the way Greve fought me in order to save me ... those moments hit me straight in the chest. If it wasn't for him, I would be a shell. Or I would be dead. The guy I was supposed to put in jail ... the guy I was charged with stopping ... saved me. Greve is complex; that much is true. But he has changed in such a way that I didn't even think was possible.

He is not the arrogant, heartless boy he likes to portray himself to be. Greve and I are one and the same. We are the by-products of our demon parents. We struggle with the reality of what that means. Greve and I are stronger than what our parents have planned for us.

Greve begins to cough in my ear. The noise brings me back to the situation at hand. We are in a tub filled with my mother's venom. The venom almost turned me. It almost killed the real me. Thanks to Greve, I can think straight again.

I rise up out of the water, hoping to have enough strength to maneuver Greve out with me. He can't stay in here, and neither can I.

His coughing gets worse. His breathing is slowing. I've got to act fast because I don't know what shape he will be in when he wakes.

Holding his arms, I pull him into a sitting position. My body aches in protest. It's been through too much, and it's not willing to do more than what is required.

I blow out a sigh of concentration. I'm weak, but I'm not useless. He will come out with me. He's got to get by the fire and dried off so that he can begin to heal.

"All because of me," I say looking into his face. "You passed out because you were holding onto me. I'm not leaving you here."

I go behind his back and push up, hoping for better results. Greve's body leans over the edge of the tub just enough so that I can pull him out on the other side. One more pull, and his body topples over the side and onto the bathroom floor.

I cut the water off from the faucet source, which is something I should have done the moment I woke up. Water is everywhere. It covers the bathroom floor, making puddles all the way into part of the living room and kitchen.

I should feel *something* because I'm still standing in water. Pain or dizziness or even nausea. My body has stopped having reactions to the water. That's a good sign that all the poison is out of me.

Taking Greve by the arms, we scoot across the water to the part of the apartment that is dry. The fire still burns in the hearth, which is something close to a miracle. "Finally, something goes right," I mutter under my breath.

He's got to get dry, and he's got to get warm. Those are my main two concerns. Forget me. As long as Greve is all right, then I will be. I will find a way to be okay.

I place him by the fire and prepare myself for the next task at hand. My heart hammers in my chest. Sweat drips off my forehead, and it feels like butterflies are dancing in my stomach. His clothes have to come off.

"Just do it," I say out loud. He's already seen me so what's the big deal? Plus, I'm still sitting here naked. So much for modesty. Modesty went out the window a long time ago.

My hand brushes against his face before I decide I will just have to get over this whole thing. I was trying to throw myself at him because of the imbalance, and now, I can't imagine seeing him that way. I hate this. I hate all of this and how *she* is trying to control me.

"The hell with it ..." I mutter in frustration. My hands take what's left of his shirt and pull until the fabric comes apart. Sounds of clothing tearing fill the air until Greve is shirtless in front of me. Next comes the pants.

Okay. I will have to do this too. Biting my lip, I work on the button of his jeans. It comes loose so that I can slide the jeans all the way off. Now, all that's left is his boxers.

Right. Okay. Do they really have to come off? I mean ... he'll be all right if I just push him closer to the fire ...

No. They have to be removed, too. Not one single drop of water can remain on his skin. I can't be a wuss. He's risked so much for me. It's time I do something for him.

Making a noise between a sigh and a cough, my fingers touch the edge of the fabric and pull down. My gaze wanders away from his body. I won't look at him. Not in that way, and not when he's unconscious.

When the boxers slide off, I take that as the perfect opportunity to snatch a blanket and cover him as quickly as possible. The blanket comes to the middle of his stomach and covers all the things my eyes are telling me not to see.

I find the clothes nearest to me that will fit. Black pants and a silver t-shirt are the closest, so it's an easy decision.

Now that his clothes are taken care of, I can rest a little easier. Greve seems to be okay. I seem to be okay. Maybe the worst is over, and I can go home. I would want nothing more than to never see my mother again.

After scooting Greve closer to the fire, I lay down beside him. Fatigue sets in after a few minutes, and my eyes start to droop. One minute, I'm thinking about what's to come, and the next, my eyes close into darkness.

🐦

I dream of him. His lips on mine. The way his hands move along the curve of my spine. His lips kiss the outside of my ear and travel down to my throat. Greve presses me close so that I can't get away. He laughs when I try to wiggle away from his touch.

"Where are you going?" he teases. "You can't get away from me."

I shiver when his breath reaches my face. "I don't think I'm ready to go any farther," I answer. "Let's just stay like this."

Greve smiles at me. "You can't keep acting like you want more from me and then change your mind. I will have you *now.*"

"What? What are you talking about?" My words collide into one big question.

"I'm not going to fight off the urge anymore and neither are you. I want you and you want me so ..."

I push my hands up against his chest. "No, not like this. I'm not ready."

Greve won't budge. "You wanted to have me before I put you in the water. Maybe I should have kept you that way."

My eyes connect with his, and all I see is red. Red-filled lust and desire. "You said you wouldn't take advantage of me," I mutter. "You said we wouldn't."

Greve presses his body closer, causing my hands to become trapped under his weight. He looks right at me. "I lied."

Adrenaline starts pumping through me. My body is telling me it's time to fight and fly. "No! Get off!"

"Make me," he says while trying to raise my shirt.

"Help!" I cry out. "Don't do this!"

A laugh escapes his throat. The sound takes my breath away because it does not belong to him.

Shrill, heavy laughter fills the air. "See what I can make him do to you? See what I can make anyone do?"

I look around Greve to see her. My mother is standing close, holding her arms out to me. "If you don't come with me, more things like this will happen. I will break you. I swear to it."

"Never! You're a monster!"

My mother chuckles. "You are part of me. Who's the monster now?"

My own screams jar me awake. One glance at Greve sleeping shows me all that was just a dream. My heart slows down to a semi-high pace. She's everywhere. I can't escape her. Not even in my dreams.

The tears fall before I can even register what's happened. I let them come. Sobbing is all I can think about doing. How can I get past this? How can I get past her?

I don't know if I can.

"You won't get past me," comes a voice from behind the main door. Chills go from my head to my feet at the sound of my mother's voice.

She's back. It's too soon. I'm not ready. I'm not healed enough to handle this.

"Come with me," she says opening the front door. Mother holds her hands out to me like she did in the dream. "You've survived the first test. Time for number two."

I glance at Greve still sleeping on the floor. He's out, and there's nothing more I can do for him. But I don't want to leave or go with her. I'm terrified, right down to my bones.

"I'm not going," I spit out at her.

Jade walks up to me quicker than my eyes can register. "You'll come, or I will call Edgeman on your love toy. Would you want him terminated?"

"You said you can't kill him," I point out.

"No, I can't. His father has that right. Would you like to see if his daddy wants to do the honors now? I believe you know what will happen if you don't come with me."

Greve will die. I might die, and then it will be over. No do-overs. No option of escape or freedom. We will be just two broken teenagers who died at the hands of their parents.

"Fine. I will come. Don't hurt him." I take one more look at Greve before getting up. If anybody gets out of this alive, it will be him. He won't die because of me.

"You expect me to make that promise?" Mother shifts toward the door. "Edgeman can do what he likes with his spawn, just as I can with mine."

My body walks toward her as I start to feel her presence. She pulls me close with her mind. My physical body loses all control, but mentally, I am still me. "I am your blood! Does that not count for anything?"

Mother shrugs, her face pulled tight. "You would already be dead if you weren't. Does that make you feel any better?"

My eyes connect to hers. I know that eye contact is a mistake. I've given her the easiest way to control me. But still … she needs to see that I am not just her toy. I am *me*. And I will fight to stay me.

"You are a monster," I respond trying to sound strong.

Jade spins to look at me. She smiles. "Yes, I guess I am. It's funny how things turn out in the end. Before long, you will be just like me. We can be the mother-daughter duo you've always wanted."

My hands form into fists at my side. "I'll never be like you. I'd rather be dead."

Mother places her hand on my shoulder and squeezes. Her mouth touches my ear. "Wishful thinking … now move."

And I do. I move to wherever she plans on taking me. Inside, my heart is screaming. It's pleading for a quick resolution. But my mind isn't hearing me. It's too busy following the soft commands of my mother's voice as she whispers for me to keep walking.

"Obey. Obey. Obey me," Mother commands in my ear.

Her orders flow through me. They numb me and deplete me.

"Obey?" I mumble.

"Obey," Jade agrees.

Chapter Thirty-Three

Ireland

Jade keeps her hold on me as we walk through town. Her nails dig into my shoulder as she talks to me, never slowing down enough for me to break free.

Everyone around me seems blurry. Their chatter seems muffled. I'm not getting a clear sound out of them. The only thing that is loud and clear is my mother.

"Can you feel them, Ireland? Can you feel their sorrow? Humans are so weak. I barely have to make an effort if I want them to do something. They don't question. They don't fight. Humans aren't worth much, but I do enjoy the entertainment they provide."

"Hmm," I say in hopes it will be enough for her.

The public stares at us as we walk down the street to wherever Jade has in mind. They know we are different, even if they don't want to believe it. And they are too timid to try to do anything about us. That's probably a good thing. I don't want someone to die because of me.

"In fact," my mother continues, "their entertainment value is about to go up another level."

I want to question her, but she's not allowing me to. Instead, she tells me to stop walking. We stand on the outside of the central hub for clubs and bars. Mother waves a hand, and a taxi zooms in to pick us up.

"We will be back here later," Mother whispers to me. "There's something else we must do first."

She pushes me into the taxi and climbs into the seat beside me. Her energy pulses around me. She's hungry.

"Where to?" a young girl about nineteen says from the driver's seat.

"Take us to the corner of Smith and Allen. You've got five minutes. If you don't get us there in that time, I will kill you."

The girl swings around to look at Jade and me. Her eyes grow in shock. I flinch at the way she looks at me. I feel her terror, and Jade feels it, too.

"But ... that's across town," the girls says.

Mother licks her lips and smiles. "I know."

Hurriedly, the girl drives off into traffic. She doesn't want to believe what my mother says is true. I know, though. Jade isn't kidding.

The next five minutes are the longest in my life and quite possibly the shortest for our driver. We don't even make it two miles before the girl's five minutes are up.

By the time my mother commands her to pull the car into the nearest alley, the girl is sobbing hysterically.

"Don't," I plead.

Jade is too concerned with the girl to remember to keep me silent. Mother's red eyes focus on me. "Shut up, girl!"

I drop my gaze, feeling completely numb. I can't just sit here and let this happen. What can I do when she has me in this mental hold?

The driver tries to make a run for it, only to be caught by her hair halfway out of the car. She is dragged back in by her shirt and hair. My mother gets beside her victim, wedging herself between the front seat and the steering wheel.

"Tell me your troubles," she purrs into the girl's face.

"Please don't kill me!" the girl cries.

Jade tsks at her and then places her forefinger on the girl's forehead. Their eyes connect at her touch, and Jade opens her mouth to speak. "You will be complacent. No moving or fighting. Be a sweet little thing for the last few minutes of your life."

The girl stops then and becomes silent. Jade's body starts to vibrate, and all different types of emotions come pouring out of the girl. Her name, I find out, is Bethany. I hear her name repeating in my head.

Bethany. Twenty years old. Has a son named Houston. Boyfriend named John. She's an addict. Cocaine is the drug of choice. All of her bad choices seep into the car and find their way to me.

My body shakes from the impact. I don't want to know about her, and I don't want to feed off her energy. It's an act of violation, and while I know I've done it before, I no longer want to do it again. The desire is gone. My mother, however, is just becoming more eager.

"Come here," she says to me while not taking her eyes off of Bethany.

"Never."

Jade snatches my hair and pulls me toward her before I can register what happened. A sharp pain starts at my temple from her touch. "I didn't ask," Mother hisses at me.

The pain begins to shoot through my arms, causing me to feel weak. She's doing this to me. I can't live through this again. Not this type of pain.

"Stop it," I make myself say. "Stop!"

Jade grips my hair tighter, ripping some out in the process. "Feel her. Taste her misery. You will embrace the demon blood in you one way or another!"

She pushes me so that my skin touches Bethany's head. Immediately, harsher things pour out of her and into me. Bethany's life plays out in my mind like a movie. Scenes of poor choices and mistakes flow out of her until I catch a set of green eyes looking at me. Then comes the name that I've already heard before. Those green eyes belong to her son, Houston. He was her salvation and her reason to keep going. Houston saved her in every way possible.

I shake my head, trying to get free of her. My mother's hand forces my head back down. She is un-relenting.

Bethany's heart begins to slow, and her breathing becomes staggered. This is it for her. I don't know how I can tell, but I do. Mother is killing her. She's tak-ing her soul.

The sound of screams fills the car. It's me. I'm screaming for me. For Bethany. For Houston. For eve-ryone's who's ever been in a situation they couldn't control.

When Bethany's heart stops, the last few scenes of her life filter out of my head and disappear. My hands touch her face because I simply can't believe my mother killed her in front of me. The girl is dead just because my mother was hungry. She wanted her to feel pain, and she wanted her to die.

Worst of all, I can feel the heat returning to my cheeks. The familiar sensation of need and want burns through my veins. No ... No!

"You feel it returning, don't you?" my mother whispers in contentment. "Embrace it because you will never escape it. It's who you are, who you should want to be. Demon blood is powerful. It's sacred, and you will learn to love it. Even if I have to force the angel part of you into submission."

It won't go away. It *can't.* "I feel nothing," my voice brings the coldness right out of me.

Jade looks at me, smug. She knows I'm lying. "You will start to feel it return whether you want it or not. Now, get the human out of my sight." She waves her hand at me as if she can't stand to touch the lifeless human in front of her.

I consider arguing with her, but I know she would dispose of her in the most unhuman way possible. "We are getting out anyway, aren't we? Let's just leave her in here."

She needs to be left here so that someone can find her and bury her. I look up at my mother, waiting on a response.

"Fine. You can ride with her until we get to where she was supposed to take us." Jade throws Bethany's lifeless body right on top of me before getting behind the wheel.

My body shudders from the contact. I've never seen a dead person up close. It's not something I want to remember. Silently, I push her off and lay her next to me on the seat. "I'm sorry," I whisper, making myself look at her.

"She can't hear you," my mother says to me. "Does sorry bring her life back?"

"No," I mutter while trying to hold back my emotions.

"Demons don't apologize for killing humans."

"I'm not all demon," I say even though I know she already knows.

Mother's eyes catch mine in the rearview mirror. "And angels don't kill humans."

"You killed her!"

Jade lifts her eyebrows in surprise. "Ireland, you killed her. I just helped. You read her thoughts. *You* were so greedy that you even took her soul! That heat and longing you feel is because of her. It's because the demon in you needed her." She laughs at me then. "Pity. Doesn't that mean that you can't return to heaven? Killing humans is against all the rules. Your father won't want you. You are becoming too much like *me*."

Chapter Thirty-Four

Ireland

Bethany's body slides off the seat as Jade rolls the car to a stop. My stomach rolls from the sudden impact. And because I can't stand the thought of having Bethany's body lying face down on the muddy floorboard, I hoist her body back up into position before my mother can say otherwise.

Jade opens her door, not caring to say anything else. She gives me one look to let me know I must follow her.

I murmur a silent prayer to whoever will listen before exiting the car. Cool air greets me as soon as I stand outside. My mother grumbles about something, but I try to zone her out. Maybe, if I pray hard enough, I will find myself in a much better situation.

Jade whistles at me, much like I'm her pet instead of her daughter. My face flushes with insult.

"We are going in there," she points to the building to the right.

My eyes glance to the structure in question, and my mouth gives an involuntary gasp. It appears to be a two-story brick building with no windows. There's one door, exactly in the center, that would provide a way of escape. The bricks are broken in places, and some of the mortar has been chipped away. It looks more like a horror house that I can't escape from if I go in.

Mother sees the panic on my face and takes that as a good sign. Her nails dig into my arm as she drags me inside.

"I have a bit of a surprise for you," she whispers. "But in order to get the full effect, you are going to have to be a good little demon. Think you can do that for me?"

I want to say no, but I'm scared to. If she beats me too much, I won't be able to even attempt to escape. "Yes, good little demon," I respond in hopes that it will be enough to please her.

My mother takes me by the elbow and drags me into a room adjacent to the hallway before I can say anything. White light blinds me as we walk in. Every surface of the room is white. My eyes water from the effort of taking it all in.

The smell of bleach and antiseptic fills my nose, making it burn. My mother is indifferent to the room as she makes sure the door shuts behind us.

She clears her throat to talk. "Demons should never be nice to others without some motive behind it. So, this afternoon, I've decided to show you what happens when you are kind to humans and the like."

We stare at each other for a couple of seconds, with her seeing if I will say anything, and me wondering what this will lead up to. The door clicks open, bringing our eyes away from each other.

Entering the room are two male humans, both with hands bound behind their backs. Metal handcuffs stretch over their skin so tight welts are beginning to form along their wrists.

My world stops when I recognize who they are. This can't be happening. I never wanted this for them.

Jade jerks her head toward the back of the room as a means to communicate where the men are supposed to go. They go without one word and stare numbly at me once they get there.

"You recognize them," my mother exclaims after taking another look at me. "Very good!" Jade snaps her fingers at me. "These men are here because of you. Imagine if you would have just left them alone."

"They didn't do anything wrong," I say in the strongest voice possible. "So, let them go, and I will make a mental note not to ever ask for a ride again, and I won't alter an addict's way of thinking."

"Mental notes are useless. Especially yours." Jade makes her way over to the men she's captured.

She grabs the first one by the chin and looks back at me. "I will get through to you one way or another. Being around death will change you easily enough. Seeing it and being the one that causes it is the quickest way to get that angel switch to turn off again."

My eyes narrow at her, silent. I figure it's best to not talk at the moment. That way I might buy some time for all of us.

"Your boy toy is making things harder for me. Greve got all the poison out. Too much of it, in fact, and now you are back where we started. I can't be having that, so I decided to go to further measures and move forward with the second step in the process."

"What's this got to do with Dylan and Levi?"

"Everything. You made a point to touch their lives in some way. Now, it's time to touch them permanently," Jade hisses at me.

"They are just bystanders. They did what I asked because I read their minds and gave them orders!" My voice becomes close to shrieking range. "I will not hurt them!"

Jade moves to Levi and snatches his head back to expose his neck. He whimpers under her touch. "Oh, yes you will," she says simply. "You will do more than hurt them. You will kill them on my orders."

"No! No more! I won't! I can't! They are innocent." They have family, and if I have to go through watching someone else die, I will lose my mind.

The negative and positive thoughts start to collide inside me. I'm so scared of losing who I am. I'm terrified of killing them. What if I can't get away? What if I will never get to go back home? The reality of what Mother is asking takes another toll on me. The once hardened wall of security around my mind starts to crumble more than it ever has before.

Kill them. Don't. Kill them. Don't ... My blood pulses through me with a sense of betrayal. Part of me wants to see the suffering, and the other half wants to save them.

Innocent. Guilty. Innocent. Guilty. Don't. Kill them. Don't. Kill them.

I'm so wrapped up inside my own mind that I don't see her coming until she's already in front of me. Mother places a small pistol in my hand. She looks me right in the eyes, her voice finding its way through the wall I've so desperately tried to build.

"Aim it right at their head. Pull the trigger. You do this, and guns will no longer be an obstacle. You kill them, and you might live to see another day with your thoughts mostly intact."

Her voice makes my brain switch into overdrive. She's ordering me to kill them. She wants me to hurt them, which is one of the worst things an angel can do. Hurting them means shame among my people. Killing the humans means an automatic damnation. There will be no going home ... no wings. And certainly, no freedom and no escape. Not to mention the fact that I will be a killer of innocents and that will forever be what I'm known for.

"I will do anything. *Anything* else for you! But I will not be a killer," my voice shakes from mentally fighting her demands. "Spare them and punish me."

Jade throws her hand over my mouth to silence me. Her breath crawls over my neck to finally rest above my ear. My body shakes as I try to fight back a scream. Just her touch can send me over. Visions of her nails cutting my skin circulate in my mind. I shudder from those thoughts and make myself remember that part is over and in my past.

"My dear, punishment is what you deserve. Killing them would serve as a terrific reminder. You will learn to never feel for anyone. What is important is our cause. We will take down the human race one governor, one leader, and one president at a time. They will do whatever we want because they will have no choice but to do what we tell them. That's the beauty of mind control."

Jade makes a noise that I mistake for a scream. She's laughing at me, the humans, and anyone and everyone she deems beneath her. It's a cold, disheartening noise that sends shivers down my spine and makes men everywhere duck for cover.

"I won't say it again." Jade takes my face in her hands. Her eyes find mine and circle their way into my soul. "Kill them now, or I will kill you. If you don't kill them, I will make the spy deliver your father to Earth. He will be hunted down like an animal, and I will wait until all his angel presence is gone before I torture him. You can help me. It can *totally* be a bonding experience.

"You choose." Jade smiles at me before forcing the gun back into my hand. Her eyes find mine again, and this time, I know I'm gone before she says her last words to me. Her desire hits me straight in the heart, forcing me to believe I want the same as her.

"End them. They are not innocent. Humans are *never* innocent," Jade whispers, cold and final.

She lets me go and walks toward the men to make sure she's in place for the show.

The words sink in, forming the brutal realization of what must be done. The bad in me is overrunning the good. My blood flows wild and strong with the desire to please her. The angel part is losing focus ... again. Back and forth my mind goes, fighting against itself and what I have been ordered to do.

Killing those men means my father will live. Hurting them means maybe the hurt can stop for me. But they are innocent. No one deserves to die. No one should be killed because of what they are.

Kill. Kill. Never feel. Innocent. Let them live. Jade commands blood. Kill. Kill them all ...

My hands shake as the gun is pointed at Dylan. Even through my mother's commands, I make myself look at him. He's crying to the point of hysteria, and I'm not too far behind him. The sweat from my hands makes the gun hard to hold. Dylan and I stare at each other, both feeling hopeless and tortured. I can't do it. I can't. I won't be the one she wants. She will just have to find someone else.

Working through her demands is brutal. But I am determined. Blood rushes to my head when I close my eyes. Hoping ... trying ... finding ... the one thing that she can't touch inside me. And when I find it, she's there waiting to shove me back out.

A scream fills the room. It takes me a minute to realize the sound is coming from me. My knees feel on the verge of collapsing. My head is exploding in pain. Can't fight her. Not strong enough to take control.

I feel Jade on me again. She takes my hand in hers, lifts the gun, and pulls the trigger in one swift motion. A body falls. And when the gun goes off a second time, I'm too gone to fully hear it. My knees give out as the second body hits the ground. Darkness closes in on me.

Panic. Can't breathe ... vision fades ... everything is blurry. Losing who I am ... I'm fading ... fading ... *gone.*

Chapter Thirty-Five

Greve

Waking up naked and alone is a confusing process. It is especially confusing because Ireland isn't here next to me like I thought she would be. My muscles strain as I raise myself up and away from the hearth. Somehow, I am here when the last thing I remember is being in that tub. I tried so hard to get that poison out of her. It had to be done, but I wasn't strong enough to see the process all the way through.

Once the water hit my system and stayed around, I was out for the count. It pisses me off that my body couldn't handle it. Ironic to think that as a demon, I can read minds and control people. My body can run faster than any human. But I can't handle a little water invading my system.

Which brings the topic back around to the fact that somehow, I am not dead, and I was brought back to the fire to heal. No doubt Ireland got me out. No one else around here cares enough about me to do that.

The problem is that Ireland is no longer here, which means she was taken by force. She wouldn't go off alone. Not after returning to her former self, which would have happened after the poison left her. Too much has happened in so little time. Her mind is in a delicate state and any major issue can send her to the point of no return.

"Damn it! Fuck!" I force myself up and get dressed in jeans and a t-shirt. Jade is after Ireland full force, and there's only one thing I can do to save her. She's got to go back home and the quicker the better. Jade took her again. I can feel it in the pit of my stomach.

She's not going to break Ireland like she's done with all the rest. Hundreds of hybrids have come through me. They trained with me, and I taught them all I know. It was always for my father or to keep my mother or myself alive. Never did I care about them until Ireland's sister came along. She restarted something inside me that I lost along the way. Slowly, the shell around me started to break when she was around. I found that I could smile and laugh again. I had gained a friend. But that all faded after her death.

The shell grew back ten times stronger than before. Never again, I told myself. I won't allow the hurt and pain of being close to someone just so my father can kill them. And I was doing fine until Ireland.

Ireland cracked the shell completely in two, and as a result, I've never felt more alive. In my heart, she's healed me. Now, it's time for me to try to heal her in return.

With shaky hands, I take the box out from where I hid it and cradle it. It's time to see what this box can do. The only thing left to do is open it. Whenever happens, I trust it will be for the best. "Now or never," I mutter.

My fingers pry the lid open, and immediately, the room explodes in color. A projected light zooms in close to show a blonde-haired, blue-eyed girl smiling at me. Her face seems familiar, but I can't place where I've seen her before. I can only assume this is someone in heaven who's been waiting for this exact moment.

My eyes narrow in on her because she's not Faith. The girl becomes unreadable as soon as she realizes Ireland is not with me. "Hello. Does Ireland need assistance?" she says as her voice projects through the light to me.

"You're not who I was expecting. What's your name?"

The girl tosses her hair back from her face. "I should ask you the same thing."

"I need to talk to Faith on behalf of Ireland. Is she around?"

"Faith should be back soon. She's a little tied up at the moment. I was told to be here just in case Ireland sent word she was ready to give up and accept defeat," the girl answers dryly.

Defeat? "Excuse me?"

The girl takes a step back from the light. "Oh, dear. Not defeat. That came out all wrong. I'm so sorry." She pokes out her lip.

"Look, can you help Ireland or not? If Faith is not around, I need someone to come get her within the next couple of hours. It needs to be someone capable and only within your group of friends. There is someone there who wants Ireland to die. Keep her hidden if you must."

"We've been waiting for her call. It's all organized. We do have one problem, though. It would appear that her tracker system was destroyed within her first day or so of arrival on Earth. We will have trouble finding her. If I can get your location, we will be able to find her easily."

"That's because I destroyed it. We didn't want you all to get in the way of Ireland's mission. Funny how things change, huh? I admit I have a bit of a problem, too. Ireland is currently not in my possession. She will be, and then I can relay the place back to you."

The girl beams at this news. "Well, great! We will be looking for you to reappear soon. Don't worry. Ireland is in great hands with me."

"She better be," I respond in all seriousness. "I'm only doing this because I've spoken with Faith. She has assured me that Ireland will be taken care of properly. Before I go, I want your name as a token of trust."

I really want her name so that if she ever appears on Earth, I can track her. If she does anything to hurt Ireland, I'm going to take note and take care of her if she comes down here for anything.

"You first," she says, almost bored.

"Greve. Now you."

"Everyone calls me Gabriella. Last names don't really matter up here. We are all angels here." Her smile seems a little too tight across her face.

"Thank you, Gabriella. I never forget a face as long as I have a name. Talk to you soon."

"We'll be ready," Gabriella answers before the light shuts off.

❦

I expected to feel better after the video feed disconnected. That isn't the case. There's a strong nagging feeling in my gut I can't quite get rid of. The best thing to do is talk to Ireland about this Gabriella before anything else happens. She will know her for sure.

With the so-called backup plan out of the way, it's time to put all my energy into finding Ireland. Finding her should be easy. It's what happens afterward that has me worried.

I pull her name out of a long list of people I've come in contact with and match it with her face. Thoughts appear, suddenly, like a generated map inside my head. I can't explain the sensation. When I was old enough, Edgeman took me aside and activated that part of my brain. Most hybrids think of it as one or two things: cool genetics or flawed DNA. Most of the time, I call this locator part of my brain a curse. But not right now. Today, this generated common locator is the best gift my father ever gave me.

Ireland's signal comes in from a few blocks away at what appears to be one of the clubs I took her to before. Let's hope it's as easy to get her back as it is to locate her.

Chapter Thirty-Six

Greve

The sound of cries and screams permeates the air as I approach the front door of the club. Ireland's screams are not in the mix of sounds coming from inside. Bracing myself, I slowly slide the door open and creep in.

Immediately, the scent of blood fills my nose. There's blood everywhere. Spatters appear on the floor, the bar, and the walls. Bodies lie on top of each other in a big pile in the center of the room. Some have bullet holes in their heads, and others have various cuts and lesions. Saying that this is a murder scene would not give it a good enough description.

My body hums as a result of all the lives lost. My eyes start to turn red. It's a sickening feeling. Part of me wants to go through the bodies to see if any souls are left, and the other part wants to see if there's any way I can save them.

Movement catches my eye toward the back of the wall, and then not long after, I hear a scream. Her scream shatters me. It's enough to make me break away from the bodies.

Jade smiles as I run to see how badly Ireland is hurt. "Your father and I knew you would come for her. Unfortunately, it's too late. She's too far gone to do anything with, so I will terminate her and move on to the next kid. I believe she has a half-brother the spy can send down for me."

"What did you do to her, Jade? What did you make her do to all those people?"

Jade hovers over me, blocking out everything but her face. "Ireland did all that of her own accord. I merely helped her realize what type of experiences she's been holding out on. Whether you like it or not, the moment you stepped in here, you wanted what was left of them. Ireland took most, I admit, but I'm sure I can find some other human for you to feast on."

"No," I respond even though the desire to have a taste of someone's soul lingers. "I'm not that person anymore. Ireland is definitely not, so whatever mon-ster you are trying to create, you need to go looking for someone else."

Jade backs away from me. "I can see the desire in your eyes. How I wish you were my child. Even on your best behavior, you are still more demon than Ireland ever will be. Take one look at her. Such a disgrace."

Jade moves to show me what's left of Ireland. My breath catches at the sight of her. Her body rocks back and forth against the far wall of the club. Her hair is matted with blood, her eyes bloodshot with desire. Ireland sees me and starts rocking harder against the wall, muttering incoherent sentences. Her fingers tear at her nails, which have grown several inches over the past couple of hours.

Nausea forms in my stomach, and fear forms in my heart. What the hell happened to her?

"What's wrong with her?" I dare not get too close to her for fear of setting her off.

"Isn't it obvious?" Jade laughs at Ireland who's still rocking back and forth against the wall. "Her mind is beyond repair."

I force myself to swallow the sickening feeling inside me. "No. I can help her. Let me help her."

"Not without a price. I have no use for her. She's too strong-willed to stop fighting, and I've grown bored with her. What I need is a strong hybrid that will bend when given an order. That will succumb to being who they are. Forcing and beating it out of someone doesn't always work. Sometimes, the results are this." Jade points to Ireland in disgust.

"Like it or not, the world will bow down to us demons, eventually. We've been shunned for too long and have had our minds set to take over the weak humans for some time. Why would demons bow down to something as fragile as humans when we can take over and do what we want? We can eat as many of them as we like. We can control their nasty breeding and only leave enough to use for our survival. Humans will live, breathe, and die at our command and control, and they won't really even realize what's happening."

Jade walks over to Ireland and pats her on the head. Ireland flitches at her mother's touch. "Imagine more of her at the hands of us. Everything can and will be ours. It's just a matter of whose side you are on."

"I take no sides. I'm caught in the middle. Having a human mother and a demon father will do that to you."

"So it would seem. Looks like you've got nothing to offer me, then. Go on and let me finish her off, or would you like to watch me again?"

"No watching. What's your price for Ireland's life?"

Jade narrows her eyes at me. "You."

My heart starts to drum loudly in my chest. "Excuse me?"

"You heard me. Give yourself up to me and I will let Ireland go. I need a strong, faithful hybrid that's already been through the tests and been proven to be successful."

"That's not possible." My eyes grow wide. "Edgeman has full control of me."

"Edgeman is a dying demon. He caused bodily harm to poor Ireland here. That is *not* allowed in our world. We do not harm each other's spawn. Doing that calls for severe punishment. That's why he hasn't been back around. Your father is awaiting his fate among our kind. It's very possible he will be jailed for years. You might even be dead by the time he's released if he lives through the punishment."

"So ... what you are saying ..." I sputter, "is that basically, I'm free from him? He won't be around to order me to do anything?"

"What I'm saying is that you renounce your father's protection and then claim your loyalty to me. It can be done. It's not known among your kind because, ultimately, what benefit would it serve?"

"But it can be very beneficial to some," I mutter through clinched teeth.

Jade laughs at me. "Not for you. Honestly, I'm giving you a chance to make things right. You care for Ireland? You think you can save her and ease some of that human guilt? Fine. But first, you will renounce him for *me.*"

"My freedom in place of hers? That's basically what you are offering."

"Don't make it sound like it's a death sentence. This is the girl you swore to protect, right? You've failed before, and you know you can't mentally afford to do it again. Isn't Ireland worth more to you than that?"

"She is worth ten times the value you could ever place on her, Jade. If I agree, it will be understood that I've done it for her. Not me or you. Her. Ireland is the reason, got it? And if I do decide to, I want your word that I can deliver her safely home without any intervention."

"Fine," Jade agrees. "I'm sick of looking at her. If you become mine, I can find you whenever I need you. No more running away, Greve. You've reached a dead-end."

"So does this mean if Ireland ever comes back to Earth and is back to normal, that you won't bother her? You said my life for hers, after all."

"I didn't say that. She's still mine. What we are doing is exchanging your life to save hers *now.*"

Ireland starts to scream as if she knows what Jade is hiding. Her body rocks harder and harder against the wall. Her bones sound like they are being crushed with every movement. Over and over, she screams and cries out. With each piercing sound, my heart starts to overrule my head. Each second she's here, the more likely she will not come back to herself. I can't let that happen. Surely, I will find a way out of this once she's safe. I'm stronger than being someone's call boy. They will see. All of them will see how much a hybrid can really endure.

"Better make a decision," Jade says with no emotion. "Ireland is causing real harm to herself."

"Tell me how to do it. I accept renouncing Edgeman. Get on with it so that I can get her home."

Jade comes back up to me, fire and desire in her eyes. "Excellent."

Chapter Thirty-Seven

Ireland

*H*is eyes stare into mine as he carefully comes my way. My breath catches from being scared. No. Don't touch me. Hands are too rough. No human should touch me. Filth. Vile creatures that should be controlled. Can't allow flesh-on-flesh contact. Don't speak. Do nothing.

"Ireland," he says. "It's okay. I'm going to take you home. Your real home so that you can see your dad."

His voice is reassuring, and I want to believe him, but I can't. He's half human, and humans are not worth talking to.

"Please," he whispers. "Jade is gone. It's over, and I will help you."

Jade. Jade? I scream at the sound of her name. Must rock to avoid her. Must tear nails to keep from becoming her ... Rock ... Rock. Blood drops from my fingers. Rock ... Rock. Pain in my back. Pain everywhere. It surrounds me, torments me.

"It's okay," he claims. "Do you remember me? I'm Greve."

My body says I know him. My mind fights to remember. "Maybe," I respond.

"Maybe is better than no," Greve responds, still looking at me. "Do you think you can trust me?"

Trust? Can't trust. Trust causes pain. Uncontrollable gut-wrenching pain. Demons don't put their trust in anyone or anything. Can't. Shouldn't ... my head begins to ache. I want to rock again. I want to escape this pain forever.

I shake my head no because I can't find my voice to speak.

Greve's face falls just long enough for me to see before he hides behind a planted smile. "You want to get out of here? To a doctor maybe? Tell me where you want to go and I will point you in the right direction."

"Just want to die," I hear myself say. "Leave me to die."

I want to ... rock. Rock against the wall. Sway. Fight the tears that form. There's too ... much ... pain ... bloodshed ... guilt ... anger. And not enough faith ... hope ... love ... forgiveness ... strength ... to keep me balanced.

Greve bites his lip. "See, that right there is a big problem. I'm not here to help you die. I'm here to help you live."

"Don't know how to feel," I whisper.

Greve rubs my head while pulling the matted strands of hair out of my face. "Then don't feel. Don't think or listen to all the voices in your head. Just follow me."

His eyes meet mine, and it's in that instance that my whole world stands still. His eyes burn crimson when he looks at me. We are both one and the same. Two lost souls. Two kids who don't know what the future holds. Two hybrids who are linked by an ever-growing desire to be free.

I nod and take Greve's hand when it's offered to me. He grabs onto me tight to keep me from falling. I'm weak from fighting the demon inside me. I shake my head to try to clear it, but that only makes the sickness worse. My knees give out from the dizziness, and my body starts to fall.

Greve's hand attaches to my waist as he pulls me back up. The feeling of his hand on me sends butterflies to my stomach. I like that he's touching me. I'm not so sure that I should. There are too many mixed feelings bubbling up inside me to know what I should feel and want I shouldn't.

"It's okay," Greve says as he pulls me against him.

Together, we walk slowly, and when we get to the front room with all the bodies, Greve leans my head onto his shoulder to shield me from them. His touch comforts me in such a way that I can only describe it as relief.

I grip Greve tighter as we walk outside the club to face the mob of people milling around, oblivious to what awaits them inside. We hurry along out of the way before people start asking questions. There are a few eyebrow raises and mumbles from the crowd, but one look from Greve shuts them right up. He has that effect on people. He can welcome them in or shut them away with just one glance.

"Over here," Greve says as he guides me into an alleyway. We go back as far as we can to get away from the public scrutiny. A chain-link fence blocks us from going any farther, and we stop and rest alongside two brick buildings.

My breathing slows along with my heart rate. Greve helps me to sit and lean against the wall before he sits down beside me.

"I'm going to tell you something, and I don't want you to freak," he whispers.

"Okay?" I can't bring myself to look at him. Greve is terrifying in the sense that my heart knows him, but my mind is so unsure of who he really is.

"Don't do that," Greve says while placing his hands on either side of my face. "Don't be scared of me. Ireland Grace was never really scared of me. You are still her in here." His hand touches my chest, right above my heart. "Once you get back home, you will remember everything. I'm so sure of it."

"Do I want to remember? Seems like my past was filled with terrible things, and that's why it was so easy to let it go."

Greve places his hand back on my face and pulls me close. "You had no choice but to let everything go. Jade caused that. Ireland, you've been through so much just in the past couple of days alone. You will get yourself back. You are already halfway there. You get home, and it will all fade into the background and solve all the questions you have."

"How can you be so sure? How can *I* be so sure I want to remember anything at all?" My voice sounds hoarse because I'm trying not to cry. Tears are creeping just above the surface, and I don't know if I can hold them in anymore.

A tear escapes despite my efforts and begins to run down my cheek. Greve wipes it away. "Because I've done it, and you will too. I can't say that you won't regret remembering it all when it comes back to you. But I can promise that all the harsh, horrible things you will be reminded of won't replace all the good things that make you who you are. You need your father just like I needed my mother. He will help you to balance it all."

"And what about you?" I whisper. "Why do you care so much? All I remember is *her*. Jade's destroyed me. She's weakened my mind beyond anything I've ever known. My heart tells me to trust you, but I barely have any recognition of who I am, much less anything else."

"Now, here comes the reason why I said I didn't want to freak you out," Greve answers while pulling me closer. "I realize that I can't say I love you. That would be too much to process and so little time to do it. So … I'm … not going to say that quite … yet."

Greve smiles. "Believe it or not, you have brought me back from a harsh place. I hope you will remember our time together, but do me a favor, okay? I am terrified that you will remember the me from *before* I really knew you. Before I cared what happened to you or anyone else. I am *not* that man anymore. So, when you start to remember who really I am … take into consideration that you've changed me into a person that I thought I would never see again. That is the reason *why* I care so much."

Greve leans over to kiss my cheek. His lips feel hot as they reach my skin. Before I register what I am doing, my head sways in his direction so my mouth can connect with his. Our lips touch and move in such a way that tells me I've kissed Greve before.

Greve takes my cue as a good sign. Soon, his mouth caresses my bottom lip, slowly and surely, in an effort to not go too fast. We stay like that for a while, just holding and kissing until he slowly breaks free from me.

"We've done that before." Greve backs away from me.

"It feels like we've done that a lot of times before," I say under my breath with a slight smile. I can't explain the thought process of kissing someone I think I know but can't really *remember* for sure. It's daring and frightening. But on the other hand, the act seems so normal, as if his arms are where I've always belonged.

"I want to continue to kiss you every minute of every day," Greve announces, so sure of himself.

I look away, embarrassed at his words. Has he really fallen in love with me? Before I can say a response, Greve lets out a suppressed breath. All good emotions have been replaced with ones that have turned his face cold and stern.

"Fuck. Your mother is calling me," he says in a growl. "I wanted more time with you."

"Why is she calling for you?"

Greve pulls away from me completely, to fish something out of his pocket. "Don't worry about all that," he answers as he takes out a small wooden box.

"You might not recall, but this box was given to you as a way to get back home. I figured out how to call some of your friends. They will be here as soon as you open the box and tell them where you are located."

The fact that Mother is calling for Greve feels off. How come I don't feel her? "I don't like this. Deep down my gut is telling me something is off. You won't tell me, will you?"

Greve hands me the box and then places his hands over mine. "You will know why when you are mentally able to handle it. Please don't take that the wrong way either. Ireland, you may think you are getting better here ... and I might be able to get you past what happened *today*. I will not be able to get you through what has happened a few days ago ... weeks ago. What your life has been like before me. Your mind is delicate right now, and the best thing I can do for you is to let you go so that you can go home and be healed. Then, I'm hoping you will come back to me, and I can explain further."

"What will you do if I decide to never come back? You are so sure that I will want to." I jump up to get closer to Greve. Then soon regret my decision. Immediately, my head begins to spin, and my knees go weak. Greve catches me before my body hits the ground. He kisses my forehead as he brings me back up, level with him.

"If you don't come back, I will have no choice but to continue on. Either way, you've changed me, and there's nothing you can do or say that will ever make me regret it. Now, open the box before your mother splits my head in two with her wailing. I'm confident I will see you again. Trust me when I say that."

Greve leans over so close that his mouth touches my ear. "You'll want to come back. It might not have anything to do with me, but I know you better than you know yourself right now. You'll come back to prove yourself."

Deep down, the inkling is there telling me that Greve is right. Whatever happened here, I'm going to want to find out. I *deserve* at least that. "Fine, I will open it." I point my finger into his chest. "Just to let you know though, I'm trusting you."

With shaking hands and a nauseated stomach, I flip the box open. A projected light comes on, showing a blonde-headed girl staring back at me. The girl's eyes reflect surprise as she takes me in.

"Hello. Where is your location, Greve?" The girl doesn't even bother to look at me once she sees Greve in the background.

Behind me, I can hear Greve mutter some town and street address to this creature. Her face seems to glow in delight, and behind her, I see a beautiful, ivory cloud of feathers extending from her shoulders. Wings. She has *wings*.

"What's your name?" I hear myself say a little too harshly than intended. My heart rate picks back up at the sight of her and those wings. Wings are what I wanted, isn't it? And this girl gives me the creeps ... there's something about her. Did I know her before?"

"Her name is Gabriella," I hear Greve say in my ear. "Faith is waiting on you," he adds for good measure.

Unlike Gabriella, Faith's name fills me with calm. "I want to see Faith," I announce to Gabriella through the screen.

The girl pulls back from the screen. "You will see her soon, I promise. She's preparing for your return." Gabriella's hand hovers over a button right beside her. "We can't wait to see you," she says before the screen disappears.

I turn back toward Greve to face him. "This isn't right. She's not a friend. I can feel it."

"Faith is though. She says Faith is waiting on you. I've met Faith and read her to be well ... willing to help you."

"She wouldn't present Faith to me. How do I know if she's really there?" My hands clench his arm. "Something is off ... something is wrong."

Greve takes my arm and pulls me close. "Okay. If you feel this strongly, then we need to move before she comes."

We take off in an effort to get out of the alleyway. Greve runs in front, as a means to guard me, while I struggle to keep my hold on him. He gets ready to turn the corner to lead us out when he stops so suddenly my body collides into the back of him.

"Going somewhere?" calls the voice that appeared on the screen.

Greve slides his arm across my chest as a way to shield me. I feel a little pull inside my pants pocket, only to look down to see Greve sliding something inside. He looks at me as if to say, "Not now."

Confused, I try to make a mental note to check my pocket later. Now is not the time to check it out.

By looking over Greve's shoulders, I can make out Gabriella walking toward us. She doesn't even bother to hide the fact that her wings are protruding from her back.

My breath catches at the sight of them. I've never seen anything more beautiful. Ivory feathers cascade from her shoulders all the way to her lower back. They look as soft as cotton and so alluring. Looking at them fills me with envy.

"As a matter of fact, we are," Greve answers for me.

Gabriella walks toward us still. She's decided to ignore Greve altogether. Her eyes penetrate into mine before she giggles at what I have become.

"Oh, Ireland! You've been down here for weeks and still couldn't complete this one simple mission." Gabriella's voice mocks me. She puts her hands on her hips before continuing. "*He* would have gone to jail for me. Honestly, it's like you don't know how to do the easiest things. This guy"—she points at Greve—"would have gone so that I could have been rewarded with my freedom. But noooo ... that's not the way you do things, is it?"

"Just shut up! None of it matters now. I'm not going with you," I say as loudly as I can.

Gabriella pulls her lips so tight it looks like she swallowed a lemon. She catches herself and then places a big fake smile on her face instead. "Yes, you are. As I said, Faith is waiting for you. She's been waiting for days."

"Let's go," Greve says while pulling my arm.

"And as for you"—Gabriella motions to Greve. "Jade has something special planned for you. You'll find out what it is any second now."

"I'm going to kill you!" Greve lets go of me to run to Gabriella. He gets about halfway before doubling over in pain. "Ahhhhh," he screams, gripping his head.

"Greve!" My body jolts into action to see what can be done for him. "Oh, god. Greve! What's happening?"

Gabriella tugs me away from him in one swift motion. "Leave him. Your mother is in need."

"Noooo! Greve! Don't!" I can't stop the tears from forming in my eyes.

He looks up at me with pain behind his eyes. "It's okay," he says weakly. "I'll find you ..."

I'm pulled away before I can hear anything else. Gabriella takes me by both arms and swings me into her arms. Her feet jump off, and soon, we are in mid-flight, racing back to the place I once knew as home.

She looks down at me with disgust. "I would drop you, but I'm commanded to get you back no matter the costs."

"Screw you," I say for lack of anything better.

"Not the best choice of words given your predicament." Gabriella smirks. "You know, I'm *quite* tired of hearing your voice. Let's get you a nap."

She leans her head back and butts me in the face. Stars dance in front of my eyes along with blurs of clouds and blonde hair. Blood trickles out of my nose, which is a side effect of impact and of being down on Earth too long. I am no longer immortal without a trip to heaven to regenerate myself.

Gabriella looks down at me. "Huh, that always works. Let's try this instead." Her hand clenches the side of my neck to put pressure on my main artery. I know in a matter of seconds the blood flow will be cut off to my brain. She presses and presses until blackness forms in front of my eyes. I look up one last time to see nothing but her cold eyes glaring back at me. Then the darkness swallows me whole.

Chapter Thirty-Eight

Ireland

My body doesn't jolt me awake as soon as Gabriella and I make it back through the drop-off. It's only when she drags me down the stairs through various levels that my body finally recognizes that it is home.

The familiar brightness welcomes me like a spotlight. All eyes are on me, and I can't decide if that's a good thing or a bad thing. I'm thinking bad by the way people are looking at me. There's not a single friend to greet me along the way to whatever destination Gabriella has in mind.

And while my body recognizes the familiar feel of this place, my mind is slow on the uptake. I *know* this is home, but do I really feel like it's home anymore? Not to mention the fact that my whole body aches along with my head. I've gone through the wringer, and I fear that I've spent so much time on Earth that whatever power I had inside me to magically heal myself is gone forever.

Gabriella stops at a door on level three just to push me through the threshold without any other warning at all.

My eyes blink from the sudden blackness that swallows the whole room. I hear murmured voices all around me, begging me to run. The sounds come at me all at once, all jumbled together in one terrifying tone.

Gabriella snatches my arm just as I turn to run back out the door.

"Not so fast! We've been waiting days for you to come back to us. You won't be leaving anytime soon." Her arm pulls mine as she drags me across the room.

My feet stumble over bodies lying on the floor. Each time I trip, sounds escape their mouths. That is enough to at least let me know that whoever they are, they aren't dead.

"What is this!?"

"You'll know soon enough. Though, I suspect you won't like what you hear." I can hear the happiness seep through her voice.

With one final jab to the arm, Gabriella pushes me down to the floor. She binds my hands and feet together, making sure I'm as uncomfortable as possible.

"I want to ask you something before I go. This might be the last chance for me to find out …" Gabriella's body shifts away from me. She doesn't wait for me to say anything. "Tell me, Ireland. That Greve guy … he is pretty hot. Did he live up to your expectations?

I flush. "Fuck off."

She shrieks out in laughter. "Because I plan on getting to know him once you're dead. I wanted to know if he was worth my time. With the way you answered, *clearly* he is."

"If I die, he will know you are involved. He would kill you before you get five hundred feet near him!"

"I'm not afraid of hybrids like you," she says as she walks out of the room.

The door clicks closed, leaving me with bodies of people I don't know.

"He's *mine*," I say to anyone willing to acknowledge my dedication to a guy I can't remember that well.

A noise comes from across the room. Someone is letting me know they hear my exclamation. The problem is that I don't know if they are calling me out for being stupid or calling me out in support.

The thing is—I don't care. In the back of my mind, things are sketchy about the past few weeks. My memories are slowly coming back to me now that I am home and out of my mother's reach. Jade almost destroyed me mentally and physically. She tried to make me something I refuse to be. And when the moment of self-destruction was imminent, I opened my eyes to him.

Greve was there, staring back at me. He talked with my mom and got her to agree, somehow, to let me come home. Without that intervention, I would still be in that club, staring into space, with no hope whatsoever.

The thought makes shivers go down my spine. Greve let me go, thinking I would get the one thing I've always wanted—my freedom. What he didn't consider was that the higher authority was never going to give me anything.

"So stupid," I mutter into the darkness. "It's all been a lie."

Voices around the room all mutter in agreement. Phrases like "yeah really" and "we are going to die" fill the room with chaos.

Everyone is too busy screaming and muttering that we don't hear her enter until the door's already wide open. Gabriella pushes a teenage boy into the room and places him down a couple of feet away from me. My eyes do a double-take when I see his face. Red hair comes down just above his mismatched eyes. One blue eye and one red eye stare right back at me. His nose matches mine, along with the way his mouth forms a thin line when he's angry.

"Get over yourselves!" Gabriella yells to everyone in the room. "Everything will be explained very soon. In the meantime, SHUT IT before someone dies earlier than intended."

"How about we kill you, and then we won't have to worry about someone killing us?" says the guy who has to be related to me.

Gabriella's hand whizzes by just before the sound of a slap silences the room. The guy grunts a little from the impact of her hand colliding with his face.

"Stop it!" I shout. "Stop! Don't hurt him!"

Gabriella flicks her eyes at me. "Oh, please. You are such a martyr."

"Stay out of this, Ireland," the guy adds while rubbing the place Gabriella hit.

My breath catches. "How do you know my name?"

The guy rolls his eyes at me. "Everyone knows your name. You're the topic on everyone's lips. We can't go half a day without the mention of your name."

"Alright." Gabriella waves her hands in the air. "Everyone is here and accounted for. The countdown begins. I cannot explain the joy I have in knowing that you all will be leaving us very soon. Especially you, Ireland," Gabriella adds before walking out the door.

Darkness takes over as soon as the door is shut all the way. I don't have to see in order to feel their eyes on me. Suddenly, I feel like bacteria under a micro-scope. Everyone wants to examine me to figure out if I'm the good type of bacteria or the bad. Am I going to wreak havoc or am I going to assist in fighting off the dangers we face?

"Okay. Seriously ... how do you know my name? How is that possible when I've been shunned to the lowest level my whole life?"

"Shunned for security, more like," mutters the guy. "Your father is one of the reasons the rest of us are in here."

His words hit me square in the chest. "What ... what ... did you say?"

"You heard me. Did you not ever consider that there were more hybrids than you? Or did you think that magically you were the only one?"

I swallow hard in hopes of making my voice stead-ier. "Look, *guy*. I've always wondered, and I've always hated the fact that I was made to feel alone when clearly, I'm not. But what you said about my father is impossible. There is no way he could be a part of this. Whatever this is ..."

"Whatever this is?" The guy's voice rises louder. "*This* is it. The end. A time of cleansing from the im-pure, of the filth that we are. We are scheduled to be dropped out of the sky, with no wings! And your dad is one of the guys heading the operation!"

"No … no … no! You've got it all wrong!" I strain my body against the restraints, to try to get closer to the guy who is calling my dad a traitor. "He hasn't been on the higher authority since my birth. We are the same as you. If anything, he will help us. My dad wouldn't let me die. He wouldn't let any hybrid die."

"He let you go to Jade, didn't he?" I can feel his eyes on me without seeing anything. "Your father is just like the rest. He let you go to see if you could pass the tests your mother gave you! And you must have failed if you were brought back. We are all failures. The angels can't use us because we are *tainted*. We will not conform to the way they think. The demons won't use us because we are too *weak* to fit into what they consider their "norm." We don't fit anywhere or into anything. It's dark in this room, but you are not blind. Ireland, *feel* us in your mind. You can do that, can't you?"

"Father didn't want me to go. He … practically forbid me to go …"

"But you went, and yet here you are," the boy says to me for the first time with pity in his voice.

"I don't believe you. You mention knowing all about Jade and my dad. Well, tell me how you know about them. Tell me something because all I know is some random stranger spouting out lies."

The boy sighs. "We might be strangers in person, but not by blood. Jade is my mother, too."

My breath catches at his words. In truth, he looks like he could be related to me. When he walked into the room, it was like looking at a male version of me. Seeing him should give me enough proof that he is who he says he is. Then again ... words are just ... words, until proven otherwise.

"If we are half-siblings, how come you never came to look for me? You act like you've known about me for years. Here you are spouting out things about me, but in reality, you never cared to see if what you heard was the truth."

"Ireland," he whispers, "I never intended on knowing anything about you. Not really. Your father came to me as a small child and forbid me to come looking for you. He said you were superior to me, and if I did come looking, he would have me killed." He laughs sarcastically. "Obviously, he intends on killing me anyway."

"He never told me about you, and I'm sorry for that. If I had known I had a half-sibling brother, I would have come looking. I don't believe my father is responsible for what's happening though. He is so gentle and kind. There must be another explanation."

"Good luck finding it," he mutters under his breath.

"I will find out what's happening. And when I do, I will come for you. You and them"—I nod to all the others in the room even though I know they can't see me.

"Don't make promises you can't keep," he says so quietly I almost don't hear him.

"Brother, I intend on keeping this promise. Our mother left me to die, crazed out of my mind. She tortured me both mentally and physically. She's forced me to kill innocents, and when I got so lost in myself, she left me. No part of her cared for me, and she is our mother. You have a similar story to tell, I'm quite sure." My voice quivers.

I continued, "Even if we didn't share the genetics of our mother, we share similar stories all the same. I don't intend on leaving anyone to go through something alone. Blood or not."

"Okay, well … no offense, but I don't need you to try to save me. Just stay out of my way, Ireland. I aim to kill anyone who tries to hurt me."

"I won't leave you," I repeat even if he doesn't believe me.

"You don't get it. I've been perfectly fine without you in my life all these years. I will be fine without you now. So let's enjoy our last few minutes as brother and sister before they come in to save you and then kill me."

His words cut me like a dull knife. It takes a while and a lot of effort to cause damage, but once the wound is there, it bleeds and hurts all the same. I suppose that is what he wanted. I won't leave him without knowing his name at least. "Give me your name, brother."

"If I do, will you leave me alone?"

"Yes. I won't say anything else to you while we are in this room."

My brother sighs, defeated. "Dad named me Enoch. It means *dedicated*. Joke's on him though." Enoch laughs. "I'm far from that. Don't call me Enoch. If you want me to answer you, call me Elah. Elah suits me better."

"And what does Elah mean?"

"I thought you weren't going to say anything else to me."

"Give me the definition, and I won't say anything else."

"Fine. Elah means a curse. That's what everyone sees me as. Either I'm a curse in their life or a curse for not doing something right. So, that seems fitting. Don't you agree?"

There it is again. The familiar feeling of hurt flows through my veins. This time, his words don't hurt me. They are made to hurt him.

"No, I don't agree. Hybrids are not curses on our people."

"Just stop talking, okay? I gave you want you wanted. Now, it's your turn to hold up our deal. I'm not in the mood to argue about our self-worth. You obviously value yourself a bit more than the rest of us," Elah snaps at me.

"Nice knowing … err … never mind." I stop myself before finishing what I wanted to say. To tell Elah that it was nice knowing him would solidify what he thinks of me. Plus, I wouldn't have meant it.

"Die fighting," he says loud enough for everyone in the room to hear.

Voices echo him in reply, "Die fighting. Die fighting!" Soon, the whole room vibrates with shouts of all the hybrids condemned to die.

Goosebumps form on my arms from the impact. They will all join together when it's time. These hybrids have all but given up. They want to die fighting our enemies. I can understand that. We've been singled out, used, and tossed away when others thought we could serve no purpose.

They have plans to take down as many of our enemies as possible because to them, they will die no matter the costs. It doesn't matter to them as long as they can take down some of the pure angels, too. But I can't bring myself to join them in their war cries. Die fighting? No, I don't want to die fighting off my ene-mies. I will fight to live.

~ 330 ~

Chapter Thirty-Nine

Ireland

It's been hours since the chanting died down. The tension in the room could snap a rubber band and send it flying into oblivion. Everyone is set to fight to the death, except me. I intend on doing more than die, and in order to do that, something else needs to happen besides me sitting in the dark with all these people.

Luckily, it doesn't appear I will have to wait any longer. Shadows just appeared under the doorway. A combination of fear and curiosity fills me as the door opens.

My heart beats so fast I might get sick from the sensation. A man appears at the doorway and his voice sends chills down my spine. "Ireland? Are you in here?"

A sigh of relief escapes from my mouth as my dad's voice slices through the silence in the room.

"Dad! Help me! Help us!"

"OH, IRELAND! Sweet Ireland. Thank god." Dad's voice cracks as he rushes to me. "How did you get in here? I only just heard that you've returned."

His arms wrap around my waist to embrace me. His familiar scent relaxes me along with the feeling of him being this close again. Seeing him now makes me realize how much I've missed him and how hurt I will be if Elah's statements about him are true.

"Gabriella put me in here with the rest of the hybrids. Dad, you've got to help them! They said something bad will happen to them."

Dad shakes his head. "I told Gabriella to inform me when you got back. This is unacceptable." He tugs at my restraints while producing a key to open the lock. "Come on. Let's get you out of here." He takes my hand and pulls me to a standing position.

"But ... didn't you hear me? I said we need to help the others. You've got the key; just unlock the rest of them."

Dad tucks the key into his pocket before replying. "The deal is that I only take you. If the other parents don't come to dispute on their child's behalf, there's nothing else to be done for them."

Elah clears his throat. "I happen to think there's a lot more that can be done for us. Isn't that right? Quit lying to her. Don't you think she has a right to know everything so that she can make her choice?"

"Who are you?" Dad asks a little too sharply.

Elah laughs. "You know who I am!"

"Dad!" I put my hand on his arm. "He claims he's my half-brother. He seems to think you have something to do with all this. Is that true?"

"We will not discuss this here, Ireland. I must say that questioning your own father is not a desirable trait to have."

"I just don't want anyone to die. You shouldn't either."

"I don't, but right now, we have to get you out. Then I will come back for them." Dad looks at Elah suspiciously.

My eyes shift toward Elah. He shakes his head in disbelief.

"Promise me," I whisper. "Promise you will help them."

Dad bends down and puts his hands on my shoulders. "I will do all I can."

"I ... don't ... know ..."

He takes my hand and starts to pull me away from Elah. "We cannot wait here any longer. Come. NOW!" Dad pulls me along as I struggle to break free.

I'm like a naughty toddler being dragged for scolding. My cheeks become hot with embarrassment. "Stop! Let me go!"

"Shut up, girl! You'll get us both killed," Dad hisses at me.

"You have never acted like this! What's happened?"

"That man is gone. It has to be this way in order to save you." Dad stops pulling me to kiss me hard on the forehead. The effect feels like sandpaper on my skin. Our eyes connect in one fleeting moment of panic. It's over as quick as it came. Dad's eyes form back into the cold, hard shell he's become.

Is this what I will be one day too? A cold, heartless person all because of this place? I can't. I *won't*. Thoughts and pictures form in my mind. The ones featuring Greve come first, then Faith, the humans who I've helped, the humans who ... I've ... *killed*, and it all ends with Elah.

Even in my mind, seeing Elah is like looking at my reflection. Every fault, need, worry, and desire that shows on his face, I also see on mine. We *are* connected by blood. We are intertwined by fate. We are bound to every hybrid in creation.

If he dies, then a part of me will die, too. In reality, we are two different people, but in society, we are the same. Hybrids—the result of all things wrong.

I cannot leave knowing that if he dies, another hybrid's death is added to the list. One less hybrid means one more piece of me destroyed. It will keep happening until the only hybrid left is me.

Then what?

They let me live just to honor my father's request? I don't think for one second that will happen. The higher authority will kill us all. No matter what my father thinks, I know in my heart it is true.

"Give me the key."

"Excuse me?" Dad crosses his arms, impatient.

I reach out my hand. "Give me the key," I say again.

"Stop playing games, Ireland. There is no time. We need to get out of here alive. You and I. Not us and *them*. You set them free, and we go down with them. Things are bad here. Worse since you left."

Dad's body begins to tremble. His cold exterior is gone for the second time in a matter of minutes. "Even some purebreds haven't been seen lately. Hybrids have also gone missing ... like Faith. She was one of those who disappeared. No one has seen her for two nights. And if they aren't missing, they end up in there." He points toward the room we just walked out of.

"What a minute!" I squeak. "Faith is gone?!"

"Yes," Dad answers, solemnly. "Adam reported that he expects she just ran off. But don't worry about her. Adam says he will find her and bring her back home."

"That's not possible. Faith wasn't supposed to leave. Not without me."

"I saw her a few days ago, and she didn't look like herself. Her face was flushed, and she looked worried. I asked Adam about her and whether he knew what was going on. Adam said he didn't but would send someone to check in on her just to be sure."

"Like I'm supposed to believe that. Someone or something made her go. Otherwise, she would have never left."

"Then it's a good thing we're reporting to Adam. He's waiting to see you just so he knows you are okay. After that, you will go into hiding until I understand exactly what's going on here."

"Yes, take me to Adam so that he knows I'm here. I can take my place alongside the people who will fight on behalf of my kind. There will be no hiding while others are killed," I say with determination. "We've known Adam for years. If I can't trust him, then I can't trust anyone." Not that I *do* trust him ... however, there doesn't seem to be any other option. He has to know where Faith went.

Dad smiles. "Atta girl! Come. We will go see Adam right away."

"There's just one more thing I want to do," I whisper before leaping next to my father. My hand takes the key from within its hiding place before Dad can react.

"Ireland, NO!" Dad shouts at my back while my feet carry me to the prisoners' door. An alarm sounds, blaring and unforgiving, as I open the door and slide the key into the room. Bodies shuffle around to find their means of escape. Elah's voice registers above the alarm, giving me hope he is the one who found the key.

Dad reaches me to take my arm in his. "Go. Damn it. Before they catch us!"

Our steps echo as we run out of the hall toward our means of escape. Dad maintains his hold on me, seemingly forgetting all about the key and the other prisoners. Right now, all he cares about is us. The sirens screech above us as we race in and out of various doors and closed rooms. My heart rate escalates the farther we get from an actual exit. Dad should know his way around this place, but it seems all he is able to do is take us in circles.

"You should know your way around here," I whisper. "I thought you were taking us to the way out."

Dad looks back at me. "I am. We are going to the only way out."

"Adam?" I ask to be sure.

"Yes."

"Lead on then."

We continue through several more turns and rooms while seemingly not getting any closer to where we are supposed to go. My head swims from all the turning and backtracking. All the rooms look the same, which means I will not be able to get out of here without some other assistance if I need to.

Finally, after about a dozen more turns, we reach a bland, white door. Surprisingly, the paint is peeled halfway off, which is something unheard of when it comes to an authority member. They always have the best of things, after all.

"Alright. Right through here, and Adam should be able to talk to us."

"Sure …" I say, thinking that won't be the case at all.

Dad knocks five times before waiting for the person on the other side to answer. The handle turns just as Dad places his hand on my shoulder to push me through the doorway.

Tangled blond hair and white, powdery wings fill the room before me. My heart sinks as her voice pierces my ears. "Ireland! I was beginning to think we might have lost you." She smirks.

"Apparently, Father was making sure you wouldn't," I say, my voice coming out strained. Shit. That's not the way I want to sound at a time like this. But knowing that my father is involved with her … well … how can things be so messed up? And how could I not have seen it?

"Careful..." Dad says at Gabriella. "We are here, per our deal. Take what you need from her, and we will be on our way"

"Yes, about that." Gabriella tsks as she moves closer. "Benjamin, we might have had a slight change of plans. But I will let you talk to Adam about it to see for yourself."

"What is she talking about, Dad? What deal?"

Ignoring me, Dad follows Gabriella's lead to where Adam is. Seeing the back of Gabriella's wings makes me want to pluck her until she resembles a skinned chicken. For some reason, I find myself ignoring my desire to skin her, and I follow them at a safe distance. Everything is so confusing. Father should not be involved with her. This is the girl who head-butted me and stuck me in with the prisoners, for crying out loud.

Mother put me in a place of total discord, which involves not even realizing who to trust and who not to anymore. She wiped me clean of everything except my demon counterpart before Greve got her to let me go. Now that I am back home, things are coming back to me ... slowly. It's just not as quick as I would like it to be.

"Dad, I don't think we should ..."

A hand slides over my face before I can finish my sentence. My body tenses at the contact from their body sliding into place behind me. "Shut up," some throaty voice says to me.

Out of the corner of my eye, I see Dad is in his own struggle. A man I don't recognize has successfully pinned him to the floor. Wings and bodies take up the room ahead. There are too many wings to count and way too many bodies, most of which are not in a desirable state.

"Might as well grant you a final wish. Adam waits for you," throat-voice says without a drop of remorse.

Throat-voice pushes me through after Dad is restrained next to other random bodies in the room. My eyes search for the man who's supposed to be letting us go. The man who's been my father's best friend for years. Shock fills me when I finally find him.

He's part of the body count on the floor. His naked body lies in the most unforgiving position. Hands tied to toes. Head meets his knees. Bruises cover him, which is more shocking than anything else. He is a pureblood angel ... in heaven. How can he look like this when he has the gift of immortality?

"I can see a lot of questions forming in your simpleton mind," Gabriella taunts me. "Let's get started in answering some of them."

She takes the back of my neck in her hand and pulls my hair out of place. I scream and thrust against her in hopes it will make a difference. Laughing, she zaps me right on my head. A jolt of electricity runs through my veins before my legs give out, and I topple to the floor.

Wheezing, my legs struggle to get up so that I can get my hands around Gabriella's neck. Immediately, she throws me off and right onto Adam.

Somewhere in my head, I hear Dad scream.

"You wanted to talk to your bud, Adam. There he is. Enjoy it while it lasts."

My body screams in protest as my arms try to push off of Adam. My head throws me for a loop, causing the room to spin. Gabriella slowly goes out of view, and the last thought I have before surrendering to my body's desire is that instead of plucking her, ripping out her wings would serve much more justice.

Chapter Forty

Ireland

Once upon a time, all I wanted was my own set of wings. To have them meant I could be free to enjoy life with my dad. We would no longer have to worry about being on the lowest society level. We wouldn't have to deal with the looks and the snarls from others because we would finally be the same as everyone else.

Funny how after only a few weeks, that dream doesn't seem obtainable. And now that my life is endangered, having them seems so trivial. I'm such a stupid girl with such a silly dream.

With a throbbing head, I look around to find Dad is gone. Adam remains by my side, semi-awake in a fetal position. Seems as though they have connected us together by cuffs and conveniently moved us around while I was unconscious. A small chain gives me about a foot of space away from him. My stomach turns at this new predicament. This whole time, I was certain Adam was the spy. It looks like he isn't someone to worry about after all.

And to make matters worse, we are the only ones left in the room. The bodies, which were here when I first entered, are now gone. Are they free? Not likely. Have the bodies been disposed of? Probably so, being that they all looked, at best, severely injured.

My body gives an involuntary shudder. All this time, we were taught that angels, even a hybrid, would be immortal while in heaven. That was one less thing to worry about. Not to mention that is one big perk of putting up with our peers. Death is not supposed to be possible. Now, it is a very real possibility that Adam and I are next in line to see how this whole death thing will play out.

"Adam?" I whisper in hopes that eventually, he will respond. I can't take another minute inside my thoughts. It is all too depressing.

"Wake up! It's me. Ireland."

After repeating myself another five times, Adam's eyes start to flutter. "I ... ur ... Lannnnddd ... mis ... take ..." His lips are so swollen that his speech is somewhat questionable.

"Pardon?"

"Getoutofhere," he says hurriedly.

"Doesn't look like that's a feasible suggestion, Adam." There isn't a way out that I can tell. The room is sealed tight. My eyes search over him. He meets my stares with an unfamiliar expression.

"You need to concentrate, please. I can see you are hurt, but I need to know what's happening. What happened to you? Who did this?"

Adam shakes his head. "Not enough time." He tries to move closer to me, only to stop short from apparent pain. Moaning, he slides back over without saying anything else.

My mouth opens to start on him again. As I begin to plead, footsteps echo outside the room.

Knots, which feel like rocks, fall to the pit on my stomach. The door opens to reveal someone I least expect. Someone who was supposed to wait for me. Someone who, I'm beginning to think, isn't at all who she said she was.

Faith enters and smiles at me. "Hello, friend."

" ... Hi."

"Let's get you out of here." Faith circles me like a vulture. "This is *all* wrong. Who put you in here?"

"Guess ..."

Faith comes at me with a key to get me loose. "Oh, yes. *Her.*"

Adam fixes a glance over at us. As soon as he registers Faith, his eyes grow as big as saucers. "No ... ere ... land. Don't," he tries to speak.

"Listen, Faith ... I've now been cuffed twice since returning home. Whatever's happening, I want to know what it is. And I also want to know what happened to Adam and my dad. Moreover, you were supposed to wait for me. Now, you show up after I've been told you ran off. What the hell?"

"All in due time, I promise." Faith takes me by the hand and pulls me up.

We make our way toward the door mainly because Faith is leading me. Not that I trust her fully. I can't trust anyone. Well ... maybe Greve, but he isn't here to help me.

With one last look at Adam, I follow Faith out of the room and into the hallway. Faith glances back and smiles. "So tell me what happened on your mission. Did he go to jail?"

"I don't want to talk about it."

Faith tsks while walking on ahead. "Pity. I was rooting for you."

"Yeah, well. Seems as though we have much bigger problems than my mission. That was a set-up anyway, as you know. The higher authority never wanted me to have my freedom. My failing is just something else to use against me. Now, there isn't any reason to let me stay."

Faith comes to a stop at a wooden door to our right. Her forehead wrinkles. "We need you here. In fact, we need all the hybrids. You all have an important job to do, and I'm not talking about missions down below."

"I'm not following," I reply.

"Let me show you what I mean. I've been busy. Come, friend. I am very excited about this." Faith turns the handle and opens the door.

Wary, I shuffle my feet toward the entrance. The room is ghostly white with low lighting and plenty of movement. Several medical beds line the walls and each contains a body. A few of the bodies I recognize just in passing.

My stomach churns from the smell coming off the beds. These people smell of disease and death. The knowledge that angels can get hurt here is enough to physically make me sick. Add the actual smell, and there's no possible way to keep from puking.

Searching for the nearest trash can, my body gets rid of any food that might be left in my stomach.

"This is where the failures go," Faith says, suddenly next to me.

"What?" I ask, making myself look up at her.

She pats my head. "At first, it was only the hybrids who failed at their missions. However, we've decided to eliminate the whole lot of you. It's such a *terrible* inconvenience, really."

I jerk my head away, not quite understanding. "You talk as if you are behind this."

Faith jerks her head toward the opposite way we came. Immediately, two males come to her side and fall in place behind me. My knee comes in contact with the first guy's stomach in hopes that it will affect him in some way. It doesn't. Apparently, he's a full-blooded angel. And by the way he looks at me, he is grateful to be on the other side of this genocide.

My hands get placed behind my back with my wrists pinned together. It takes both of the men to hold me down. I'm sick of this, and I'm sick of being the girl who gets taken advantage of.

Faith snickers at me. "This is the fun part. All of you have a lot of fight before the end. Adam especially. That's why he's still in the holding cell. We aren't done with him—yet," she says this as if I'm supposed to know this information already.

"At least tell me who the hell you are before you do whatever it is you want to do. You owe me that!"

"I owe you nothing," Faith says while pushing the hair out of my face. Nevertheless, I suppose I made your dad a deal. He drove a very hard bargain, but in the end, we came to an understanding."

"Interesting, as Dad hasn't shared this deal with me."

"He doesn't have to. You're not of age, therefore, he can choose what happens to you. All in due time, of course."

"Let me see him! Let me see my damn father!" I scream while pulling away from the guys behind me.

They struggle against me until a sharp object slices my face. Intense stinging starts soon after the impact. Blood trickles slowly down my cheek until the gash heals back together.

A small knife stays knitted inside Faith's hand as she bends down to look at me. "You stupid girl. Benjamin doesn't want to see you. All he sees when he looks at you is your mother. Do you know how annoying it is to constantly see the face of a demon looking back at you?"

Faith motions for the men to walk me forward. Leading the way to some unknown destination, she continues to talk. "You hybrids are all the same. Selfish and dangerous. You can never be ready or able to carry our wings. And what is really unfortunate is the fact that your mother had the chance to get rid of you, and she didn't. Frankly, this whole thing is getting to be too much. Demons and angels aren't supposed to work together."

Turning around, her eyes make contact with mine. "Your mother has been bossing me for years. She only wants her *children hybrids* as soon as they are of age. Doesn't matter that we've dealt with you all since infancy!"

Faith's boney finger pokes my chest as she continues to ramble on. "Your father was in on it, too. Let's control the *humans*, they said. Let's work *together* to expand our territories. The demons couldn't stand to see the inferior humans walk free to breed and pollute what could become their home. So, they devised a plan, and with the angels' help, we got together an assembly if you will—hybrid children who could read minds and control the humans basically without killing the demons' food supply. I'm sure you have found out what happens when demons try to control themselves?"

My body gives an involuntary shudder thinking about Mother's devouring of humans while she was around me. Even worse, I think about when I did it. All those people died because I couldn't keep my demon desires at bay.

Faith laughs at the look on my face. "Yes. You know exactly what happens when the demons run amuck. Those filthy beasts. Bloodshed everywhere. Hell, there wouldn't be anyone left if all the demons came out of hiding at once. No humans. No food. Demons can only survive on fire for so long. If there is anything a demon hates the most, it's loss of control."

"What's the point of me knowing all this if you intend on killing me?"

Faith shrugs. "Guess there's really no point. And that's the beauty of this whole thing. Jade picks out the mate she wants, and they come together to make the perfect hybrid combination. They did it on purpose, you see. Angels brought you up only to have the demons kill the angel part of your soul. You go from one assembly line to the other as we mend and mold you to become exactly what *they* need. Free-range controllers is what the demons call your type. Control the humans willingly. Get to their leaders. The leaders will enforce what the demons want with the help of the free-range controllers. Humans arranged like cattle to form labor camps and the like. Demons slowly take over to consume the Earth all while having the humans for whatever they need or want. Once the movement starts, it should be quick with little loss of human life."

Faith turns around and beckons me to follow. We continue to walk. "You would think with all this human reproduction that there would be enough to sustain demon life for eternity. That's not the case. There are too many, and if the demons get out of control, human life would be gone in a matter of months. Not even a year."

Faith laughs. "Dumb fools need the humans to survive. They need you. But angels don't need anyone. I fail to see what's in it for us. To have you mingle in our lives, even from the lowest level, will cause more harm than good. You can corrupt the purebreds. Who knows ... even start your own allegiance with each other. Why continue on? Why continue to give a shit about anyone else? They want to give us land? We don't need it!"

"You may think so, but what's to say the others will agree with you?" I ask. "Seems to me, they wouldn't want to mess up a good thing. Everyone has been happy at the expense of the hybrids. Why change that now?"

Faith stops walking to take in the view before her. The entrance to our destination is straight ahead. My heart sinks as the drop-off comes into view.

"Ireland, you asked about my mother once. I've been around for a long time. Too long. My mother was in the original group with your father to come up with this treaty with the demons. All was fine until Mother started to change. I don't know how to describe it, but she was no longer mentally capable of handling her-self. I suspect a demon was the cause of it. Much like what you had to endure recently. Do you remember how close you were to completely losing yourself? If it wasn't for that boy, you would still be down there with Jade or dead. Backtrack to years ago and replace your-self with my mother. The difference is that the demon waited until her immortality wore off to torture her. She was pure. So pure. The demon caused me to lose her," Faith whispers. "She might as well be dead."

"Maybe there's a way to help her become stable again," I respond. "Let us help you and her."

"Oh, you are going to help." Faith smiles, showing her teeth, "More than you probably want to."

For the first time, Faith doesn't look like a girl my age. All her innocence is gone. All the likeness of what I used to see in her has disappeared. She's showing me who she really is. A person filled with revenge and spite. She's someone who I never thought would present herself this way.

"Take her," Faith orders the men. "The others will be arriving soon."

The men take me by the shoulders to drag me to the drop-off.

My back collides with one, knocking him to the ground. We shuffle around while I try to break free. My elbow zeros in on the other guy's gut, causing him to momentarily lose focus.

"Just tell me where to go, Faith, and I will go. But you are not going to have me tied up again!"

Faith looks at me first and then the men, assessing the situation. "Your effort is honorable. At least you fight for what you want. Go over to the drop-off ledge and stand. The men will be right behind you, so don't try anything."

I nod, feeling a bit of satisfaction. The men follow me over as I stand close to the ledge of the drop-off.

My body gives an involuntary shiver, wondering what it would be like to fall to the grounds of Earth below.

Chapter Forty-One

Greve

Seeing Ireland leave was equivalent to someone ripping my heart out and stepping on it with sky-high heels. That someone wearing the heels just so happens to be her mother, of all people. Jade appeared right after Ireland's feet left the ground.

We watched her go, but to my surprise, Jade didn't seem bothered at the realization of Ireland's departure. By the look of her face, she is more pleased to have me.

"Luck was on her side. If it wasn't for you, I would have killed her," Jade says with no remorse.

"I'm aware. It was probably something you planned as soon as you got my father in jail." My voice comes off agitated.

Jade whips around to take a swipe at me. "Things are coming together, I'll admit it. Most of my children do not make it past the first stage of meeting me. I knew Ireland wouldn't. Just like her sisters and brothers who all came before her. Your dad just screwed up this time, which allowed me to take the bait and make a trade. Overall, I'm very pleased with my new son."

Folding my arms around my chest, I respond with, "I bet."

Jade smiles. "Glad you are being compliant."

She keeps looking at me until an all too familiar sensation begins making its way into my head. It starts with tingling and quickly moves on to pain. It only hurts when you fight the outsider who's trying to come in.

Jade narrows her eyes at me to force her way through my shield. If I let her in, the person I am might not ever come back the same. She'll pick and pry until my brain is flexible enough to allow her to take control.

You will have to kill me because you will not be able to change me. I won't let you. My declamation can be heard loud and clear in my mind.

Jade's eyes turn into slits as she tries to penetrate farther into my head. "They all comply, in time. You will be no different."

In spite of the pain, I smile. Because of Ireland, I am able to find peace. Because of her, I can let go of the guilt of not being able to save her sister or the other hybrids. *She saved me.* The boy who's made too many damn mistakes. Greve, the *traitor*, as I've been called by other hybrids I've met along the way. And the sad thing is, they were right. I was a traitor. Traitor through and through from the moment Father ordered me to start programming humans and angels alike. I didn't care about anyone. Not really. Just as long as I could survive and make it another day.

That one-track mind almost cost me everything. Shit, I was practically dead inside. A muted version of a person, hiding behind rage and self-devastation. Jade will not break me. She can't. I won't allow her to. Even if Jade tortures me every day for the rest of my life, I'll keep going for all the others who couldn't.

"BOY!" Jade screams, breaking my thoughts.

My eyes refocus her face. Jade looks at me with an expression I've never seen before. Her fingers point to the box Ireland left behind. A soft light comes from it to project a familiar face into the sky.

Confused as to how Jade acquired the box, my mind backtracks to when she came to take me. She must have snatched it off the ground, and I didn't realize it. She obviously knew it could be of help. Jade wasn't counting on this, however. She looks as confused as me.

My heart sinks from the box's display. Gabriella has dragged Ireland to her side, in preparation for whatever she needs to tell us. Even from down here,

Ireland's state is concerning. Her hair is matted on top of her head. Her eyes are unfocused, and her body language tells me all that I need to know. Something has gone to hell, and Gabriella wants the demons to know.

Ireland pulls out a piece of paper and starts to read. Gabriella stays at Ireland's side to peer over her shoulder.

"Get away from me, Gabriella. I'll follow the script." Ireland shifts her weight. She moves over to make space between them. Clearing her throat, she makes her announcement.

"Greetings to all demons. My name is Ireland Grace." She looks up from the paper to peer at the screen. "I was told to read this word for word, but this isn't from me."

Gabriella pokes her. "Get on with it before we are both punished!"

"Not my problem," Ireland replies. "I'm already dead."

"Just read the paper, Ireland!"

"Fine." Ireland sighs. "The time has come to end everything. No treaty is worth helping demons or hybrids. I speak on behalf of all pure residents of heaven, which henceforth will no longer go along with housing hybrids. They are vile creatures, taught by their peers to take advantage of, hurt, use, abuse, or even kill others. We no longer care how you are handling Earth or Hades as long as you take your filthy hybrids when we drop them from the sky. Think of them as a parting gift. These hybrids will become what you already are. They'll rot from the inside out. Just like what you are doing to this world—killing it from within and leaving nothing but poison behind."

Ireland drops the paper. "I'm done."

Gabriella flashes her teeth. "There's more left."

"I said I'm done. You can read the rest or the person who will be responsible for this genocide can."

"Oh, my god!" Gabriella snatches the paper out of Ireland's hands to finish reading it herself. She clears her throat. "Jade, we know you are seeing everything right now. You have the box Ireland left behind and we can see your red eyes glaring at the screen. You have a unique opportunity your fellow demons do not get to have. To witness it will be a beautiful thing."

My heart sinks as Ireland appears back on the screen with two musclemen behind her. For a moment, our eyes lock onto each other through the screen. Not knowing what is going to happen, I want to cry out for her. She needs encouragement. She needs *me*, and I can't help her.

"We've got to do something," I mutter to Jade, desperate for some reprieve.

"You're right," Jade agrees while finally breaking away from the broadcast. "We are going to hunt down every single hybrid left on Earth. They are no longer disposable if our stash is getting killed up there."

My eyes grow hot. "That's not what I meant."

Jade snatches my arm, causing pain to shoot through me. "Ireland is not my problem or a priority. She's not yours either. The time you spent with her has made you soft. Have you forgotten why you're still alive?"

"Of course not," I hiss.

"It's not because you're a trainer, although you seem to think that's the only reason ..."

"You need me. I'm the only one who can do it," I say, daring her to elaborate more.

"But you forget that you are mine, and you will do what I say regardless of whether you like it or not."

A commotion on the other side of the screen breaks our exchange. Jade and I both look up to see Ireland struggling with two men behind her. They bind her hands and feet together in front of her before leaning her against a wall.

"Greve, if Faith ever comes down to Earth again ... kill her!" Ireland says, knowing full well I can still hear her. "It's too late for me, but you promise me. Promise me you'll kill her for all the hybrids."

"Faith? Faith the girl in the cab? She's behind this?" Greve says.

As if right on cue, Faith enters the screen from the side. Her voice rough, she says, "The fact that I slipped right under your radar that day must bother you terribly. Greve, your name is on the edge of everybody's tongue as being the most ruthless trainer/tracker in the demon world. And yet ... you picked up nothing from me the day we talked. Why is that?"

Her eyes flick toward Ireland. "Never mind. I already know."

"I was not myself. It was a temporary lapse of character."

When Faith nods her head, the two goons holding Ireland bring her toward the screen. "And that *lapse of character* will cost *her* everything."

"Shut up!" Ireland shrieks. "This is not his fault!"

"I never expected this to work out so unbelievably well." Faith smiles. "Two lovers blinded to see what's really going on around them. Couldn't have planned this better, but nonetheless, it's time for you two to say goodbye."

A glare of light catches my eye, causing my stomach to turn. Gabriella holds a metal syringe in her hand and is pointing it right at Ireland's neck.

Losing all control, my knees give out. "Don't do this! Please don't do this!"

Jade pipes in beside me, "If you kill the hybrids, do not show your face around here again."

Faith snickers. "You won't have to worry about that."

"Greve," Ireland interrupts. "Go. I don't want you seeing this."

"I'm not leaving," I answer, searching her face for a reaction.

"If I survive, I won't be the same," she says, fearful.

Oh, god. "Doesn't matter." My words slip out slowly. "I'll be here regardless. If you come back, I'll find you. I'll search to the ends of the earth to find you again."

"Promise?" Ireland asks, crying now.

Looking straight at her eyes, I say, "Damn it. On my life, I promise you."

Chapter Forty-Two

Ireland

Staring back at him, I think that maybe, just maybe, Greve loves me. He cares enough to acknowledge that I've got a chance to survive this. I thought for the longest that survival would happen. But seeing all these other hybrids getting sick and dying brought me back to the reality of it all. Which brings me back to the needle pointing straight at my neck.

"So sweet," exclaims Gabriella.

"Give me that," Faith roars, snatching the needle out of Gabriella's hands.

The tip of the needle almost pricks my skin.

"It's time, and I'm doing it," Faith says.

"NOOO!" screams a familiar voice. The sound is followed by a body barreling into Faith and knocking her to the floor. Coughing and wheezing immediately follows as the bodies roll against the ground.

"Get him off!" Faith demands of the goons beside her. They come running to her rescue but are stopped short as more footsteps echo off the stairs leading to the staircase just outside the drop-off.

More commotion ensues as all the other hybrids run into the room with my brother leading the way.

"How?" Faith squeaks as she sees him coming toward me. Her moment of confusion is all it takes for my rescuer to gain full advantage. Adam wraps his arms around her throat to stop her from making any sudden movements.

Elah comes toward me with a knife and slices my hands and feet free.

"Thanks," I murmur, shocked at the scene before me. I look up at the screen to see nothing there. Greve and Jade are no longer on the other side. My heart stings at the thought that I might never see him again.

"You left us with a way out. We are returning the favor," Elah says. He takes my hand and pulls me up.

The goons take a swipe at Elah, nearly whacking him on the side of the head. Elah tackles one. Their bodies collide, with a bunch of grabbing and pulling. The next man makes a jab at me, pulling my hair and taking me to the ground.

"Ahh!" I wheeze, the pain throbbing against my scalp.

"Don't!" Adam begs. "Don't kill my daughter!"

Daughter?! I scan the room looking for the man who raised me as his. Benjamin is nowhere to be found. Adam's face, ghostly white, draws me away from my search to look at him. Faith holds the needle to his throat, the contents already injected.

"Ireland," he murmurs, losing ground against Faith. The poison he was injected with finally taking full control.

Faith slips away, cackling and smiling with triumph. "Surprised?" Faith asks, still holding the needle.

I don't know if I escaped the goon's hold purely on the flight or fight technique or if it was because Adam claimed me as his own. Either way, my body found new strength to wiggle my way to him.

Elah comes up from behind, apparently finished fighting with the first man from Faith's army. "Get Gabriella and any other angels you can find," he commands to the array of hybrids who have joined him.

Most run off to do his bidding while a few stay behind to hold off Gabriella. Elah turns to Faith, ready to pounce.

Adam's slow breathing causes me to focus only on him. "Please, you can't be serious," I whisper in his ear. My hands hold both sides of his head.

"Deadly serious," he answers. "I'm sorry I couldn't tell you. It was part of the condition that I didn't. They said if I raised you, I would be a terrible influence, so they gave you to Benjamin. None of the hybrids here are being raised by either parent. Lies. Everything here is just lies."

"None of this makes sense," my voice croaks under the pressure.

Adam coughs again, his whole body shivering. "I always watched over you, and I've always loved you. Every parent meeting, I was there, remember?" He smiles weakly.

"Yes." Tears fill my eyes. "You were, and now you're dying because of me."

"No, never because of you. All because ... of ... angels," he says as his eyes roll into his head. "Get out of here and don't come back. Find the boy. He ... will ... keep you ... safe."

"Adam? Dad?!"

Adam's eyes look at me, but there's no life left in them. My arms wrap around him, saying goodbye. I know, now, that I'll kill Faith or die trying.

"You! You monster!" I spin around to face Faith. Elah backs off, respecting my need to take care of her on my own.

If Faith is afraid, she doesn't show it. "You're wrong," she says. "Hybrids are the monsters."

Our bodies collide as I ram her. We fall to the floor with Faith landing on her wings. Fluff fills the air as I frantically pluck out as many feathers as possible.

"I'll rip these off of you!" I scream. My hands reach and pull anything and everything I can get ahold of. "I was never getting my wings. If I can't have any, you aren't keeping yours."

Faith screams unintelligible things while I go at her. Then suddenly, she jabs the needle into my arm. My breath catches as I process my momentarily lapse of judgement. How could I forget she still had it?

Before she can push the plunger down, I take ahold and pull it out of my skin. "I don't plan on dying today. I don't mind if you do, though."

Looking at Elah for guidance, he nods his head. Getting my answer, the needle connects to Faith's neck and she gasps in shock as the poison fills her veins.

She wiggles away from me, struggling to breathe, and I let her. I glance down at her, wondering what went wrong. We went from classmates, to friends, to enemies in just a short period of time. I can't wrap my head around it.

The other hybrids run back in, pushing several angels along in front of them. "What now?" I ask Elah because he obviously has a plan, and I don't.

He points to the angels and Gabriella. "They are flying us out of here."

"Are you crazy? Those of us with demon parents will be killed on sight if we go back to Earth!"

"I know a place they can't get us. We'll be safe there. Come, and I will show you." Elah reaches for me.

"Let me do something first," I say, remembering the note tucked in my pants. I pull it out and open it in case the demons come for me as soon as my feet touch Earth.

"Ireland,

Your mom is my mom now. My dad is your dad. Don't question, just know I did it because I want to make things right. No matter what happens or how much Jade changes me, bring me back. I'll remember you—Greve."

Not believing what I just read, I tuck the note back in my pocket. Later, I tell myself. Surely, he didn't. He wouldn't. Not for me.

"Ready?" Elah asks.

I nod, taking his hand. Gabriella is rushed over to the drop-off along with other angels and hybrids alike. "Drop us off together and say nothing," Elah says to the group. "We'll keep Gabriella with us. She's one that I cannot afford to let go of. The rest of you

can return here, but if you try anything or send anyone for us, we'll be back, and we'll kill you all. Even if
that means cutting your wings and sending you falling. Got it?"

Gabriella wails at this news while all the others
know better than to say anything at all. They nod in
compliance, truly scared of what the future could hold
for them.

Elah turns to one of the hybrids, a guy with black
hair and blue eyes. "Did you get it?"

"Yes," he answers, pointing to his backpack.

"Good, then let's move."

I turn toward Gabriella. "I guess you'll take me one
more time for old times' sake?"

"Of course, she will," Elah answers for her. He
takes one of Gabriella's arms, and I take the other. We
drag her off the ledge and wait for her wings to unfold. When they do, we glide away from our own personal hell toward the place that will be our new home.

The wind cools my face as we fall. The cold replen-
ishes my soul right down to the bottom of my heart,
and for the first time in my life, I finally feel free.

Acknowledgements

I want to thank my amazing friends who took the time to provide me with feedback on *Hades Sent*. Jennifer, Beth, Latisha, Teresa, Kristin, and Donna. Y'all joined me in my leap of faith and stuck through it to the end. Always encouraging me to continue on. I will always be grateful.

Thank you to my family who also took the time to read and give me feedback when I needed it. My sister Taylor, my mom Sherry, and my nana Claudia. I appreciate all that you do.

Jake, you are always so eager to hear my ideas and give me the encouragement when I need it. I've never had such a supportive partner. I love you.

Easton and River. My boys. You will probably never know just how much you pull me from dark places. How much you make me smile and how proud I am to be your mom. I love you.

Many thanks to my editor, Jeanne Felfe, for your encouragement, praise, and hard work!

About The Author

B.Y. Simpson hails from a small town located between Nashville and Memphis, Tennessee. She studied Child and Family Studies at The University of Tennessee at Martin. She began writing her debut novel in a journal during lunch breaks, hoping one day to see it in the hands of others. When not writing, she is working as a counselor along with being a mom to two boys and three adopted cats—Samantha, Samhain, and Tootsie (guess how she got her name).

You can find B.Y. Simpson on Facebook at B.Y. Simpson-Author for news about future projects and an occasional cat pic.

www.ingramcontent.com/pod-product-compliance
Lightning Source LLC
Chambersburg PA
CBHW051202190726

48288CB00006B/1761